Also By Francine Beaton

P O Box 2347
Pretoria
E-mail: beatonfrancine@gmail.com
www.francinebeaton.com

EYE ON THE BALL

A Playing for Glory Romance

FRANCINE BEATON

© Text: Francine Beaton
© Publication: Francine Beaton
P O Box 2347, Pretoria, 0001
E-mail: beatonfrancine@gmail.com
www.francinebeaton.com
Cover Design: German Creative
Typography Setting: Francine Beaton
First Edition: 2018
© Copyright: 2018

Eye on the Ball
ISBN 978-1-990902-01-7

To everyone who believed in me and supported me, who forgave me for many ruined dinners, and brought me hundreds of cups of tea: thank you. I couldn't have done it without your support.

CHAPTER ONE

J akes grunted when he slid into the booth. When he could stretch his injured leg on the bench and rest his back against the wall, he was almost out of breath. He tried to breathe through the pain, but it wasn't easy to do when he gritted his teeth at the same time. Unfortunately, the compression sleeve chaffed against the bruise on his leg, which increased his discomfort. He knew he shouldn't complain about it, as it was for his own benefit, but it would be a relief to remove it.

"You should've taken the painkillers."

"No," Jakes scowled, "I need to tough it out. I'll take it when I go to bed."

"You know that's stupid. That's why you got them. You just came off a ten-hour flight. It's not to say you're weak to take the bloody painkillers."

Jakes shook his head. "Believe me, Michael. I used enough of the stuff in the last couple of days. I anyway took some before the flight."

"Which was hours ago!" Michael scowled. "You should've

taken one earlier to ease the pain but it's now too late for that. Let's get you something to eat then we can go back to the apartment."

Jakes learned in the last year not to argue with Michael. The head physio for the Buffales anyway was right, as you would've expected from a man with his experience. Jakes could admit it, though: he had been stubborn in not drinking more painkillers, but he was too scared to take that chance. One of his former teammates got addicted to the stuff. It could happen so quickly, and he didn't need addiction as well. His life was already too complicated.

He flushed, now uncomfortable under the older man's scrutiny. "Sorry. I just feel sorry for myself. If it hadn't been for this injury, I would've been preparing for tomorrow's test match."

Michael almost sounded sympathetic as he nodded. "Yeah, it's a bummer. As I understand from the Bok training camp, you would've started this week. It would've been your first full Cap starting for the Springboks."

Jakes didn't even attempt to hide his disappointment. He would've loved to play in the rest of the test matches, but it wouldn't help to grumble about it now. "I'm not done. I would do anything to get back on the pitch again."

"Anything?" Michael asked with a sly smile.

Jakes studied Michael's face, now dubious. Michael looked way too self-satisfied for his liking. His grin, most likely in gleeful anticipation of what he would put Jakes through in the upcoming weeks, was obvious. Michael proved Jakes right when he warned, "The therapy is intense, Jakes."

"I don't care. I'm not afraid to work hard. I'd do anything you asked."

Michael smiled. "I know. At least you didn't need an

operation. But, let's wait until Monday and see what the new scans show. It might be better news than we first thought."

"I hope you're right," Jakes mumbled as he picked up a menu. He knew he was stubborn in not drinking more painkillers, but he was too scared to take that chance. One of his former teammates got addicted to the stuff. It could happen so quickly, and he didn't need addiction as well. His life was already too complicated.

He wasn't hungry, but he needed to eat before he could take the medication. He scanned through the menu, finding a few options he might like. Michael's attention was still with the menu long after Jakes made his choice. He leaned his head back against the bench and closed his eyes.

His thoughts drifted to his injury, which happened in the mid-week friendly game against a combined English counties team. The injury couldn't have come at a more inopportune time, just before he could play himself into the regular Test squad.

When Tom Brady, the Buffaloes' head coach and Michael's father, suggested that Jakes joined Michael at the rehab centre here in Denver, Jakes didn't think twice. He wanted to be fit and ready for next season when they played in an exciting new competition. It was also a World Cup year.

The cheery voice of a server interrupted his thoughts. He almost groaned. Cheeriness was the last thing he needed at the moment. Cheerful people most often than not expected you to respond in the same manner he was not in the mood for that now.

Jakes listened to Michael giving his order, his eyes still closed. Only when Michael drifted off as a sign that he finished giving his order, Jakes inhaled deeply before he opened his eyes.

Luckily, he had because the woman nearly knocked the breath straight out of his lungs. Her blue eyes, as bright as the

Free State sky in winter, first caught his attention and then it was her wide, welcoming smile. Those blue eyes stared directly back into his.

Time stood still. A strange calmness took hold of him and for the first time since his injury on Wednesday, Jakes forgot about the pain in his leg.

Nice. Really nice.

The thought surprised him. It came to an abrupt halt when Michael jumped up. He dragged his gaze away from the woman to Michael who was now scowling at the woman. "What are you doing? Can't you see the glass is already full?"

Jakes follow Michael's movement, not sure whether he should be amused or not. Michael grabbed a bunch of serviette and dabbed haphazardly at the water tumbling over the rim of the too-full glass. Maybe it was better to suppress his sudden bout of humour as he witnessed Michael's futile attempt. Those serviettes didn't have a snowball's chance in hell to mop up the water. Still fascinated, Jakes followed the water's progress as it spread over the surface. That was, until it trickled closer to the edge, then over and onto his lap.

When the waitress tried to dry the water from his lap, Jakes galvanised into action. He grabbed her hand in the nick of time before it came too close to a part of his anatomy Jakes had sworn no woman would touch. Well, not anytime soon.

"For heaven's sake, woman, stop!" Flustered, he grabbed the cloth from her hand. He couldn't even look at her. Maybe she could read minds and then she would know where his thoughts went.

Her movements stilled and she stepped back. She didn't say a word before she turned and walked away to fetch another cloth and more serviettes. After she returned, she dried the rest of the table still without saying a word. When everything was as dry as it could be, Jakes pushed the wet serviettes and cloth to the side. Only then did he glanced at the waitress again.

Not that the woman even looked in his direction. Her face was set as she picked up the damp cloth and the soaking mess of serviettes and left to dump them in the kitchen. When she returned, she appeared calm, but she didn't fool Jakes. He could swear her eyes were shooting daggers in his direction as she waited impatiently for him to give his order.

Without even realising it, Jakes kept on staring at her. Maybe he did for too long as she sent a furtive glance in his direction. Fascinated, Jakes followed the movement of her tongue as it slid over her bottom lip in a nervous gesture before her straight, even teeth started to nibble the one corner of her mouth. Jakes' jeans suddenly felt too tight but still he kept on staring.

Oh, man, if it wasn't that he...

No, no, no.

No way was he thinking about a woman like that. Not now, nor for the next six months. His natural instinct was to retreat, because he knew by now that he wouldn't have done anything about it, but this woman was far too tempting.

Focus, Jakes, focus. Eye on the ball, and all that.

When she looked up again, waiting for his order, Jakes scowled without even realising he did it because he was so busy concentrating on his mantra when he mumbled his order.

Her face scrunched, clearly confused. If Jakes hadn't been so uncomfortable, he would've thought it was cute.

That was, until Michael chuckled, "In English, Jakes."

Had he not spoken English? Geez, the jetlag must affect him more than he thought. His English wasn't that bad. Sometimes, when he was nervous, he might have a stronger accent, but he didn't usually make mistakes like that.

When he caught Michael's amused expression, Jakes growled, "What's so funny?"

Michael said in Afrikaans, "Stop frowning at the poor woman and repeat your order, but this time in English."

Jakes grunted, "A cheeseburger and hot chocolate."

"Tell the lady, not me," Michael grinned again.

Jakes turned back to the waitress. Had the effect of the painkiller he took before the flight still not worked out of his system? Why else would it feel as if his tongue stuck in his mouth and his brain hadn't caught up with his surroundings?

He shook his head to get rid of the feeling and repeated his order. This time he ignored her face. He focused on her notebook instead.

When she walked away with their order, Jakes let out his breath. He took a deep gulp of the remaining water, still irritated with himself. It wasn't as if he and Michael usually speak Afrikaans to each other. Then it would've been easy to understand why he got confused, but they spoke English. They always had.

Jakes' last years with the Blitzbokke gave him enough opportunity to speak English. He wasn't that bad.

Jakes blamed it on the waitress. She had this effect on him. He had been avoiding women for the last eighteen months, and he was getting good at it. He knew the warning signs. When he felt the sudden rush of heat when she bit her bottom lip? That was a warning in big red and bold letters. He should do well to heed it.

Jakes saw through Michael when he asked with fake concern, "Are you okay?" Michael still tried to hide his amusement.

"I'm fine."

"I wondered. Your face is flushed. I hope you didn't catch a nasty bug on the plane."

Jakes wondered the same thing. He knew his excuses were lame but it was the best he could come up with at such short notice. "It must be the altitude or something."

"Or something, yes." This time Michael openly laughed at Jakes.

Jakes rather ignored Michael and pretended to take in his surroundings, something he didn't do when they arrived. It was a sports pub and restaurant with a few big-screen televisions scattered throughout. Several showed highlights of previous rugby test matches.

"I didn't expect them to show rugby here," Jakes said, breaking the awkward silence.

Michael grinned. "You'll be surprised. Rugby is getting more popular in the US. There are quite a few clubs in Denver. The rehab centre where you'll be getting your therapy is associated with one club, the Denver Black Bears. The rehabilitation facilities are on the same grounds and state-of-the-art."

Jakes still didn't dare look at the waitress when she delivered a new container with cutlery and serviettes.

Unfortunately, when the waitress returned with their drinks order shortly after that, but Jakes' was coffee instead of the hot chocolate he'd ordered. Maybe he should've told her nicely she brought him the wrong drink. Even better, Jakes should've kept his mouth shut, but his irritation level was already high. He still blamed it on the fact that she rattled him so much.

Jakes shoved the cup rather clumsily back to her, splashing coffee all over the side. He mumbled, this time at least in English, "I ordered hot chocolate."

Only after she picked up the cup and disappeared in the kitchen's direction, he dared to look up. His eyes followed her until she reached the hatch and picked up the drink he ordered.

Jakes had felt cooped up on the plane. He thought it was a

good idea to get out of the apartment but now he was regretting it. When she reappeared with the drink he ordered, Jakes accepted he made a mistake. He should've stayed at the apartment. If he had to judge the service they received from the waitress so far tonight, it would be a long night.

The waitress put the hot chocolate on the table in front of him with a flourish. Jakes could almost *see* the sarcasm in the gesture. He looked up and saw the spark in her eyes, but it wasn't the cheery one as it was before. Jakes couldn't blame her. Uncomfortable, he dropped his head.

Michael continued to enthuse about the rehab facilities but Jakes kept on searching for the waitress. He didn't want to speculate about his reasons for doing so. He quickly lowered his gaze when he noticed she was on her way to their table with their food.

Disappointment enveloped him when she put the plates in front of them, and he noticed the contents. "What's this?"

The look she gave him spoke volumes as if he was stupid. Her answer was nonchalant, "Your order."

Jakes shook his head. "I didn't order this."

The waitress took out her notebook and studied it. She glanced at their plates and flushed. She grabbed the dishes in a hurry and delivered it to the right table. As soon as she finished, she returned to their table.

Maybe he should've let Michael handle the situation. Better yet, he should've allowed her to apologise. Jakes did neither. He frowned at her, "You wrote it down. Couldn't you at least check?"

Michael cleared his throat and stared at his phone, suddenly very busy. "You got a problem?" Jakes glared at him.

Michael shook his head, but Jakes saw the grin. It made him even madder.

When the waitress walked away, Jakes mumbled, maybe louder than necessary, "How the hell does she still keep a job?"

It could be the pain in his leg that made him act like a bear with a sore head, but Jakes knew that wasn't the truth. Those blue eyes were unnerving, making him feel things he shouldn't even contemplate. He had two options: fight or flight. Fleeing was out, so he had opted for the first.

Fight? That surprised him. It was something he hadn't done in years. Panic suddenly got hold of him when he realised it. He put his hands under the table, his fingers finding the rubber band with ease. With his eyes still on the waitress, Jakes tugged at it, breathing deep.

She stopped at the hatch where she took out her notebook and spoke to the person on the other side. She sighed then flitted a nervous glance in the manager's direction, then at Jakes before she disappeared.

Time dragged on and on without the woman reappearing with their food. Jakes had calmed to such an extent that he had stopped playing with the rubber band a while ago. He tried to shift to a more comfortable position, but it didn't help. Each movement made him realise he should've taken the medication. His leg was hurting like hell and his body drooped from fatigue. e now agreed with Michael that it was stupid not to take the medication. He needed a painkiller before he passed out.

When at last he couldn't hide it anymore, Jakes knew he had to do something drastic. He glanced around one more time hoping to find their waitress, but she'd done a vanishing act. Since she'd disappeared, she hadn't come back and it didn't look as if she was planning to return soon.

He grunted to Michael through clenched teeth, "You don't have to tell me I told you so, but you're right. I should've taken the meds, but I can't go on much longer without it. Where's that woman with our food?"

Michael glanced around and shook his head. He turned to Jakes, taking in Jake's white face and clenched jaw. His expression clearly said, "I told you so," but at least he didn't say it out loud.

Michael sighed, lifting his hand to signal for another waitress. An older man appeared. He introduced himself as Bob, the owner, and asked, "Is there something wrong, gentlemen?"

Again, Jakes should have let Michael handle it. Before Michael could open his mouth though, Jakes glared at the man. "What *wasn't* the problem, you mean?" and rattled off the mistakes the waitress made. "Can you send someone who knows what they are doing, please?"

Jakes only listened with half an ear to the man's apologies before he called another waitress. "Clara, could you please check these gentlemen's order?"

The waitress disappeared to the hatch, spoke to the chef, and held up one finger to the older man. It might mean it would be only a minute and Jakes sincerely hoped so. He could deal with a minute, but not much longer. He suspected that the food might have been ready for some time and might now be cold, Jakes sighed. It wouldn't matter. He would eat it and get out of this place as soon as possible.

Clara arrived almost immediately with their food. Both Jakes and Michael accepted it and didn't take long to finish eating. While Michael signalled for the bill, Jakes glanced up. Their waitress had at last re-appeared.

ANGIE SPLASHED her face with cold water. What had just happened with that foreigner? Getting lost in his eyes was the weirdest experience. Not that anyone could blame her. His eyes were an unusual shade of moss green, but still: it isn't something that happens often.

She looked up at the mirror, noticing her reflection as if for the first time. She knew she didn't look her best tonight. She had dark circles under her eyes, which even her best efforts couldn't camouflage. That was what lack of sleep could do to you, she surmised, but it was all for a good cause.

Even her eyes looked tired tonight. Most people complimented her on her eyes, but Angie wasn't sure it was her best feature. It wasn't tonight. She was so used to them, as both her brothers and father had the same blue eyes. Electric blue, as one of Jesse's ex-girlfriends, called it. Tonight, she felt as if they were on dim.

She grimaced at the ponytail. It made her feel like a schoolgirl. She preferred to keep her long, dark, curly hair hanging loose so it could frame her face. She always thought it formed a nice contrast with the paleness of her skin and the blue of her eyes. Those contrasts appealed to her artist's eye.

Angie felt her smile was her best feature. Well, it had been when she smiled often enough for people to notice. She loved the way it softened her face. Recently she hadn't had many reasons to smile and tonight was no exception.

She sighed and glanced down at her uniform. She knew this job and this uniform were two of the biggest reasons she didn't smile anymore. It was killing her soul. The clothes looked dreary, and so unlike her usual style of flowing skirts and bright colours.

She lifted her hand to brush the hair that had escaped her ponytail back from her face. Her engagement ring caught the bathroom light, and she sighed again.

That might be the most significant reason she'd lost her smile. She knew she had to decide soon. She needed to be happy again.

She glanced back at her reflection and smiled, just for the hell of it. Yes, definitely her smile. Angie vowed she would do anything in her power to get it back.

To her relief, Angie saw the two men had finished eating when she returned to the restaurant. One of them signalled for the bill. She didn't realise she had been in the bathroom so long and lost track of time—again.

She picked up the check and went across to their table, trying to avoid eye contact with the enormous man.

JAKES PUT on his jacket before he slid his injured leg out in front of him. He managed to push himself upright with the help of the table and the back of the bench. A jolt shot through his injured leg when someone walked into it. Curses rolled off his tongue, but he couldn't stop it at first. He only managed when he breathed in a mixture of flower and apple. His heartrate accelerated as he tried to push away the woman before she injured him any further. When he could breathe through the worst of his pain, he took another deep breath before he opened his eyes.

He should've known. It could only be the waitress who got him in such a flat spin. For several seconds their eyes held. Heat shot through his body when she nibbled her bottom lip, a blush spreading over her face. He had to breathe deep before he could push her away. His voice sounded low and husky when he mumbled, "You're a danger, woman."

ANGIE THOUGHT the man was enormous earlier, but now that he was standing, she noticed how massive he was. He was well over six-feet-three or four, with muscles in all the right places. Under her hands, the Henley shirt underneath his jacket clung to well-defined muscles. His voice sounded husky, sending ripples down her spine.

When he pushed her away, she realised what she was doing. She almost let out a groan but managed to stop it in time. What more can go wrong tonight, with this customer?

The man turned away to accept crutches from his companion. Without looking at her, he pushed it under his arms.

Oops! Crutches! How embarrassing! No wonder he didn't get up when she spilled the water all over him.

He turned back to her. His eyes dropped to her mouth, and then they narrowed. Angie suddenly felt warm but then the man frowned and swung around abruptly. Without saying goodnight, he turned and hobbled out of the restaurant.

Well, that was it. That man was the rudest, most obnoxious man she had ever met. This time she couldn't stop herself from calling at his back, "Thank you and good night to you too."

He didn't react. Not that Angie expected him to. When the door closed behind him, Angie turned away muttering "Creep," even though he couldn't hear her anymore.

CHAPTER TWO

As soon as she turned around, Angie caught Bob's signal to join him in his office. She didn't have to guess to know what was coming. She should be used to it by now, as the elderly owner had regular talks with her in the month since she started.

When she entered the office, Angie knew this time was different. Bob wasn't smiling tonight as he usually did. His face was grim when he motioned for her to sit. His next words confirmed her fears, "Angie, my dear, I'm sorry. You and I must agree—this job is not for you. After tonight's fiasco, and the two gentlemen's complaints, I have no other choice."

"You're letting me go?" Angie whispered.

Bob grimaced. "No, not yet, but this is your last warning."

Angie sighed and closed her eyes. She just had to try harder. It's only a few more weeks. She looked up at the kind old man and mumbled, "I'm sorry, Uncle Bob. I'll try, I promise."

"I know you will, my dear. I know why you're doing this, but I have a business to run. I can't afford you chasing away my customers."

"I understand, Uncle Bob. Is there anything else I can do?" Angie knew she sounded desperate.

"Let me think about it. Clara told me Thomas was sick and you stayed up with him. It is admirable that you are so loyal to your friend and take care of her son, but you can't carry on like this. Take the weekend off to catch up on your sleep, and we'll talk on Monday."

"Thank you, Uncle Bob. I appreciate it," Angie smiled relieved. She hugged him goodbye and rushed out to get her bag and jacket from the staffroom.

The rest of the staff all knew she wasn't a good waitress and gave her sympathetic glances. She didn't have to say anything to Clara. Her best friend already knew something happened as her encouraging wave said it all.

Angie tried to think about the positives as she strolled to her car. At least she would be home earlier and could relieve the babysitter. She still had her job. How she kept it for so long, she didn't know. She was sure Bob kept her on because of his friendship with her father. Bob had always been a softie.

She was *so* tired. After spending the previous night looking after Clara's sick toddler, she'd only had a few hours of sleep. She could blame her lack of concentration on that, but she knew it wasn't the whole truth.

If she could keep her mind on her job, she wasn't a bad worker. Unfortunately, her brain didn't work that way. She always got lost in a new project, a painting, or just her over-productive imagination. She didn't even feel comfortable in a kitchen, so being a waitress in a busy restaurant was ten times worse.

Angie realised soon after she started that waitressing wasn't one of her better ideas, but she wasn't prepared to admit it to anyone, but she didn't have to. Her family knew her well enough.

She would never admit it to Chris. She would not give him a chance to make nasty comments or blame Clara as he usually did.

Maybe she should teach again.

Angie shuddered, remembering her first teaching job. She didn't mind the teaching, but not all the kids wanted to be in the class. Some made her life a nightmare. If she could teach kids who liked art, it might have been different.

When Clara came in from her shift, they cuddled under blankets with a mug of hot chocolate each. Clara didn't wait long before she asked, "So, what happened tonight? I know you can sometimes get lost in your own world, and it's kind of cute, but tonight you didn't concentrate at all."

Could she tell Clara about her argument with Chris before her shift started? Clara already knew how Angie's fiancé felt about her and Angie's insistence on helping her, but she didn't want Clara to feel guilty.

Angie couldn't understand Chris' attitude about her helping Clara. Why could he not see it as she had? It was only for another few weeks. Chris criticised her for her soft-heartedness and said Clara was abusing their friendship. It couldn't be taking advantage of your friendship when you offered, could it? She couldn't convince Chris, and he didn't want Angie to help Clara. The strange animosity between her fiancé and her best friend bothered her.

"I had an argument with Chris earlier," she admitted but didn't elaborate.

Clara raised her eyebrow. They had this discussion several times since Angie moved in with Clara. Clara urged Angie to speak to Chris, but Angie always postponed it.

"I know how you feel about Chris, and I know you wouldn't say anything. Since I came back from Boulder, things are deteriorating between us. The rift I felt is getting worse but after today's argument..."

Clara frowned, then showed how well she knew Angie when she said shrewdly, "But that's not all. What happened? Why did Uncle Bob let you come home early?"

Angie didn't answer but she didn't have to. "Why are you blushing?" Clara asked, sitting up straight.

Angie hadn't even realised she blushed, but she did react this time, "Did you see the enormous man with the crutches?"

Clara gave her a saucy grin. "Yeah, me and all the other women in the pub. You could almost hear how all the ovaries in the pub stood to attention when he walked in."

Angie's mouth dropped open. "Clara!" was all she managed.

"Oh, come on, Angie. Don't tell me you were immune? You had to admit, that is one of the most gorgeous men you've ever seen," Clara argued.

"That might be true, but he was rude. And he was the reason Bob gave me my last warning," Angie snorted.

Clara's eyes widened, "Him? Why?"

With a sigh, Angie told Clara everything that happened. Thinking about it now, she was getting angry again. It wasn't such a big deal for Bob to almost fire her!

She looked up at Clara's concerned face and reassured her friend. "Don't worry about anything, Clara. Uncle Bob said he would find something else for me to do. He told me to take the weekend off so I can babysit Thomas."

Clara shook her head. "I'm not worried about Thomas or myself, Angie. I'm worried about you."

Angie blurted, "You need not worry about me. I still have my job."

"That's not what I meant, Angie and you know it."

Angie knew what Clara meant, and she couldn't postpone

it for much longer. Her reaction when she looked into the stranger's green eyes, Angie knew that her engagement no longer worked. Had it ever?

ON THE WAY to her father's consulting rooms the following Monday, Angie stopped at the notice board outside the Community Centre. She went through the vacant positions with the vague hope that there would be something suitable for her between the vacant positions advertised.

It might be fate because hidden between the others was one position listed for a temporary art facilitator. It was only until the Holidays, but it was better than nothing. That was the kind of job she was looking for. She hoped that, as it was in her field of study, she could keep it. The less than a hundred hours wouldn't be enough to get her certification, but at least she could still help Clara. She could also tell her family and Chris she had a job in her line of study. It would mean even less time for painting, but she could work harder on her own art when Clara was self-sufficient again.

SHE HADN'T BEEN as nervous in a long time and, to settle her nerves before her interview the next morning, Angie first stopped for coffee at the restaurant at the centre. To divert her attention away from the meeting, she used the time to catch up on her text messages. She first thought it was her imagination when she felt as if someone was watching her. She shrugged it off and finished reading the message from her sister-in-law.

When she still got an uncomfortable feeling, Angie glanced around. There were a few people in the coffee shop, but Angie didn't have to look far to find the watcher. She recognised him as the man from Friday night. He had a curious look on his face while he studied her, but when their eyes met, Angie knew he recognised her.

In horror, she noticed he was preparing to get up, his eyes still fixed on her. Oh no, that was not going to happen. She grabbed her bag and waved to the surprised waitress on her way out. At least she had settled her bill when she ordered, so she didn't have to wait. She heard a man's voice calling "Wait!", but there was no way she would confront that man again. Definitely not now. She wanted to be in a good mood when she arrived for her interview, and he would be enough to spoil her day.

Angie crossed her fingers while she made her way to the part of the community centre, where she had to report for her interview. It had to go well today and she took extra care with her appearance. She chose her favourite blue skirt and peacock blue top, which brought out the blue of her eyes. She complemented it with boots, jacket, and scarf. Her hair was hanging loose, held away from her face with a hairband to match her skirt. She even wore makeup, something she rarely did.

When she arrived at the interview, she put all thoughts of the man out of her head. She needed to concentrate and didn't need him to distract her. When she left the premises an hour later, she grinned with relief. She'd worried unnecessarily. She could start immediately, and Angie guessed it counted in her favour.

Tomorrow, she was starting her new job.

JAKES SHIFTED to get more comfortable, but it wasn't easy on a bar stool. It was the Wednesday after he arrived in Denver and he could feel how hard Michael had worked him in the last three days. He still had to rely on the crutches for a few more days, but soon he wouldn't need them anymore.

He didn't complain about the toughness of the rehab, as he could feel the difference already. He could now manage most of the time without the painkillers. He wouldn't say his leg didn't still hurt, but he hadn't expected to be doing what he did today.

Apart from the stretching exercises he did in the High-Altitude room, he also had daily massages and Electro-Therapy. The rest of the time, he did upper-body strength in the gymnasium. Today he also managed water therapy. He was eager to get back into his usual exercise routine, though.

No, he should clarify that. He was keen to get back on the pitch with the ball in hand.

Jakes came in every night since the previous Friday hoping to see the server he had mistreated. He had had no luck so far. He thought he saw her at the coffee shop yesterday, but it might not have been her.

A group of men came in, which interrupted his thoughts. Their Bears tracksuits gave away that they were all members of the local rugby team. He'd watched part of their training tonight and envied them. He wished he could've been on the pitch with them. If he hadn't sustained this injury, he would still have had a full month of training and test matches with the Springboks.

Jakes signalled to the barman and settled his bill before he hobbled towards the men's room. Turning into the narrow alley leading to the bathrooms, one player blocked his way. He must've noticed Jakes, even though he was deep in conversation. He moved out of the way without lifting his eyes from his shoes. The man ended his call, but his phone rang again. Jakes heard his sigh, but he answered the call anyway.

Jakes thought he was mistaken when the man said, *"Hallo Ma, hoe gaan dit?"* and almost stopped. It sounded like Afrikaans, translated as, "Hello Mum, how are you?"

He didn't want to listen to the man's conversation and as

soon as the man confirmed he indeed spoke Afrikaans, Jakes continued to the bathroom. When he came out later, he was in time to see the man sigh. He rolled his eyes and promised his mother he would behave, leave the girls alone, and eat properly.

Jakes couldn't stop the chuckle that escaped. The man frowned in Jakes' direction. He glanced down at his phone to end his call but then pulled his head back sharply to look at Jakes, the surprise evident on his face. Jakes apologised in Afrikaans, "I'm sorry, I didn't want to listen to your conversation. I didn't expect to hear Afrikaans here. I'm..."

The man shook his head and with a laugh exclaimed, "Jakes du Plessis!"

He grinned and continued in Afrikaans, "I know who you are, but what are you doing here? Oh, sorry, I'm Rayno Botha," and immediately held out his hand to Jakes.

Jakes was surprised that someone recognised him here in Denver, but Rayno just laughed, "I may have lived here for a while, but I still follow South African rugby. Don't tell me you're coming to play here?"

Jakes shook his head in denial and lifted his leg, still in the brace, "No, I'm here for therapy. I'm going back to Pretoria before the season kicks off."

They drifted back to the restaurant, chatting in Afrikaans. When Rayno established Jakes was alone, he invited him to join them, "Come, I bet it will thrill these guys to meet a Springbok."

When Jakes corrected him, "Only a one-time Springbok," Rayno shook his head, "It doesn't matter. You're a Springbok."

Jakes followed Rayno to a table where his friends gathered. None of them had taken their seats yet, as they were talking to the group that came in before them.

Jakes stopped behind Rayno. He stood upright, balancing himself on one crutch. His tall and muscled body towered over the other men, even his fellow South African. He took the chance to study them while they continued their conversation. He judged them all to be about three or four years younger than him.

When Rayno said he wanted to introduce them to a fellow South African, they turned towards him and studied him with the same interest. One of them looked Jakes up and down and muttered, "What the hell do they feed you guys in South Africa?"

Jakes and Rayno looked at each other and said at the same time, "*Pap en vleis.*"

The other man frowned, "What's that?"

Their frowns clearly meant that they didn't know what it was, so Rayno explained with a laugh, "If you translate it into English, it is porridge and meat. Lots of meat."

One of the men grimaced, "Can't you guys eat junk food like everyone else?"

Rayno replied with a smirk, "Mike, you're so skinny, you should maybe try it."

The others turned on Mike, "Yeah, Mike, you should."

Mike was probably used to their abuse and showed them a rude sign.

When the other group disappeared to their table, Rayno turned to his friends. As he made the introductions, Jakes concentrated on remembering their names. Mike Cutt was the man who first spoke. The second man, Jesse Summers, looked familiar. The last member of the group was Chris Johnson.

They settled at the table and Clara came to take their orders. When she returned with their drinks, Jakes glanced up to thank her. He noticed the dirty look she gave him. Jakes frowned, not sure what he'd done wrong to deserve such treatment but he pushed it to the back of his mind when Mike asked, "So Jakes, what brings you to Colorado in the middle of the winter? I don't think it's a South African's first choice as a holiday spot ."

Jakes grimaced, "It wouldn't have been my first choice either. It's freezing here. I can hardly feel my toes." He rubbed his hand over his leg and admitted, "I'm here for therapy at the rehab centre."

Jesse turned his head and frowned at Jakes, "I should've known. You're a rugby player, aren't you?"

Jakes nodded but didn't elaborate, and Jesse probed again, "So what happened?"

"Hamstring strain. Our physio is here learning new techniques, so my club sent me here."

Jesse ignored Jakes' short answers and asked, interested, "Is it working?"

Jakes pondered over the question before he admitted, "Ask me next week. I'll wait for the MRI on Monday and the doctor's decision, but it looks promising."

Jesse grinned, "My father wouldn't take any chances. He would give you the go-ahead only when he's convinced you're ready."

Jakes had a light-bulb moment. No wonder Jesse looked familiar. He nodded, surprised that he hadn't recognised it earlier.

Jesse wasn't shy with his questions and asked again, "So, apart from playing rugby, what do you do?"

Jakes flushed, "I have little time for anything other than rugby at the moment."

Mike frowned, "Are you a professional? Who do you play for?"

"Yes, the Buffaloes, a team from Pretoria."

Before Jakes could stop him, Rayno announced, "Jakes is too modest. He's a Springbok in both Sevens and Rugby Union."

Jakes shook his head, "You don't get Springbok colours playing for the A-side. I only played from the bench against Australia. I don't feel as if I can call myself a Springbok yet."

"It's still good to become a Springbok after one season back in Rugby Union," Rayno argued. "And anyway, everyone speculated you would've started the first test if you hadn't suffered an injury. I still can't figure out why they let you play the midweek game if you were in the test squad," Rayno grumbled.

Jakes agreed. He wasn't happy about this injury happening now when he had realised his dream to play a full test for the Springboks. He shrugged, "Too many injuries in the squad."

Rayno smiled, "You had a dream debut. I mean, you scored a try within minutes of arriving on the pitch." Rayno congratulated him.

Jakes flushed, mumbling, "Thank you."

Chris contributed for the first time to the conversation when he asked Jakes, "Sorry that I ask, but how old are you?"

"Twenty-eight."

Chris frowned, "Aren't you old to make your debut for the national squad?"

"Maybe," Jakes admitted. "Some people may think that, but if you're good enough, it doesn't matter how old you are. I have three teammates between thirty-two and thirty-eight. They're fitter than many of the younger guys."

"Rayno mentioned you played Sevens too. Did you enjoy it?" Jesse asked.

Jakes nodded. "Yeah, I did. I played all my senior rugby for the Blitzbokke in the World Sevens Series. I only returned to Rugby Union at the beginning of this year. I had a good run with the Sevens. The only reason I left was that I still had a dream to become a Springbok in the Fifteen Man game."

Jesse asked, "Is this why you came here for therapy?"

"I don't want to be a one-time Springbok," Jakes admitted. "I want to be fit and ready for next season. It's a World Cup year and might be my last chance. With our Head Physio here, the club suggested I join him. I jumped at the chance."

Clara returned with the food, saving Jakes from a further inquisition. When Clara had left, the conversation changed to other subjects.

When Chris realised no one was listening to their conversation, he asked Jakes, "Was it difficult to change between the two codes?"

Jakes shook his head, "Not difficult. There are things to adapt to, like numbers of set pieces, and pace, for example."

Chris glanced at his friends. When their attention was still elsewhere, he asked, "Could I pick your brain sometime? I need to decide."

Jakes studied Chris. He was cautious. There was something about Chris he didn't like. It might be his abrupt way of speaking. Not wanting to cause a scene, he agreed, "Yeah, that's fine."

He hoped it would never come to it though. Chris Johnson might be the type of person Jakes usually avoided.

He turned his head towards the other occupants of the table, making it clear the private conversation was over. Although he didn't contribute much, he listened to the easy banter between them.

Jakes surprised himself by enjoying the time with Rayno and his friends. Maybe it was because he felt the same camaraderie he experienced with his own teammates and friends. For the first time since he arrived in Denver, he relaxed and realised how much he had needed it.

When they got ready to leave, he even exchanged numbers with Rayno and Jesse. Outside, while Jakes waited for his cab, Jesse asked, "What are you doing Friday night?"

Jakes shook his head and grimaced, "Not really. I usually have dinner here and then go home to watch television until I'm too tired to stay awake," Jakes muttered. "Not much different from what I do at home."

Jesse laughed, "Well, come and join us at our clubhouse. We have a pizza and beer night. You can play pool or darts or whatever tickles your fancy."

"And maybe you can meet a nice girl," Mike added when he and the others joined Jakes and Jesse.

The others groaned dramatically. Jesse pointed out to Mike, "You need to find fresh blood, man. You know the only women who would be there will be the staff and the other boys' partners. Find your own."

Jakes wanted to laugh at the consternation on Mike's face, but he didn't need to think too long or hard about the invitation before he agreed. It would be good to go out to get out of his head. He had too much time on his own to think, and he accepted Jesse's invitation. He didn't need one more night thinking about things that should stay buried...

CHAPTER THREE

Angie checked the time. She was running late. She'd made it to the clubhouse with only a minute to spare before her shift began but she could only blame herself. She needed time after her last patient left to recollect herself. Neither Angie nor the psychologist expected the young boy to open so soon about the abuse he suffered at the hands of his stepfather. Luckily they recorded the sessions. If they hadn't, they could've missed this unexpected development.

No amount of training could've prepared her for the things she heard today. She had to put it to the back of her mind. Angie knew that. She couldn't dwell on it the whole night. One of her professors at college ingrained that rule into them. You couldn't take your work home.

Angie stacked the plates and cutlery onto the trolley in the storeroom so she could set the tables while the players were still training. If she hurried, she could be finished before them.

Luckily Uncle Bob *had* found her something else to do. It might not be the most glamorous job, setting tables here and at the restaurant, but she didn't care. It meant she didn't have to deal with the players. Since Uncle Bob took over the clubhouse, some boys ate dinner here. Others preferred to go back to The Whistleblower, their usual hangout.

She bumped the storeroom door open with her hip and pulled the trolley through, muttering under her breath. It didn't matter which way you steered it, it often went its own way. The wheels were sliding in a different direction than you pushed.

All her concentration and attention were on the trolley. She didn't see the other person turning into the corridor ahead of her until it was too late. The cart crashed into the man's leg before Angie could control it, and she heard soft swearing.

Angie didn't have to look. When she heard the voice muttering in a foreign language, she knew who it was. She still turned her head to confirm her suspicion but then she had a second look, then a third.

Wow, if she wasn't panicking right now, she would've drooled over the sight in front of her. Nobody would've blamed her. She thought the stranger had a fabulous body when she saw him in the Henley shirt, but this? Just wow!

He only wore a tank top and training shorts with his trainers. A thin layer of sweat glinted over his smooth, tanned skin. Angie could do nothing other than admiring the well-developed muscles of his arms, legs and the tight backside, but then she noticed a brace covering his upper left leg. It was the same leg he was clutching while he sank down on the carpet.

She stepped around the trolley and would have stepped even closer if he hadn't looked up at her, scowling. He was so angry he didn't even realise he wasn't speaking English. Although she didn't understand a word, his body language and facial expressions said it all. No, the safest way to avoid his anger was to step away and get help. She noticed with concern he had closed his eyes and was taking deep breaths.

When she heard voices, Angie realised help was on its way. She panicked, grabbed the trolley, and rushed into the clubhouse's direction. She should've stayed and made sure he was okay, but today she wouldn't have been able to cope with his rudeness. She still felt too vulnerable. She might have burst into tears at the first harsh word.

She snorted rather unfemininely. He probably had already uttered several. It might be better she couldn't understand him.

Why did she always have to appear clumsy when that man was around? First, it was the water accident, and now, not yet a week later, this. It would be better to avoid him. If she couldn't see him, she couldn't do any damage. The sudden flash of humour surprised Angie, but it evaporated when she remembered the man's anger. She might have deserved it, but she should focus on her work instead.

Five more weeks. That was all she needed to help Clara through her apprenticeship.

In the clubhouse, she set the tables in a hurry. Preparing the last table, she glanced through the window with a view on the training pitch. The players were leaving the pitch. That was the sign for her to do a disappearing act into the background.

Angie promised herself to speak to Uncle Bob about the stupid trolley when she struggled to push it back to the storeroom. They needed to get the thing fixed before she did any more damage with it.

JAKES BELIEVED that his unsuccessful attempt to apologise to the blue-eyed waitress should've been a sign. He was far better off avoiding her. He had too many moments when he thought about her and it made him uncomfortable. He couldn't afford that.

He now wished he could've avoided her for longer. Much,

much longer. Hell, he warned her on the first day she was a danger, and now she'd done what he feared most. He could only hope and pray that she hadn't done serious damage, but the pain wasn't a good omen.

He tried to bite back the swear words rolling off his tongue. The woman should be thankful she didn't understand him. He scowled at the woman who now stepped closer to him with a look of concern.

He closed his eyes and sank down on the carpet, clutching his leg in both hands. Before he could add anything nasty, he heard voices behind him. The woman might have heard it too, as she grabbed the trolley and disappeared in a hurry. If he wasn't in so much pain, he might've admired the speed with which she'd done it.

Michael and one of the other physios knelt concerned next to Jakes. He accepted their support to stand, but when he tried to put weight on his leg, a sudden shot of pain made him feel dizzy.

Jakes needed no one to tell him she *had* done damage. He could only hope it wasn't as bad as it felt.

"I need the Doc, Michael," Jakes managed through shallow breathing.

Michael shook his head in dismay and asked, "What happened?"

In deference to the other physio, Michael spoke English, but Jakes reverted to Afrikaans when he mumbled, "That woman who spilled the water on me in the restaurant? She's a danger with a trolley. This doesn't feel good."

The physio studied him and sighed, "Let's get you to the medical rooms before we jump to conclusions. Do not put weight on it," Michael warned.

Jakes grimaced. There was no need for Michael to warn

him. There was no way he would put any weight on it. He would not do any more damage to it if he could help it.

He swore again at the woman while he hobbled with Michael's support to the doctor's rooms. He had been so confident. His rehab had gone well, and Doc said he might start light training in the next week. He had been so relieved his injury wasn't as severe as they'd first suspected in London, and now this. He could wring the woman's neck.

Hours later, his mood hadn't improved. He was still angry with the woman. When Doc Summers gave Jakes the verdict, it was better news than expected, but Jakes was disappointed. He had put his heart on playing again soon. There were no fractures or sprained muscles at least although the bump had resulted in more inflammation of his already battered leg. The fact she hit him at the same place as his previous injury didn't help.

When he'd arrived from London, his leg had been bruised and swollen. That had caused more discomfort than the strain itself. It was understandable considering that a prop weighing over two-hundred-and-sixty pounds lands on him. The strain was borderline grade two, but Doc Summers didn't want to take any chances. He treated it as a full grade two tear until the swelling disappeared. With the inflammation clearing up within a few days, Jakes healed quicker than expected.

Jakes had enough experience dealing with injuries and pain to last him a lifetime. He also had enough experience with self-doubt to know how to deal with it. The sooner he got back on the field, the better.

Since he'd met the Bears players last week, Jakes spent most of his time with them. He realised he could help the squad while he was here. He spoke to Jesse, their captain and when Jakes mentioned that he might start training again, Jesse invited him to train with them.

Jakes had thought it would be an excellent test. Both Michael and Michael's father, the Buffaloes' head coach, had agreed. Jakes wouldn't have done it without the doctor's approval, but even Doc Summers agreed.

Now he had to wait another couple of weeks before he could return to full training.

ANGIE AVOIDED the giant foreigner in the week since she hit him with the trolley like he had the pest. She heard he became friends with her twin brother. She now knew his name was Jakes and that he was South African. Apparently, he was also helping Jesse's team.

Angie tried so hard to avoid any social situations where she could bump into the man that Jesse was getting upset. At least Angie was busy enough to justify her excuses. Between her two jobs and helping Clara with Thomas, Angie didn't have much free time anyway.

Since nobody had confronted her about Jakes' injury, Angie relaxed. Jakes apparently told everyone that his injury was due to a freak accident.

The team played a friendly match against one of the local clubs on Saturday afternoon. Angie was busy in the storeroom stacking the trolley. She looked up when she heard Chris' voice behind her, "Hey Babe, what are you doing?"

Angie frowned as she turned around. Chris never called her Babe. He should know by now she hated it. Angie realised that Chris wasn't talking to her. He didn't stop at the storeroom and she listened as his voice faded away. Angie leaned out of the doorway. She caught a glimpse of him before he disappeared around the corner, talking on his phone.

Who was Babe?

Angie pondered about this development. She suspected

that Chris was cheating on her the past few weeks, but she had been so busy that she hadn't even had time to think about it.

No, that wasn't the truth. She had, as usual, did everything to avoid confrontation but Angie now didn't have any choice. She had to confront Chris, but today wasn't the time or place.

When Angie finished her duties, she went to sit above the tunnel leading to the locker rooms. She sat there at every home game, so Chris and Jesse knew where to find her. Her eyes drifted to where the team stood in a circle on the pitch with the coach.

Her eyes widened in surprise because it was Jakes talking to the squad, not the coach. Her gaze slid over him in appreciation. Geez, but the man had a body to die for. He was tall and had a powerful physique with all muscles in proportion. The shirt he wore clung to his chest and arms, and the blue jeans moulded his thigh muscles. He most certainly did not carry an ounce of extra fat.

She heard he was causing a stir amongst the local women supporters. It wasn't a surprise considering his physique and attractive looks.

Angie remembered the bright moss-green eyes, strong face and the full mouth which didn't look as if he could smile. And his voice? Oh yes, his tone was rich and deep with a guttural accent...

Angie shook her head, disgusted with herself and turned her eyes to her fiancé, where he stood next to Jakes. There couldn't be a more significant contrast between the two men. Chris looked almost like a boy compared to the South African. Where Jakes had a tan with dark hair and stubble, Chris was far shorter and slimmer with blond hair, blue eyes, and a clean-shaven face.

The game finally kicked off, and Angie had to concentrate on following the game. The first half flew by and at the end of it, the Bears was in the lead. The players all went off the pitch and disappeared into the tunnel. Jesse grinned up at her and Angie smiled back at her twin brother before he followed the squad. Chris was just behind Jesse, but he didn't even make an effort to glance at her.

All thoughts of Chris' behaviour disappeared when Jakes followed the team down the tunnel. For one, or two, maybe three, brief moments, he glanced up and held her eyes without a smile. Angie couldn't look away. They broke eye contact as he disappeared in the tunnel, and Angie blew out her breath.

"Wow, now that was a potent look," Clara observed when she sat down next to Angie.

"Hah, rather a dirty look if you asked me," Angie snorted.

Clara gave her an inquisitive look and Angie realised she might have to come clean. Although still reluctant, Angie told Clara about the trolley incident. She regretted it when Clara couldn't stifle her giggle.

"It's not funny," she glared at Clara. "If you heard how much the guys complained about his 'freak accident', you wouldn't think it's funny. I wanted to apologise, but he was so angry I'd rather avoid him. I'm now glad that I work in the back instead of serving them."

Clara grimaced, "Hm, I have my own ideas about that. I thought Chris upset you, but I'm sorry, Sweetie, tonight you have little choice."

"What do you mean?" Angie asked, confused.

Clara frowned, "Didn't you look at the schedule? You're supposed to work with me in the clubhouse tonight."

"U-ugh," Angie groaned. "You serious?"

Clara nodded, "I know you don't like it, we're two waiters short."

Angie slumped back in her seat. She knew she wasn't a good

waitress. The only reason she did this was to help Clara. For Clara's sake, she would grin and bear it tonight.

After the game, Angie tried every trick in the book to avoid Jakes. Not all of them worked. He stood deep in conversation with Jakes when she delivered Jesse's beer. Jesse grabbed her arm and said, "Angie, may I introduce you to..."

Angie ignored Jakes as she told Jesse abruptly, "I have to go. Speak to you later."

Angie saw Jesse's confused expression and she didn't blame him. She couldn't be friendly to the man when he had been so rude, but she can't explain that to Jesse now.

She heard Jesse's apology to his companion, "I'm sorry, I don't know what it is with Angie. She's not usually so offhand."

Two hours later, Uncle Bob beckoned Angie. She felt wary when she followed him into the office behind the bar. As far as she knew, she had made no mistakes. Bob didn't hesitate, and as soon as he closed the door behind him, he started speaking. Shocked, Angie could only stare at him when he finished, "You're firing me? Why?" she asked, confused, "What did I do?"

Bob looked uncomfortable, "I'm sorry, Angie, but I already gave you your last warning. Management heard you hurt someone. The man is both a patient at the rehab centre and helping the club. They asked that I replace you. As I have nothing else for you... I have to let you go."

"Did he...?" Angie stopped. Of course, the big brute complained. He probably told everyone now what happened.

The... the... Angie couldn't think of a word to describe the man and what he did to justify what she was feeling now.

She took the envelope from Uncle Bob in silence. She wouldn't grovel for this job. She had to make another plan. She grimaced, "I guess you want me to leave now?" she asked.

Bob nodded, "Yes, I'm sorry, Angie."

Angie didn't reply. She left to pick up her bag in the staff room next to the kitchen. She didn't leave, though.

Maybe she should've thought about it more carefully, but she was too angry. On the way to the door, Angie picked up a pitcher with ice water and stalked to where Jakes was sitting with Jesse, Chris and a few others.

Angie heard Jesse asking his companions if they wanted more beer, and they all turned to her to order. Even Jakes lifted his head to look at her. Angie couldn't place the look he gave her. Was it guilt or embarrassment? Well, it didn't matter anymore. He got what he wanted.

His voice sounded completely different from the other times he spoke to her. If she hadn't been so angry, her mouth would've dropped open, but he would not fool her. She hissed, "You can fetch your own beer. I have something else for you."

Angie lifted the jug and poured the ice-cold water over his head. Her brother and his friends protested in shock as Jakes inhaled in shock. Angie dumped the pitcher on the table, turned and left the clubhouse, suddenly calm. The place was quiet apart from the South African's muttering and her brother's protests. Angie didn't care what they thought. She felt so much better for it.

It might not have been fair to Jakes. He wasn't the only one who caused this rebellion. She should've saved some of the water for Chris. *He* might need it to cool down another part of his anatomy.

JAKES DIDN'T KNOW what he'd done to make the woman so angry, but he didn't care anymore. She'd caused him enough damage already.

"What did you do to my sister to make her so angry?" Jesse

asked as he pulled a clean towel from his sports bag and handed it to Jakes.

Confused about Jesse's comment, Jakes rubbed his head and shirt as dry as he could. He had no idea who Jesse was referring to. "Your sister?"

"Angie?" Jesse explained. "The one who poured a jug of water over your head?"

Jakes stared at Jesse. "She's your sister?"

He didn't expect that, but now that he thought about it, Jesse had looked familiar the first time they met. When Jesse nodded, Jakes sighed, "Hell, I had done nothing. I should be angry. She was the one who damaged my leg again last week. The first time I saw her, she spilled water on me in the restaurant. I don't know why she's angry."

The other men at the table glanced at each other. To Jakes' shock, they burst out laughing.

"What the hell?" he exclaimed, standing up. "I can't see what's so funny," he grunted while he threw money on the table.

"Just keep your sister away from me," he said to Jesse before he hobbled away as fast as he could.

It was freezing cold. He was away from home, and somehow, he got on the wrong side of the most beautiful woman he'd ever seen. She was engaged to the biggest asshole on the team. That gave Jakes enough warning signals.

Even though he tried his best, Jakes still couldn't understand why Angie was so angry with him. Was it because he was so rude that first night? He would've apologised a long time ago if he had an opportunity. The only time he saw him was the time she bumped into him with the trolley and again last night. When must he have apologised?

Getting into bed, Jakes realised his pep talk didn't help. He still thought the blue-eyed woman was beautiful, but the fact that she had a fiancé was enough reason for Jakes to stay away. That, together with the list of other reasons, told him why he shouldn't even think about her.

It didn't help, though. He still dreamed of Angie, as he had every night the past week.

CHAPTER FOUR

With what happened the previous night, Jakes hadn't expected Jesse to contact him so soon. Jesse surprised Jakes when he invited him to a pizza-evening at the house he shared with some of his friends. Michael had already informed Jakes he was going out for dinner. Not fancy being on his own, Jakes accepted Jesse's invitation.

Although not keen, Jakes accepted Chris' offer to pick him up. He learned during the week Chris was engaged to Jesse's sister. Since Jesse's sister was the waitress from the restaurant, it might be awkward. He anyway didn't feel comfortable spending time with Chris. It might be because he had noticed how Chris flirted with other women. He had enough experience dealing with a cheater and he didn't wish it on anyone else, even if it was the most frustrating woman Jakes had ever met.

As Jakes expected, Chris had an ulterior motive. The whole way Chris asked about the Sevens, making Jakes wonder why he was so interested. He found it strange how Chris not once asked why Angie poured water over him last night. It would have bothered him if another man caused such a reaction in his fiancée.

There were already a few cars when they arrived. Music and voices drifted through the open doors. Jakes shivered and pushed his hands deeper into the pockets of his jacket. Hell, are these people not cold? He would've closed the doors a long time ago and switched on the heating to full blast.

He followed Chris through the garage, entering through the back door. Rayno, Jesse, and Mike all turned when they came in, then gave Jakes a welcoming smile. "Jakes, glad to see you, man," Jesse reacted first.

Chris pushed a chair towards Jakes and suggested, "Sit. You need not get any taller."

Jakes accepted the invitation and the beer Jesse slid over the table to him. He relaxed when the heat of the kitchen spread through his body while he listened to the four housemates arguing about the toppings of the pizzas. Well, Jesse and Rayno argued. Mike made suggestions, but Chris stayed quiet throughout the debate.

By the time they ended their argument, Jakes had finished his beer. Mike disappeared to a different part of the house and Rayno excused himself to go to the bathroom. When Jesse took out his phone to place the order, Chris got up and invited. "Let's join the others. You want another beer?"

Jakes nodded, and Chris took out two beers while Jakes managed to get up with the help of the table and crutches. In the lounge he offered, "We'll find you a seat then I'll give you your beer. We can't have you hanging around on your crutches the whole night."

Jakes stopped behind Chris when he called, "Any space for a man with an injury?"

When a woman answered, Jakes' heart sank in his shoes. He didn't expect there to be women. Now he wouldn't stay long.

His discomfort increased when Chris stepped aside to introduce Jakes to the woman sitting alone on the couch, "This is Angie. Angie, this is Jakes."

Jakes stared at her, then glared at Jesse. He made it clear to Jesse last night that they should keep her away from him. He wouldn't have accepted the invitation if he had known she would be here.

She stared at him in disbelief before she jumped up and exclaimed, "Who invited you?"

Judging her reaction, she too wasn't happy to see him.

Jesse asked his sister, "Why are you so angry with Jakes?"

Angie answered her brother but still glared at Jakes, "He," she said, pointing to Jakes, "cost me my job."

"Say again?" Jakes asked, confused.

Jesse said to Angie, "What do you mean? What job?"

Her face flushed as she muttered, "The Whistleblower."

Jesse's glance flitted between Jakes and Angie before he asked, "What happened?"

Jakes closed his eyes, then balanced himself on one crutch and leg and rubbed his hand through his hair, "I..."

"He..." Angie started at the same time, but Jesse interrupted.

"One at a time," he instructed. "You," he said, pointing to Jakes.

Suddenly rattled, Jakes glanced around, noticing everyone watching him. He hated being on the spot like this and could already feel the panic rising. "I... You..." was all he managed before Angie asked sarcastically, "What? Now you can't string two sentences together? Don't tell me you struggled when you voiced your complaints about me ?"

Jakes shook his head, but he couldn't get a word out. He knew the symptoms. He wasn't sure if the room was so quiet, or if it was one of the usual signs of a panic attack, but he didn't care anymore. His best option was to remove himself from the situation as fast as he could. He mumbled, "I'm sorry. Best if I leave," before he hobbled out the still-open front door before somebody could stop him.

Jakes had left his jacket and keys in the kitchen, but he didn't feel the cold. He hobbled as far and as fast as his crutches allowed, but he needed to stop and breathe. He leaned against a car parked outside and balanced himself on his uninjured leg so he could get hold of the rubber band on his wrist. He tugged it while doing the breathing exercises he learned as part of his therapy. With his eyes still closed, he concentrated so hard that he didn't see the figure watching him with a concerned expression.

Jakes opened his eyes when Rayno spoke to him in Afrikaans. He had to blink his eyes a couple of times before he could focus on Rayno.

Rayno had Jakes' jacket and keys in his hand. Jakes shrugged into his coat when Rayno handed it to him, mumbling "Thank you."

"You want to leave?" Rayno asked.

"Yes, I'm sorry. I'll get a cab."

Rayno shook his head, "No worries. I'm picking up a friend, so it'll be no bother."

Jakes was quiet in the car on the way back to the apartment. Apart from being embarrassed about the panic attack, he didn't know what to say. When they stopped in front of the building, Jakes mumbled, "I didn't know she got fired."

Rayno said, "I'm not sure what's going on, but don't fret about Angie. Jesse will figure it out."

Jakes mumbled a greeting and got out. He still stood on the sidewalk and watched Rayno driving away. He hoped he could make amends, although he wasn't sure how he could if Angie didn't want to talk to him.

. . .

ANGIE FROWNED at the open doorway through which Jakes had disappeared. She turned back to Jesse to accuse him, "Why did you not tell me you invited him? I wouldn't have come."

"I knew you wouldn't have, that's why I had to get you and Jakes together to figure out what was going on. It seemed my plan has backfired," Jesse grimaced. "Why don't you tell me what's going on? I don't know you like this, Angie."

When Chris said, "You've changed since you moved in with Clara. This is only something Clara would do," Angie had to take a deep breath.

She had enough of Chris and his unfair accusations towards Clara. She glared at Chris, "Stay out of this, *Babe*," she said with emphasis on the last word.

His eyes widened and a guilty flush spread over his face. He turned abruptly and stormed to the kitchen. Angie watched him go. She needed to deal with him soon but not tonight. She turned back to Jesse and hissed, "Ask your friend what's going on."

"I did," Jesse admitted, "But he was as confused as I am. According to Jakes, he had more reason to be angry."

"What?" Angie exclaimed. "What reasons did he have?"

She didn't wait for his answer and grabbed her handbag and jacket. Jesse stopped her before she could leave. "Come on, Angie. You know you can talk to me."

Angie sighed, leaning against her twin brother. She knew he was right, but she couldn't do it now. After the sleepless night, worrying, Angie hadn't much energy left. She shook her head, "Not now. Maybe another time."

While she drove back to Clara's, Angie reflected on the evening and the events of the last few days. It was clear Jakes didn't expect to find her there. She had to admit that it was an unpleasant surprise to her too.

Angie had been impulsive before. It was part of her nature, but she had never been impulsive to the detriment of another person. She already felt ashamed of her spontaneous reaction from last night. And hadn't expected to see Jakes so soon. She was still angry that his complaints got her fired, but she could've handled it differently.

Why does he cause such fierce reaction in her? She didn't understand it. Maybe she should stay away from him. Every time he was in the vicinity, something disastrous happened.

She should do far better by concentrating on finding another part-time job to help Clara. After she'd done that, she could figure out how to deal with Chris.

Angie craved the comfort of her family. Jesse would've been her first choice, but not tonight. As Chris was there and she not in the mood to confront him, Angie took the turn-off to her parent's home.

If it surprised them to see her on a Sunday evening, neither of them showed it. It was only when they had gathered in front of the fireplace with a mug of cocoa each that Angie told them Bob fired her. Even though Angie expected their reaction, she still felt the comfort that they hadn't judged her. They knew why she was doing the extra jobs.

If it hadn't been for helping Clara, Angie would've survived. Her salary at the Community Centre wasn't bad. She was selling enough paintings at the Young Artist's Gallery. It was enough for her needs because she could still live with her parents.

"I only needed to keep it for another month. Clara will be okay then. Where will I find another job? I've been searching everywhere. The few jobs available are for waitressing, and I've already proved I'm not good at it. I think no one would hire me as a waitress after this disaster," she admitted.

"Oh Sweetie, something will come up. It always does," Mary sympathised.

Angie shrugged, "I don't know. I feel like such a failure. Why can't I keep a job?"

"Because all the jobs you took were not for you. We know why you're doing this, Sweetie, and we love you for it. But both your father and I will be grateful when it's over, so you can get back to your painting. When did you last paint?" her mother asked.

Angie admitted. "Not for a while. I'm so tired I couldn't even think about it. I'm also running low on supplies, and I can't buy more until I get another job. I'll have enough money to pay for rent and food but nothing else."

She lifted her hand when her mother wanted to say something. "I know you'll help, but I can't accept it. This was my decision, and I need to deal with it."

"You know we will help if you need it?" Mary insisted.

Angie nodded. "I know. But I need to do this." She smiled, "I only came for TLC."

Her father chuckled, "Then you're in the right place. Your mum said earlier the home is too quiet without you."

"Well, I'll stay here tonight. A night in my own room might be all I need," Angie decided. Before she could change her mind, she sent a message to tell Clara.

"You know your room is always ready. If you're not working tomorrow, you can sleep late and do what you want. You could even paint a little."

Angie shrugged. She would think about it tomorrow because she now was too tired.

. . .

ON MONDAY NIGHT, Jakes opened the door to Jesse. He stood aside for Jesse to enter and followed Jesse to the lounge and waited for him to sit.

Jesse waited until they both took their seats before he confessed, "I'm sorry for putting you on the spot last night. I wanted to figure out what's going on but went the wrong way about it. I only wanted to find out what was going on with Angie."

Jakes sighed. "I didn't know she got fired. I didn't mean to complain about her. I went to apologise because I was rude, but I couldn't find her."

"Wait. You make no sense. Start from the beginning, and leave nothing out," Jesse suggested.

Jakes rubbed his hands through his hair, took a deep breath, and talked. He told Jesse everything without looking at him. When he finished, he looked up and saw to his surprise that Jesse wasn't angry as he expected. No, the man was grinning, confusing Jakes even more.

"Jakes, don't take it all upon yourself. I've spoken to Uncle Bob, and it was only a matter of time. Even Angie would admit she wasn't a good waitress. She hated it. I know why she was doing it, and why she's so upset about losing the job. She only needed it for a few more weeks, then she would have quit anyway."

"Oh," Jakes managed. "Why did she do it then if she hated it so much?"

Jesse sighed. "To help her friend Clara. Angie and Clara have been friends since we were five years old. Clara and her sister Amy never had a good family life and spent most of their time with our family. When we were eighteen, Clara eloped to marry a guy two years ahead of us in school."

"Simon was a nice guy. He was home from Afghanistan when they eloped. Clara's family disowned her and moved away. Since then, they've had no contact with Clara. Simon died in Afghanistan when Clara was six months pregnant. Angie did everything she could to help Clara. You can't help but admire Clara. She studied and worked part-time and brought Thomas up with only Angie's help while completing her degree. She still needed to complete her internship, but it would've meant less salary than she'd earned and might not have coped financially. That's when Angie stepped in and moved in with Clara. She worked two jobs so she could contribute to the rent and food. The rest of the time, she took care of Thomas so Clara could work. Clara is almost finished with her internship. She already has a job lined up with a good salary, so it's only for another few weeks."

Jakes groaned, "Geez, now I feel bad. Can't I speak to the owner?"

"No, it won't work. As I said, I spoke to Uncle Bob. He didn't have much choice to fire her when the club management complained because she hurt you with the trolley."

Jakes frowned, "How did they find out about it? I told no one, not even your father." The realisation then hit. "Michael. He was the only one who knew what happened. I blurted it out in pain, I guess."

"Must have been him," Jesse agreed. He studied Jakes with a thoughtful expression, "I'm curious. Why did you tell no one what happened? I mean, you could have told us what happened?"

Jakes flushed. Geez, he didn't even know himself why. He had his suspicions, but there was no way he could tell Jesse that. He mumbled, "I didn't want to get her into trouble. I still feel bad because I was so rude to her."

Jakes didn't even want to think what went through Jesse's mind. He had seen Jesse's grin even though the other man tried to suppress it.

Jesse stayed quiet, thinking about something then suddenly asked, "You mentioned you wanted to take a few sightseeing tours while you're here. Do you still want to do that?"

Jakes nodded, surprised by the sudden change of the topic.

And you said you feel bad because Angie lost her job?"

Jakes nodded again. Where was Jesse going with all these questions?

Jesse did not wait long to inform him, "Then I may have a solution for both you and Angie."

"What do you mean?" Jakes asked now suspicious.

Jesse grinned, "Angie can be your tour guide. You can pay her the fee instead of a tour company."

Jakes' heart missed a beat or two. He stared at Jesse, thinking about his suggestion. At least he shook his head. "I don't think it's a good idea. She doesn't like me and..." Jakes swallowed before he continued. "I'm not good with women. I don't talk much. It'll be awkward."

"What if she said yes?" Jesse probed, "Will you do it then?"

Jakes still didn't think it was a good idea. He knew he was already more aware of her than he had been of any other woman in a long time. "What about her fiancé? What would he say?"

Jesse frowned, "He can't say much. He's not prepared to help her."

It was Jakes' turn to frown. He couldn't figure Chris and Angie's relationship out yet, but it wasn't his business. He couldn't get involved, but he got the impression that Jesse wasn't happy with Chris.

Jesse tried to convince Jakes again. "Come on, Jakes, it's the only way I can think of to help Angie."

Jakes wanted to make sure he understood Jesse's suggestion correctly, "You want me to hire Angie as a tour guide to help her. You know Angie doesn't like me and might refuse to do it?"

"It's worth a try," Jesse argued. "And you said you felt bad about Angie losing her job."

"I feel guilty, but I still don't think it's a good idea. Maybe if Angie agreed, which I doubt..." Jakes mused about the possibility.

He should have known Jesse would jump on his half-hearted agreement. Jesse didn't give Jakes any more time to protest, "Leave Angie to me. I know my sister better than anyone else."

Jakes stared at Jesse. His heart pounded louder than an African drum when he thought about the possibility. What happened to all his pep talks about staying away from the woman and keeping his focus? And why on earth did he even consider doing it when he knew it would end in disaster? He knew himself.

Though he still felt it was a wrong decision, he could feel the growing anticipation of seeing her again.

Not a good idea, Du Plessis. Not a good idea at all.

CHAPTER FIVE

Angie stared at the man standing behind Jesse. Jakes was gripping the crutches so tight that his knuckles showed white. He was clearly as uncomfortable as she was. Angie was still in two minds about Jesse's idea, but after three days of not finding another job, she didn't have a choice. At the end of next week, she had to pay her contribution to the rent.

Even after Angie gave in, it still took some convincing from Jesse for her to join them tonight for the basketball game at the University. If Rayno and Monica didn't join them, Angie would definitely have found an excuse.

How had Jesse managed to convince Jakes? If she had to judge his facial expression, he wasn't comfortable being here. He hadn't even glanced in her direction once. Sy looked down at her shoes and nibbled her bottom lip. Maybe she should leave. This was obviously not going to work out.

She looked up when Jakes' brusque voice spoke up close to her, "I'm sorry. I should rather leave."

Angie shook her head but couldn't meet his eyes. She still

remembered the effect that green eyes had on her. She wanted to turn to follow Jesse when Jakes cleared his throat and mumbled, "Angie?" Only her name, but there was a question in it somewhere.

Angie made a mistake to look up. The uncertainty in his eyes and voice hit her like a sledgehammer. She couldn't even doubt his sincerity as it filtered through in his deep voice. Maybe, just maybe, Jakes du Plessis wasn't such a jerk as she thought.

"I'm sorry you lost your job. I'm sorry I was so grumpy. It's no excuse I know, but I came off a ten-hour flight. I was tired and grumpy and in pain. I went back on Saturday, and the following week to apologise, but I couldn't find you. I also told no one apart from Michael about your involvement with the trolley. If you want to get your job back rather than doing this, I can talk to the owner."

Angie stared at him in surprise. Not only because that was the most she ever heard him speak but also because of his suggestion. Why would he do that? That question was, however, even if he convinced Uncle Bob, did she want her old job back? She shuddered, just thinking about it and shook her head, "No, you don't have to."

He still looked uncertain. Angie probably shocked him when she grinned, "I have to be honest. I sucked at waitressing. You actually did me a favour."

Wow, those green eyes that looked as if they could see straight to her soul, widened when he stammered, "You did? I mean, I did?"

There wasn't even a glimpse of a smile touching his face. Angie's laughter filtered away. Maybe she was the only one who saw the humour in the situation. It might not be so funny to me on the receiving end of a jug of cold water, and a wayward trolley.

She blushed uncomfortably. This wasn't Jesse's best idea. It was a stupid idea, and she should never have let Jesse convinced her. She had to find something else.

She didn't want Jakes to see how uncomfortable she was and turned in a hurry to walk away. She didn't get very far before Jakes called her back. Angie stopped. His voice was low and tentative, and she had to strain her ears to listen to what he said.

"I'm sorry. I told Jesse this wasn't a good idea."

She turned to face him. This time she looked at Jakes without getting lost in his eyes. She noticed the rubber band on his left hand for the first time. The thumb and index finger of his right hand rubbed with agitated movements over the rubber band. Her eyes lifted to his face, taking in his clenched jaw. He didn't make eye contact, glancing away, uncertain, as if he was ready to flee at any moment.

Angie realised what was going on. Jakes was close to a panic attack. The only reason she recognised the signs was because it formed part of her course.

That was when Angie realised. This man was close to getting a panic attack. She could only read the signs because they dealt with it during her art therapy course.

Did she cause it? It was possible.

She took a deep breath and muttered, "I appreciate your offer, Jakes, but if you feel uncomfortable, we don't have to do this. I'll find something else."

His eyes briefly flitted to her before he looked away again. "It's not you."

As he turned and hobbled away on his crutches, Angie watched his slow movements. She closed her eyes and sighed. Well, that was it then. Back to square one.

Her eyes darted open when she heard his voice. He came

back! He still looked nervous, but his voice sounded more determined. "I'm sorry. Could we try again?"

Angie was curious. "Why? Why did you change your mind?"

"It doesn't matter whether it's you or someone else. I'll respond the same with any other tour guide. I need to warn you, though. I don't talk a lot, and sometimes I need space."

Angie nodded, "I understand. Would you mind if I talk?"

"I don't mind." he mumbled.

"So, we're good?"

He took a deep breath and nodded.

Angie studied him for a moment. She had to ask, just to make sure he was really okay with the arrangement. "Okay, we need to agree on a few things."

He grabbed his backpack from his shoulder and took out a document. "I've drawn up a contract."

Angie's mouth dropped open. She hadn't expected that! She wanted to laugh, but he looked so grave that she didn't want to embarrass him. She corrected him with a smile, "Okay. But that's not what I meant."

He frowned at her, a confused expression on his face.

Angie tried to explain, "I need you to tell me when you feel uncomfortable. You must also be honest about what you like and dislike. Things otherwise may get uncomfortable."

He nodded relieved. "Oh, okay."

"And I don't want you to feel you owe me this job. If you don't want to do this anymore, tell me."

"Okay," he agreed.

Angie narrowed her eyes before she added, "And accept my apology."

"Which one?" he asked.

"What do you mean?" Angie asked, now confused.

"For spilling water on me? Or running into me with the trolley or pouring water over my head?"

Angie couldn't get a word out at first. Not because he was right and she had to apologise, but because she was fascinated with the glint in his eyes. Maybe the man had a sense of humour, after all.

Angie laughed embarrassed, cursing the flush that heated her skin, "I guess all three."

"Apology accepted," he nodded sagely.

Angie watched fascinated at the transformation when his face softened and his mouth turned up in a crooked smile.

Jakes managed to draw her gaze away from his face when he balanced himself on one crutch and held out his hand. "I guess you have a job then."

Angie didn't think twice about taking his hand to shake on their deal. The sudden flush of heat rushed from their hands through her body. Her eyes flew up to meet his green ones in surprise, and there it stayed. Had he felt it too? Probably, as neither of them broke eye contact or let go of the other one's hand until Jesse spoke next to him. Their reaction is the same and instinctive. They dropped each other's hands and looked away. Angie kept herself busy by putting the document Jakes gave her in her bag and Jakes had an intense interest in his shoes.

"I guess you two have come to an agreement?"

Angie heard Jesse's remark, but she dare not look at him. She nodded, still confused about her reaction. There was no way Angie would be able to hide it from Jesse. She heard Jakes mumble something but couldn't make out what he said. Maybe Jesse could as he turned towards the stands and called over his shoulder, "Now come on, we have a game to watch."

Angie followed him quickly. When they reached their seats, she made sure she sat as far away from Jakes and Jesse as possible. She needed to compose herself. Monica was so infatuated with Rayno that she luckily didn't notice anything amiss.

What happened when they shook hands? It was unexpected but then, maybe it shouldn't be. Didn't it also happen that night at the Whistleblower?

Whatever it was, she couldn't let it happen again. She had a job, even if it was only a temporary one and she needed to concentrate on that.

She couldn't concentrate on the game, however, as her mind was in turmoil. She was actually surprised when the game ended. She just fell in with the other's suggestion to go to The Whistleblower. She hadn't heard a word of the conversation, but she couldn't admit it now. Jesse, especially, would know that something was going on with her. He already teased her earlier when she didn't hear him asking her if she wanted a hot dog. She said yes, even though she didn't really want one. And now again.

And the worst of it all was that she didn't know what was going on with her. She could get scatterbrained sometimes, but tonight it felt ten times worse. Why?

Angie had her answer a few minutes later when they waited for the cabs outside the stadium. Angie looked up to find Jakes watching her. When he caught her eyes, he mumbled, "Uhm, you have mustard...," pointing to her face.

Angie blushed and tried to wipe it away, uncertain if she got the right spot. Apparently not, as Jakes lifted his hand and used his thumb to clear the last remnants of her hot dog away. As soon as he touched her, Angie felt a similar electric shock as she had earlier.

His thumb lingered at the corner of her mouth when their eyes met and held. She thought his eyes were moss-green, but now they had darkened to the colour of an old tree. His thumb brushed lightly over her cheek before he dropped his hand when the cabs arrived.

They still stared at each other for a couple of moments, but then they both scattered away to get into a different cab as if that would help. Nothing, but nothing, could wipe that moment from Angie's memory.

BACK AT THE WHISTLEBLOWER, Jakes sat at the end of the table, stretching his leg out in front of him. He would've felt comfortable if Angie hadn't taken the seat next to him with Jesse on her other side and Rayno and Monica across the table from them.

Jakes tried to stifle his unease. He was so conscious of Angie next to him, but now that they came to an agreement, he had to make an effort to get to know her. The problem was that he didn't know how to do it. It had been a very long time since he had to get to know a woman from scratch.

When the silence lasted too long, Jakes cleared his throat and asked, "Jesse mentioned that you work at the community centre. Tell me more about your job."

Jakes completely forgot about his discomfort when Angie started speaking. He stared at her, utterly fascinated. Yes, she hadn't lied. She loved to talk that wasn't the only thing keeping him captivated. He loved how her eyes and face lit up, her hands also contributing to the conversation. They fluttered each time she explained something.

She looked completely different from the woman he'd seen the first time. She'd then looked nervous, but he guessed he'd contributed to that. He heard often enough that he looked intimidating. Jakes knew he was the least intimidating person. It might be because of his size or because he didn't smile much —not with strangers anyway. And he had been grumpy that night which wouldn't have helped to squash that illusion. It was only when people got to know him that they realised that he was anything but intimidating.

Jesse spoke to Angie and Jakes drifted off, lost in his own thoughts. He and Angie had made peace and she'd apologised but Jakes was still wary. He had enough experience to know that apologies come easy. It had taught him not to trust easily.

He observed Angie while she chatted to the group. Her natural smile kept him fascinated. It often resulted in a soft laugh. The way she made him feel scared the living daylights out of him.

He might have made a mistake with this job thing. He realised that first night that he had to stay away from her and now Jesse managed to convince him to give her a chance. He had committed himself to spend more time with her than he should. How was he going to cope with it?

He had to be careful. He couldn't let Angie get too close.

Jakes closed his eyes and visualised the other women he knew. Most he knew only in their professional capacity like Chloe, their nutritionist and Hannah, the sports scientist. He might need to treat Angie the same way he treated them, as colleagues and only colleagues.

Satisfied with his decision, Jakes relaxed. Through the snippets of conversation, Jakes heard a song he recognised. It was one of his favourite songs and he drummed the beat on his beer bottle.

Angie startled him when she teased, "I guess you like the music?"

Jakes mumbled, "Yes." That was all he could get out.

Angie might've expected him to elaborate as she stared at him. Jakes didn't know what to say.

He still didn't trust this sudden friendliness. Last week she'd given him a hard time, and now she was as friendly as a week-old kitten. Jakes had learned as a child never to trust kittens. They look all sweet and cuddly, but their nails and teeth are sharp, and they can use them anytime.

He knew Angie was still waiting for him to answer, but he'd rather keep quiet. He had warned her. She didn't look too bothered and carried on talking.

Angie didn't let his surliness stop her. She asked, obviously interested, "I've heard the name Jake before, but never Jakes. Is it your real name?"

The question surprised Jakes and so his reaction when his mouth curled up in one corner. "No."

Wow, even to him that one-word answer sounded rude. He might need to elaborate. He took a deep breath and added, "I'm named John-Jacques after my two grandfathers. My father's name is John, so my family called me Jacques. In high school, my teammates called me Jake. One day after a match, the coach said I had such a good game it was as if there were two Jakes' on the field. The name stuck."

He drifted off again, surprised at how much he'd revealed. It could be a record. Other people had said before how talking to him was like pulling teeth. If you didn't ask him a question, he wouldn't volunteer information.

Angie caught on. Before he could retreat into his shell, she asked, "Have you thought which places you want to visit?"

He didn't miss her amused expression when he pulled another paper out of his backpack. Jakes knew himself. He had to be prepared. It was the only way he could deal with the situation. Angie could anyway plan their excursions if she knew what he liked and what he wanted to see.

She took the paper from him and studied it. Judging by her expression, she hadn't expected some of the things he wanted to see and experience. He had to thank his coach at the Sevens for that. He taught them they shouldn't only focus on the tournament. They must treat the whole experience as making memories; since then, he did just that.

Angie didn't comment on his choices in front of everyone else. It should be a good sign they might get along better than he expected.

Exploring with a local would be nice, but he still had a bad feeling about spending too much time with Angie. It wouldn't take much to fall for her. He was already way too attracted to her.

ANGIE WAS ABOUT to enter the coffee shop when someone called her name. She turned when she recognised Jakes' voice. She was even more surprised when she realised he was not using the crutches. He still walked with an awkward stiffness. A brace covered his tracksuit pants.

He must have had a shower, as his hair was still damp. A tight, long-sleeve T-shirt hugged the muscled chest and arms. Angie didn't have to look around to know that the women in the coffee shop were admiring him. Jakes was oblivious as he kept his eyes focused on her.

When he reached her, she asked, "You finished for the day?"

Jakes shook his head, "No, I have a break. I need something to eat before I have another session with the physio. You?"

"I'm on my lunch break," Angie admitted. She needed something to take her mind off the session she just had with yet another abused child. It seemed she got more than she had hoped for when Jakes asked, "Mind if I join you?"

Mind? Why would she? She noticed the uncertain pull of his mouth and suppress that thought. They knew each other and since they were both here alone, it would be ridiculous to eat alone. It would anyway give them a chance to finalise their plans for their first excursion.

When Jakes still hesitated, Angie realised that she hadn't given him an answer yet. She replied quickly, "No, of course not," and turned to walk in front of him. Angie was extremely conscious of his large frame following close behind her when the waitress directed them to a table in the corner. His reaction was swift when he reached around Angie to pull out her chair. When last had it happened that a man, except her father or brothers, pulled out a chair for her?

She mumbled thanks while she thought about it. Jakes did it without a thought as if it was second nature to him. It might be if she had to judge the way he spoke to the waitress.

He caught her look. The left corner of his mouth curled up when he admitted. "I'm not always so grumpy."

Angie laughed. "I've noticed."

An uncomfortable silence fell over them in the time it took the waitress to fetch their coffees. Jakes warned her that he didn't talk much and she boasted that she spoke enough for both of them. She thought frantically of something to talk about while she waited for the waitress to deliver the coffees. And of all the brilliant subjects she thought about, she chose to ask, "You ditched the crutches?"

Jakes nodded, "Yes, I saw your father earlier. The newest MRI showed my injury wasn't so severe. I may still have to use the crutches when we walk far, but I can start light training with the team next week.

"That's great news," Angie said relieved. Now, she didn't feel so bad about the ridiculous trolley incident. "Are you up for sightseeing then?" Angie asked.

She took a sip of her coffee while she waited for his reply. She was in two minds whether or not she wanted him to pull out. Maybe it was better if he didn't want to continue. On the other hand...

She didn't even want to think about the other side of that

argument. It was that side that made that Angie breathed an inward sigh of relief when he nodded.

She wasn't the only one who still worried about the wisdom of their arrangement. Jakes did too but for a different reason than Angie. " I'll talk to Chris to make sure he's okay with our arrangement."

It didn't look like he was keen to do that. Angie didn't blame him because if she didn't want to speak to her fiancé, why would he? She shook her head, "That's unnecessary. I already told Chris you offered me a job."

It didn't bother Chris that Angie was going to explore the city with a strange man. And a handsome man, Angie had to add. No, Chris hadn't worry about that. As usual, he only moaned because she did it to help Clara.

Jakes didn't reply as the waiter brought their food. During lunch, they spoke about the route Angie had planned for their first excursion. Or rather, Angie spoke and Jakes only agreed with her suggestions. They were still lingering over a coffee when the alarm on Angie's phone beeped.

Angie blushed when she cancelled the alarm. She had noticed Jakes frown and quickly explained, "I need to get back to work. I set the alarm before I forget."

To Angie's surprise, Jakes remarked, amused, "You're scatter-brained, aren't you?" She nodded, now even more embarrassed. It might not be a good thing to admit to your boss, even if it was a temporary arrangement.

He quickly reassured her, which surprised her even more because he offered information voluntarily and even more so because it didn't seem to bother him that she was scatter-brained. "I'm used to it. My mum's a sculptor. I guess all the arty types are all the same."

.   .   .

ANGIE LEARNED VERY QUICKLY that Jakes hadn't lied. He was a man of few words and if she meant few, it was really a few. Despite that, she also learned from his few remarks and the type of questions that he asked, that Jakes was intelligent. He was also inquisitive and interested in everything.

He mentioned that his mother was a sculptor, but he still surprised Angie when he voluntarily visited an art gallery or two. Chris hated it to go with her and was even reluctant to attend Angie's one and only opening night. Jakes, however, enjoyed it and he had a clear stance on what he liked and didn't like, and abstract art wasn't his favourite.

The discussion on what he liked followed after they visited the National Gallery. Angie had already thought that Jakes was way too solemn and decided to tease him when he asked her about her paintings. She pretended to be embarrassed when she declared, "It's a shame that you don't like abstracts."

"Why?" he asked suspiciously.

Angie suppressed her smile. "Because you won't like my work then."

His eyes widened and his face turned a bright red. He stuttered over his words, "Geez, I'm sorry. I should've kept my mouth shut."

He looked so cute when he couldn't apologise enough, that Angie couldn't suppress the laughter any longer. Jakes first stared at her shocked but when he suspected that she was teasing him, he needed to confirm it, "You are only teasing, aren't you?"

Angie nodded as she wiped the tears away. Jakes exhaled and admitted, "You got me there, but I will get you back."

The next moment it was Angie's turn to be surprised, so much so that she almost missed his warning to get her back. More than that, she was possibly drooling when his mouth not only curled up in the one corner as he rarely did. No, today it curled up at both sides in a proper smile. Her thoughts were erratic when the effect of that smile on her, rushed through her. Maybe it was not such a bad thing that he didn't smile often. The women already couldn't keep their eyes off him. If he smiled like that regularly, they would fall over their feet for him.

He had to notice that she was staring at him because that smile disappeared as fast as it had appeared. The surly man she met the first time was back. Before she could do anything, he mumbled an excuse that he needed the bathroom and fled back to the building they had just left.

Angie stared at the door when it closed behind him. Now what?

JAKES' heart was still beating fast when he stormed into the bathroom. How the hell did that happen? He had been careful, or hadn't he?

He rinsed his face a couple of times with cold water, but it didn't help. He had to face the facts.

He scrunched the paper towel he used and threw it in the bin. His mind drifted back to what happened. He didn't even have to close his eyes or think too hard about it. He can recall it quite vividly.

He could blame it on that infectious laughter that caused him to smile with her. Smile? When last had he done that and so spontaneously? And that with a woman who was not his mother or sister?

It made him realise that he was way too comfortable with Angie, and that was only after one week.

What was he going to do about it? He shook his head. He had no idea, but it wouldn't help to worry about it now. He couldn't let Angie wait outside in the cold while he hid inside the bathroom.

As the English say, "In for a penny, in for a pound." He was here. He now needed to make the best of the situation.

And *not* fall for Angie.

Tell that to the birds. The warning of not falling for Angie came way too late. Jakes realised it as soon as he got outside and noticed Angie's worried expression. If a woman gave you a warm feeling when she smiled, if you worry that you hurt her or made her worry, then it was already too late. If that wasn't a sign that he had fallen for Angie already, Jakes didn't know.

As long as he realised that that was where it would stay.

And then he might as well reassure her, which he did summarily, "I'm sorry that I kept you waiting. And because you teased me, you now owe me something."

"What?" she asked uncertainly.

"I want to see some of your paintings," Jakes answered firmly.

"Are you sure?"

"Yes, I'm sure."

Angie exhaled and mumbled, "Then come."

THEY HAVEN'T SPOKEN MUCH since Jakes insisted that he wanted to see her paintings. Angie was more nervous than she wanted to admit and she didn't even know why. Why would it matter if he liked her work or not?

But a nagging voice at the back of her mind kept on telling her that it *did* matter. She *wanted* Jakes to like her work.

Before she could ponder about it any longer, they arrived at the Young Artists' Gallery where there was still two of her paintings. Angie didn't take Jakes straight to the corner where her artwork was displayed, because she didn't want to influence him. She let him browse through the gallery and followed in his wake. Sometimes he would stop and studied one for longer or made a comment. Angie may explain more about the painting or the artist.

The closer they got to the first of the two paintings, the faster her heart beat. She kept her breath when Jakes stopped in front of it to study it carefully. He should recognise the scene even though it hadn't snowed when they visited City Park this morning as it had in the painting. As with some of the other artwork he'd seen, he expressed his appreciation, "Now this is what I like. It is something I can recognise."

WHEN ANGIE DIDN'T ANSWER, Jakes turned to her. Of course, he had to see her unnatural colouring. His eyes narrowed and he turned back to the painting. He leaned closer to read the name of the artist.

Angie didn't look at the painting but kept her eyes on Jakes. His appreciation was sincere when he remarked, "Wow! I guess you're *A Summer.*"

When Angie nodded, Jakes shook his head, "You're incredibly talented. Why do you still do odd jobs if you could paint like this?"

Angie shrugged. "My dad insisted that I studied so that I have something to fall back on if things didn't work out. I first studied for a teaching degree but didn't like it. I love helping people and art therapy was a good course for me."

"That's a shame," Jakes muttered. He turned to her and frowned, "But I heard the uncertainty in your voice."

Angie leaned closer to him and whispered, "Can I tell you a secret?"

Jakes leaned down to hear what she wanted to confess and whispered back, "Yes, of course."

"You are right. I don't want to be an art therapist anymore. My heart breaks every time I have to work with an abused child.

The older people whose highlight of the week is the hour or two I spend with them, have the same effect on me."

"You're a softie," Jakes said, nudging her arm.

Angie couldn't even disagree because he was right. "I am."

Jakes turned to her. His eyes were intense when he advised, "Follow your dreams, Angie. Don't waste your talent."

How couldn't she believe him when he was so open and honest? He didn't make any secret of his belief in and the appreciation of her art. She had enough time to witness his reaction in the other galleries. He was not pretending.

Then why did it have to be a stranger, a man she barely knew, who steadfastly believed in her when her so-called fiancé didn't give a damn?

Didn't it say something about their relationship?

CHAPTER SIX

J akes turned to the television above the bar, showing one of
the English Premier League Football Games. He wasn't a
huge football fan but watched a few games when he was
bored. He had often wondered why the round ball didn't
interest him as much as the oval ball. He didn't even try to play
football.

He had his answer when one player went down in a
dramatic fall after a light ankle tap and shook his head in
disgust. Someone snorted next to him, "Wimp." Jakes didn't
even have to look to know that it was Angie. She stared at the
TV with a frown. He had already recognised her perfume and
voice, but he still looked, surprised that she was so early.

His mouth curled up when she turned towards him, rolling
her eyes. "I guess you don't like football?"

Angie frowned for a moment, then laughed, "Oh, soccer.
No, absolutely not. The other player barely touched his leg, and
he rolled on the ground as if he'd broken it. He could get an
Oscar for that performance."

"I thought Americans like football, sorry soccer," Jakes

ventured.

Angie smiled. "Well, after baseball, basketball and American football, yes, I guess soccer is popular. But my family prefers rugby union."

Jakes nodded, "Yep, I've noticed."

Angie placed her order with the barman. When their drinks arrived, Jakes settled the bill. With their drinks in hand, they ambled across to the booth to wait for the others.

It still surprised Jakes how easy it was to talk to Angie. It came as natural to him as talking to his family and friends. He wasn't used to it, but it didn't surprise him when he answered her next question too without thinking about it.

"Have you played any other sport or have you only played rugby?"

Jakes had answered that question in many interviews before and didn't have to think about it. "I went to a primary school in a small town in the Free State. We only had a few boys, so I played cricket, and I did athletics and swimming to make up the teams. It was different with rugby though. It was the one game where I played my heart out."

"Why rugby?"

Jakes took a sip of his beer before he answered. "A few farms away from us lived a man who played for the Springboks. When I was five, my dad took me to a test match at Loftus Versveld to see him play against the All Blacks. I already knew then that it was all I wanted to do."

"When did you start playing?" Angie quizzed again.

"I played my first match the following year when I started school, and I loved it."

Angie looked so interested that Jakes didn't hesitate to answer her next question. "But why do you love it so much? What is it that draws you to the game?"

"It's difficult to explain. Maybe it's like your painting? It's your calling, or it's not. I like the physicality of the game, even though it comes with lots of aches and pains. The game has taught me so much."

"Like what?"

Jakes had to think hard on how to explain it. "Apart from the discipline, friendship, sportsmanship, teamwork and respect? I don't know. I enjoy being part of a team and the camaraderie. I even like the bantering between us, which is saying a lot coming from an introvert. It might have to do about the way we interact with teammates and opponents. It may be physical on the pitch when you tackle your opposite number hard, but then you help him up, and afterwards, you have a cold beer together. You don't always get that in competitive sports."

He took another sip before he continued, "Those boys are not only my teammates. They're my friends, my family. When I went through a bad patch, I always had rugby. It helped me to concentrate on something other than myself. That and the support of my teammates and the club..."

Jakes cleared his throat before he added, "I was a shy teenager. I still am an introvert, but rugby gave me confidence. I'll never be the most talkative guy, but when I talk about the game? It's different."

"I've noticed," Angie grinned. "When you talk about rugby, it's as if your whole face lights up."

Jakes knew it was the truth, but he wasn't even surprised that Angie had picked up on it too. It still made him wary, but since that day she took him to view her paintings, things changed. He kept on warning himself to keep a distance, but every day he spent with her, he could feel and see the boundaries sliding away. Take this afternoon as an example.

Previously Jakes would've asked Rayno's or Jesse's assistance when he realised he needed clothes more suitable for this weather. The locals said the weather was mild, but according to their standards. His thin South African blood wasn't used to it. He only took a few personal items to the UK because when you tour with the Springboks, your whole suitcase consisted of items the Springboks supplied, from tracksuits, warm jackets and both formal and informal clothes. He definitely was not going to wear that here.

When the weather deteriorated this afternoon, both Angie and Jakes agreed that it might be better to end their excursion for the day. Jakes had shocked himself when they got outside the Sports Hall of Fame and the cold hit him, that he asked Angie, "I need to buy warm clothes. Will you help me?"

As it did every time, her smile hit him in the solar plexus when she immediately agreed. "I know just the place. It is one of the many places I've worked before but didn't last long," she confided while she flagged down a passing cab.

Jakes knew how he struggled to find clothes to fit him and asked with a doubtful frown, "Will they have clothes that would fit me and be warm?"

Angie nodded confidently, "Yes, it's only for big and tall men, so if you can't find something there, you may struggle. You won't believe it, but there are bigger men than you, although they don't all have a body such as yours...."

She trailed off and a blush spread over her cheeks. She turned her face to look out of the window, but Jakes had seen it. He had to suppress his smile. That was the first time he'd seen Angie at a loss for words and embarrassed, and he had to admit, he liked it that she admired his body.

Luckily they arrived at the shop and he didn't have to analyse the reason why that knowledge made him feel so good.

Jakes had never been an enthusiastic clothes hopper. He usually lived in his kit or jeans, shorts and T-shirts, most of it sponsored. His publicist, Sue, often did his shopping if Jakes needed something for an event. His mother and sister frequently bought shirts for him, but the rest he picked up as he went along, which didn't happen very often.

Not that he had to worry about what to buy. Even though Angie might be a bit scatterbrained, she still had good taste. In no time, Angie, with the help of a sales assistant, got Jakes enough warm clothes to see him through his stay. If Jakes had to judge, she made sure he had something for every eventuality.

After he settled the bill, Angie insisted he changed into his new gear. When they got back outside, Jakes appreciated the warmer clothes. He had, on Angie's suggestion, changed into layers, and he felt the difference.

The door opened, and the others drifted in. Jakes studied Angie and Chris when he greeted her–if you can call it a greeting. It didn't have anything to do with him, but it bothered him. He had a business agreement with Angie, and it would be best if he remembers that.

Jakes sighed under his breath. That argument wasn't working anymore. In the few days he'd spent time with Angie, he could feel his resistance crumbling. He could understand why when he listened to the conversation around him. They were making plans for the weekend, or rather, Angie planned as she had done with their excursions that week. Jakes didn't mind it and would fall in with their plans.

He listened to the others discussing the weekend's plans. Jakes let Angie do most of the planning as she had for that week. He didn't mind falling in with whatever they decided.

Jesse suggested that they meet at their house the next evening. When Jesse mentioned that they could get food delivered, Jakes shook his head. He was sick and tired of takeaway food. His appetite evaporated just thinking of having another burger or a pizza and he, therefore, suggested quickly, "I can make dinner if you would allow me?"

All eyes turned to him, but for once, Jakes didn't feel

uncomfortable.

"I take it that you can cook if you make a suggestion like that," Jesse remarked then snorted. "For goodness sake, Dude. What can't you do? How must a guy compete with you?" but then he laughed, "But Bro', I won't say no to that offer."

The others chorused their agreement.

JAKES LISTENED to Angie's chatter as he chopped the chicken breasts in smaller pieces. He was grateful he had something to occupy his hands and mind from what he had witnessed this afternoon. Jakes didn't want to look at Angie now. How could he look her into the eyes and *not* tell her? Anyway, should he tell her?

When he finished chopping the chicken, he covered it in cling wrap and then kept himself busy washing the chopping board and knife, leaving them in the drying rack. He took out a clean board and pulled the bowl with the vegetables closer. While he was busy with the chicken, Angie had peeled it, although under protest.

He might play what was according to some people a violent game, but Jakes wasn't a violent person. Today, however, he had been close to hitting someone. He frowned when he remembered what he saw on his arrival. He had to take a deep breath to calm himself when he got agitated again.

He took a clean chopping board and gathered the vegetables Angie had peeled. He chopped the carrots with more aggression than necessary and didn't see Angie's look of concern. He would've if he weren't so angry. Sudden humour flashed through the anger. It was better he murdered the poor carrots than doing what he wanted to do earlier.

He frowned when he recalled the events of this afternoon. When they made the arrangements for today, Chris mentioned that he would be home at around four to let Jakes in if he wanted to start with the preparations for dinner. Jakes usually finished mid-afternoon on Fridays and since he decided on a chicken- and vegetable curry, he wanted to start early so that the curry can simmer. Michael, however, had made arrangements to go see his brother play a tennis tournament in Boulder and they finished even earlier than Jakes anticipated. Even his shopping didn't take long. The cab dropped him off twenty minutes earlier than the arranged time.

Jakes hadn't even paid the driver when the front door opened, and Chris came out of the house. He was not alone and the woman with him, her hair and clothes in a similar dishevelled state as Chris', greeted him with a passionate embrace, It was evident that they hadn't been playing cards unless it had been poker and Chris had lost half his clothes in a bet.

The woman wasn't Angie.

Chris hadn't even realised that Jakes had been watching them. When the woman drove away, he glanced at his watch and disappeared into the house. The cab driver had given Jakes curious looks when he struggled to suppress his fury.

Many people think that rugby is an aggressive game, but Jakes was the least aggressive person. Today, however, he came very close to hitting someone. The few minutes it took him to take out his shopping and tried to temper his anger, didn't help much. Jakes couldn't even remember when he put the bags down, but when Chris opened the door several minutes with the same dishevelled disappearance and a lipstick mark on his cheek, Jakes almost lost it. All the anger he built up in the last two years had come to a boiling point. He was the one man who knew how it felt to find out that you were not the only man in your fiancée's life.

The only reason he didn't hit Chris was because of years of

discipline and training. Jakes couldn't even remember what he told Chris, but it had the desired effect.

Or not.

Chris, the coward he was, disappeared before Angie arrived.

It seemed that Jakes hadn't been as successful as he thought in hiding his lousy mood from Angie. Without realising it, he had chopped the carrots with more aggression than necessary. He only realised it when she put her hand on his to stop his movement. Jakes stilled and slowly looked up into her anxious face.

"Is everything okay?" she asked gently.

For a few moments, Jakes held her eyes and then he nodded. He looked down at the chopping board and muttered, "Please keep on talking."

He almost felt disappointed when she took her hand away. He didn't have to invite her twice because she immediately regaled him with things that had happened at work that day. Jakes concentrated on her voice while he continued chopping the vegetables. It surprised him that her voice managed to calm him. Or maybe the glass of wine she poured for each of them, had also contributed to relax him.

By the time he finished with the vegetables, he felt comfortable enough to answer her incessant questions about the side dishes he was making. It was actually scary how easy it was keeping him company while he cooked the chicken and prepared the raita and sambals. She admitted not being a good cook, but she didn't mind when Jakes gave her the job to cook the basmati rice. She had one request though: he should keep an eye on it while it's cooking.

When the rest of the housemates arrived, Angie had already set the table. The aroma of the curry filled the house. Jakes and Angie were sitting at the kitchen table with their second glass of wine and Angie was still talking non-stop.

Well, the rest of the housemates arrived, but of Chris, there was still no sign. When they were ready to sit down for the meal, Rayno asked, "Shouldn't we wait for Chris?"

Jesse frowned and shot an uncomfortable glance at Angie before he muttered, "He is gone for the weekend."

Jakes kept an eye on Angie. He wished he could judge her expression. Was she disappointed, or sad or angry? All that gave away that Chris' disappearance bothered her was that her smile had disappeared. As usual, it didn't last long and a short while later, she was the Angie Jakes had gotten to know the last few weeks.

THE WEATHER FORECAST for the rest of the weekend was miserable. It limited their outdoor sightseeing activities, but Angie still had plans. Jakes and Michael arranged to watch the weekend's rugby tests at The Whistleblower with Rayno, Jesse, and Mike on Saturday morning.

To date, the Springbok tour to Europe and the UK provided disastrous results. It was only thanks to the penalty Jakes' teammate Matthew Kemp, the current Springbok flyhalf, kicked over in injury time that allowed the Springboks to beat the Scots with a mere two points. Jakes could imagine how disappointed the Scots must feel to lose with such a small margin right at the end.

After the game, they took the train into Denver where they met Angie, Monica and two of Monica's friends at the 16th Street Mall. The rest of the group went skating while Angie and Jakes explored the Mall. Angie had a field day teasing Jakes when he spent too much time and money at the shop of the local basketball team, the Colorado Buffaloes. He even bought a game jersey with his number and name printed on the back, much to Angie's amusement.

On the train ride back, Jakes listened to the banter between the friends. Jesse teased Rayno when he caught Rayno kissing Monica, telling him, "Wait for the mistletoe, my friend."

Jakes frowned confused. What were they talking about?

When his companions realised that Jakes had no clue about the symbolic use of the little, white berries of the season, they left it to Rayno to explain. When Rayno finished, Angie laughed and Jesse clarified, "Jonathan, our eldest brother, loves mistletoe. He decorates the whole house at Christmas time just for the opportunity to kiss his wife."

The mistletoe discussion led to Christmas and everyone's plans for the Holidays. Monica and her two friends were all from a town a small distance from Denver, and they were going home to spend it with their families. Angie was going with Chris to his family in Colorado Springs and Jesse and the rest of the Summers family were going to Keystone where their father owned a chalet.

Neither Jakes nor Rayno had any plans for Christmas. Jakes had, but he had to change his. He and his best friend, André, were supposed to go on holiday together but Jakes' injury changed all that. André was now spending the holidays with his family. When Jesse heard that, he invited, "Come with us to Keystone. There is loads of space."

Rayno accepted without thinking twice, but Jakes was hesitant. He was already more involved with Angie and her family than was healthy. It didn't matter if she wasn't there to spend Christmas with them was not a good idea.

"What else are you going to do, Jakes?" Jesse argued at Jakes' hesitancy.

"I don't know. My family is in Australia, so I don't have any fixed plans. I first wanted to see what's happening with my therapy," he admitted with reluctance.

"This will be a chance for you to experience a white

Christmas. Have you ever experienced one before?"

Jakes shook his head, "No, not yet."

"Come on then, here is your chance," Jesse argued. "Would there be a problem with your visa or flights or something?"

"No, my visa is still valid for another two years. My flight is changeable," Jakes admitted.

Before they arrived back in Cherry Creek, Jesse had, with Rayno's assistance and contributing arguments, convinced Jakes to accept his invitation.

Jakes hoped he wouldn't regret it.

ANGIE COULD SEE Jakes was uncomfortable. His skin is pale and he tugged the rubber band at his wrist with an increasing frequency. Angie was in two minds if she should interfere.

While she was in the bathroom, she heard the women sitting at one of the large tables discussing him. Their comments made her angry, but she felt more uneasy about the sudden bout of jealousy.

Over the last week, she'd often had to remind herself that Jakes was actually her boss. It didn't feel like a job anymore, even though he diligently paid her each week for the sightseeing trips they took. They felt more like friends now.

She now considered them to be friends. He still sometimes appeared withdrawn, but he soon started to open up to her more often. She often got glimpses of a man who could be a lot of fun if only he relaxed.

She thought he couldn't smile but the crooked smile now often made its appearance. At first, it only tugged at the left corner of his mouth, but these days it more often made its appearance on both sides of his mouth. Angie couldn't wait for it to happen.

It was ironic. That first night she met Jakes Angie realised that her own smile was disappearing. The same rude man from that day was now the one who made her smile more. Jakes had a weird sense of humour and made her laugh with his dry remarks. The first few days she wondered if it only sounded funnier with his accent. Now she didn't even hear his accent anymore and he could still make her laugh.

She enjoyed the time she spent with him, discovering new places—some even she didn't know existed. She was grateful for the work and almost felt sad it would end soon. Angie enjoyed the time they spent together, but it also made her feel guilty. She had seen little of Chris during the last few weeks. The only times she had seen him was when she and Monica joined Jesse and his friends for dinner after training. Chris, however, kept disappearing, so Angie never had time to talk to him.

She probably could've taken more effort to see him. She knew she was guilty of avoiding the situation rather than to confront it. What made it worse was that she hadn't even missed Chris during this time. That was definitely not a good sign for their relationship.

She didn't want to think about it now. She focused on Jakes and the redhead, who was leaning closer to him. She spoke to Jakes, but he didn't answer her. Did he see her? Angie doubted it, even though he stared at her. The anxious tugging of the rubber band was a giveaway. Drops of sweat glistened on his forehead, but the woman was oblivious to his distress. She was one of those women who were so confident that all men found her attractive. She didn't even realise what she was doing to the man right in front of her.

Angie noticed it before. Jakes fascinated the women but he either ignored it or was oblivious and Angie suspected it was the latter option. She couldn't blame the women, however. Jakes was an attractive man. She teased him about it once, but he made it clear that he wasn't interested. It was one of those rare moments he relayed something personal about himself. He didn't elaborate but he only mentioned that he came out of a bad relationship and was not interested in flings. He was in Denver for therapy, and that was it.

The night they'd agreed about this job, Angie already realised Jakes suffered from panic attacks. Angie wanted to know how she otherwise could help Jakes. She spoke to the psychologist at work who gave her a few pointers. She learned to look out for the signs.

The only time it happened was once when a woman approached him while she was in the bathroom. Just like this one, she flirted with Jakes and, just like now, the nervous tugging of the rubber band and excessive sweating was a dead giveaway that he was close to a panic attack. That woman disappeared when Angie returned to their table. This one didn't look like one who would easily give up.

Angie pretended then not to notice and talked about their plans for the rest of the day. Jakes was quieter the rest of the day than he had been earlier. Since then, Angie tried to run interference before the symptoms escalated.

Jakes now needed her help. Without thinking about it any further, Angie rushed towards Jakes and the woman who still hadn't let go of her target. Angie summarily pushed her away and stopped in front of Jakes to take his hand.

A MOVEMENT in the corner of his eye caught Jakes' attention. It wasn't Angie. The perfume filling his nostrils was sweet and cloying, not soft and subtle like Angie's. It was also not Angie's face that filled his vision a moment or two later. The woman had long and unnaturally red curls and bright red lips to match the barely-there red dress. He didn't know the woman, but her appearance looked way too familiar. His hand shook when the panic got hold of him. He knew the signs because he had experienced it enough at a time he would rather forget. He wanted to flee but his fear kept him paralysed on the chair.

The red lips moved, but Jakes didn't hear anything the woman said. The noise in his ears was too loud for that. He grabbed the rubber band and pulled it hard. He quickly found a rhythm and tried to concentrate on the pain and noise every time it slapped against his wrist. If he had looked down, he would've seen the welts every time the band made a red mark against his skin.

It felt as if he was in a tunnel and all sides were closing in on him. The woman's voice and the rest of the sounds in the restaurant faded away. He didn't hear the television, the gentle humming of the early Friday night crowd, the clatter of cutlery, nor the music coming from the jukebox.

He couldn't breathe, and at any moment, the dizziness would claim him. He is vaguely aware of the sweat running down his forehead into the corner of his mouth, the voice in his head and the feel of the rubber band hitting his skin.

Just when the voice in his head begged him not to disappear, and before it could die away and the world turned black, the redhead left. A dark-haired woman with blue eyes replaced her.

An angel.

Her gentle touch on his arm and then his hand prevented him from disappearing into the blackness that wanted to enfold him. Her voice eradicated the one in his head. At first, he didn't make out what she was saying, but then she laid her hand gently against his cheek. He could feel her thumb pressing into his palm and then her voice penetrated the haze. He automatically did what she asked, as her eyes kept his captive.

"Breathe, Jakes. In and out. That's it, Jakes. And again. Breathe in. Breathe out."

Breathe in. Breathe out. Breathe in. Breathe out.

Sounds filtered through the haze, began to register. *Breathe in. Breathe out.* Air filled his closed-up lungs. The tightness around his chest lifted. *Breathe in. Breathe out.* His muscles relaxed and his breathing became more regular.

Without breaking eye contact with Angie, and without letting go of her hand, Jakes concentrated on his breathing. *Breathe in. Breathe out.* He felt the sweat running over his cheek and lifted his other hand to wipe it with the sleeve of his shirt.

"How do you feel?" Angie's soft voice broke through the thin layer of anxiety still left.

Jakes took one last deep breath and breathed out.

He only became aware of his surroundings when Angie dropped her hand from his cheek to rest on his arm. His muscles contracted underneath her touch. He only realised then that where she had earlier pressed her thumb into his palm, their fingers were now entwined the way lovers often do. Their eyes held. Jakes didn't want to look away. He could read the worry and empathy in her eyes and he had to swallow hard. He tried to say something, but nothing came out. They only stared at each other in silence.

A hand slapped him on his other shoulder. A deep male voice filtered through the haze. Jakes broke eye contact with Angie and dropped her hand. He concentrated on the voice and turned his head to the sound. It was a familiar sound. A familiar language. Afrikaans. It still took several minutes for his brain to catch up. Another deep breath, another blink of his eyes and Jakes returned to the present.

Rayno, unaware of what happened, carried on talking. Jakes didn't hear half of what Rayno said, but he let the familiarity of his home language flow over him like a comforting blanket. Jakes didn't have to look to know Angie had stepped away. He already felt the loss.

How did she know he needed help and what to do? What did she think of it? Jakes didn't even want to think about it now. Anyway, the next person to speak to him was Angie's twin brother but as his sister, Jesse was only concerned when he asked, "Are you okay?"

Jakes nodded, "Yes, it was a woman who didn't want to leave me alone, but Angie saved me," he managed with a weak attempt at a smile. He heard Jesse's reply, but the rest of the group had arrived, and they got ready to leave. Jakes didn't have the opportunity to think about that moment between him and Angie before Rayno interrupted them. He would do it later when he was alone.

Jakes met Angie's eyes for a moment as he held the door open for her. He wanted to thank her for her help, but he still felt too embarrassed. He was distracted while he listened to the conversation of his friends as they strolled the few blocks to the Christmas Market. Later on, when they announced that they wanted to go to a nightclub, Jakes checked his watch. He didn't like nightclubs and he anyway wanted to get to bed early.

Jakes knew his new friends wouldn't understand, but tomorrow would be his first match after his injury. He had to prepare himself and needed to follow the rituals he always did before any other game, even though it wasn't a professional game.

It didn't surprise him when Angie also declined the invitation. Chris was absent again, and Jakes wondered how much it bothered her.

While the others searched for cabs, Jakes offered to walk Angie back to her car she left at The Whistleblower. Angie protested, but Jakes was adamant. "There are quite a few drunks around. I don't like you walking to your car alone. I'll escort you."

Angie stared at him surprised but then she pulled herself together and mumbled, "That's thoughtful of you."

Before they left the market, Jakes stopped at one of the stalls. Angie looked up in surprise when he pressed the packet of warm nuts into her hands. Maybe she had forgotten that she once mentioned that she loved it.

They walked back to her car in comfortable silence. Angie stopped suddenly and Jakes almost walked into her. His heart missed a beat when she took his hand and he realised how close they were. Heat rushed through him. Hell, did she know what effect she had on him? But not the nervous reaction he got around other women.

He had to swallow hard before he managed, "I wanted to thank you for helping me earlier."

Angie smiled and again it felt as if his heart did a somersault, "It was my pleasure. I wouldn't be a good friend if I didn't intervene."

Jakes shook his head. He looked down at their hands and noticed the red welts still visible on the inside of his wrist.

His heart wouldn't last. It nearly stopped when Angie rubbed her fingers gently over the marks. Jakes couldn't think. He almost stuttered, "Jesse says she's the resident man-eater."

Angie looked up at him without replying. Their eyes held as it had earlier. Jakes almost felt disappointed when she suddenly dropped his hand and turned, fumbling for her car keys.

He might be a fool. He should've walked home to let the cold weather cool him off, but he didn't do it. Jakes accepted her invitation to drop him off at the apartment because he realised his time with her was running out. How stupid was that?

But walking home and chastising himself wouldn't help. It was way too late. Jakes knew it should've stayed at friendship, but he had fallen far too hard and deep already.

CHAPTER SEVEN

Angie's heart was still beating too fast. She clutched the steering wheel tight to stop her hands shivering.

What had just happened? It was as if something significant happened between her and Jakes tonight.

In a daze, Angie indicated to turn left and park in front of the apartment block. She switched off the car and turned towards him.

Earlier tonight he looked surly, but now a shy smile curled in the corner of his mouth. Angie stared at it, fascinated. When he cleared his throat, she realised she hadn't heard a word he was saying. "I'm sorry. Could you repeat that?"

"I only thanked you for the ride."

The smile disappeared and he looked down at his hands where his fingers were playing with the rubber band. He made no move to get out, though. He caught her unaware when he took a deep breath then looked straight at her, saying, "Chris is stupid."

Angie gaped at him, surprised, "What?"

Jakes repeated firmly, "I said Chris is stupid."

Angie grimaced. She thought so too, but she didn't expect Jakes to think so. She wondered about it and asked, "Why?"

Jakes cleared his throat before he answered, "If my fiancée is as beautiful as you, I won't leave her alone as much as Chris did. I wouldn't have wanted her to spend so much time with another man. If I were a different man, I would've taken advantage. You're a beautiful woman and if..."

Emotions flitted over his face, from horror to embarrassment. Jakes might've realised he said too much. He fumbled for the door handle and mumbled, "I'm sorry. I was out of line."

Before Angie could react, he mumbled "goodnight" and closed the door.

Angie waited until the door closed before she switched on her indicator and turned into the quiet street. In her rearview mirror, she noticed he still stood rooted to the same spot, watching her drive off.

On the way to Clara's apartment, Angie thought about Jakes' words. She had spent many thoughts on Chris' behaviour in recent weeks. She still remembered the man who put a ring on her finger before she went to Boulder. In the year since then, things had changed between them. She now admitted that they had been too hasty to get engaged. They were way too young and their relationship too new for such a drastic step.

She might have grown up, but it didn't look like Chris was ready to settle. His infidelity was a clear indication of that.

Angie suspected that Clara knows more than she let on. Before Angie left, Clara and Chris got along. Now they can't stand each other.

It didn't bother her that Chris didn't spend more time with her and it should have. She had to admit that she actually felt relieved to not being alone with him. Their conversations always ended in a fight and Angie hated it. The intimacy she thought they had before she went to Boulder was also long gone. Chris didn't treat her even as a friend these days, so it wasn't surprising that he didn't act as her fiancé.

Maybe her pride more because she was definitely not heartbroken about it.

Did the time she spent with Jakes had something to do with it? He proved to her she needed someone who supported her and her art. Chris wasn't that man.

She was a coward. She knew that but that was just how she was. She hated confrontation and the conversation between her and Chris would not be pleasant but she couldn't postpone it any longer. She had to end their relationship before the Holidays and the sooner she did it, the better. The best time would be Saturday after the game. She should just stop procrastinating.

JAKES ENTERED the locker room way too early. He liked to be there in plenty of time to get himself into the right zone. He had seen these guys taking it easy the previous weeks, and he didn't blame them. They still played for the love of the game.

Sometimes he envied them that, but he wouldn't let himself fall into the same mindset.

He stopped when he heard a voice and realised there was someone there before him. Jakes wanted to call out a greeting when the person spoke again, and he recognised it as Chris's. He must be on the phone as the conversation sounded one-sided.

Jakes didn't even feel ashamed as he listened. He could feel the bile rising when he heard Chris said, "No, I'll see you after the game, Babe. Angie will be at dinner with Jesse and the others. They won't miss me."

Chris stayed quiet for a few moments, listening. He then

lowered his voice, "If I were there, I would lick your beautiful body everywhere."

Chris chuckled and said, "No, this won't do. You give me a hard-on, and I won't be able to play. Keep it for after the game, Babe."

Chris said goodbye and put his phone in his bag before he turned. His face turned ashen when he noticed Jakes standing a short distance from him. Jakes didn't even realise he'd moved closer until he dropped his bag on the tiles. He moved with such speed Chris had no time to react. Jakes picked him up with one arm and pushed him against the locker. Chris struggled to get out of Jakes' grip and grunted, "Let me go."

"I can kill you! How could you do this to Angie? We had this discussion before."

Chris grunted, "It's none of your business."

"That's where you're wrong. Angie is my employee and my friend. She doesn't deserve the way you treat her," Jakes growled. "Does Jesse know?"

Before Chris could answer, Jesse spoke from the doorway, "Does Jesse know what?"

Behind Jesse, Rayno, Mike and a few players piled into the locker room. Chris didn't answer. When Jesse walked closer, he saw Jakes had Chris pushed up against the lockers, he demanded, "What the hell is going on?"

Jakes glared at Chris, only noticing then how red the other man's face was. He was still reluctant when he let Chris go. Chris fell on the bench, breathing hard. Jakes grunted in his face, "You're not worth it, you bastard. Either you come clean, or I do it for you. Do I make myself clear?"

Chris glanced from Jakes to Jesse and back before he nodded, "After the game."

Jakes gave him another angry look and stalked out. If he stayed in the locker room, he might have punched the other man, and that wouldn't do. Outside, Jakes found Michael and the other physios. Jakes noticed Michael's curious look, but then, everyone could probably saw he was furious. He grunted to Michael, "Will you strap me?"

Michael nodded, and Jakes followed him to the therapy room next to the locker room. Jakes was quiet the whole time Michael massaged and strapped him. He attempted to regain his focus, pushing the other man's deceit out of his mind.

Chris was right. It was none of his business, but how could he let the man treat Angie like that? She didn't deserve it.

When he returned to the locker room, he noticed the sidelong glances of the other players. He picked up his bag where he'd dropped it on the floor and turned to Rayno, "Where is my locker?"

Rayno studied him before he indicated the locker next to him. He sat down on the bench and removed his boots and scrum cap from his bag. He glanced up when the assistant coach stopped before him and without a word handed Jakes the match kit.

Jakes almost laughed. He wondered if the man knew he could speak English. Since Jakes arrived, he'd only given Jakes instructions through Rayno.

Jakes took the kit, again realising how different it was from home. At home, their outfits would be already waiting for them in front of their lockers when they arrive. They had two kits. One is a warmup kit and the other the match kit. Here, you had one jersey. He guessed you warmed up and played in the same set.

He had forgotten how different things were between amateur and professional rugby.

As the others had already changed into their kits, Jakes stripped and did the same. The jersey was tight, but he could still move in it. He put his tracksuit back on, as he would only play from the bench. Doc Summers and the coaches gave him permission to play, but just for half an hour. Jakes wasn't happy about that. He would have liked to test his recovery with eighty minutes of hard rugby, but he didn't argue. He was too eager to get back on the pitch.

Jakes followed the players to the warm-up room and followed the instructions as if on auto-pilot before they returned to the locker room where he ignored the banter of the players. He felt the anticipation build as it always did before a game. This might only be a friendly game, but it was an important game for him.

After the team talk, Jakes managed to push all other thoughts to the back of his mind where they belonged. His teammates were far more relaxed than he was. For them, this was still a social event and might think Jakes was too intense, but they didn't know what was at stake for him. He only had one more year to play himself into the Springbok squad for the World Cup. Today was the first step in fulfilling that dream. He wanted to make sure it counted.

He glanced up when Jesse came to stand in front of him and smiled, "Dude, relax. It's only a friendly."

Jakes nodded without replying. Jesse probably realised that Jakes was not going to answer him and walked away to speak to Chris. Jakes frowned. He'd thought Jesse and Chris were best friends, but he noticed now there was tension between the two. That and his animosity towards the other man were not good for the team dynamics. Jakes promised himself to keep control. He couldn't think of the incident earlier.

Focus, Jakes. Focus.

He closed his eyes and started his visualisation exercises, ignoring the men around him.

When the manager gave the signal for them to take the field, he felt relieved. He picked up his parka and took his place in the line, behind the fullback. If he started the game, he would have stood halfway, behind the two flankers. That's how he preferred to play too, in the middle. There he could control the game from the back of the scrum and still links with the backline.

He jogged behind the others to take his place next to the field. He accepted a blanket from Michael and huddled underneath it while he watched the game. It was close, and by halftime, the Bears were only leading with two points. Jakes followed the squad back to the locker room, glancing up to where he'd seen Angie the previous time. She was there again, but unlike the last time, she smiled when she caught his eyes. Jakes nodded and disappeared into the tunnel.

ANGIE'S EYES drifted to the touchline where Jakes had been warming up. He was busy shedding his tracksuit. Angie heard the sudden chatter of the local women supporters when he stood up, dressed only in his rugby gear.

Jakes took his place next to the linesman, waiting for his signal to join the squad on the field. He jumped up and down at first, then ran fast in one place, swinging his arms. When the number eight came off the pitch, Jakes joined the lineout in a flash.

Angie's mind drifted as usual, but a shout from the crowd interrupted her thoughts. Jakes held the ball in his one hand while he ran. For such a big man, he was fast on his feet and strong. He pushed first one, then two more players away from him before they could tackle him. He briefly glanced to his right and passed the ball to Chris close to the try-line for the Bear's first try of the second half. It happened so fast the opposition looked stunned. His teammates celebrated, but Jakes ambled back to the halfway line without a smile on his face.

The rest of the half, he dominated the scrums and stole balls on the ground. He even took a few balls in the lineout. His runs were impressive, and it looked as if his play was rubbing off on his teammates and the team suddenly played with more enthusiasm. Every time they stopped the game, he spoke to his teammates, especially Jesse.

When the final whistle sounded, the two teams walked off the field. Angie caught Jesse's smile. When Jakes caught Angie's eyes this time, he gave her one of those smiles with his lips curled up on both sides. Her heart somersault when she watched him disappear into the tunnel. Angie only then realised she hadn't even noticed when Chris had left the field.

She flushed and got up to make her way to the clubroom where she met the others.

The boys were in high spirits when they met after their beer with the opposition and their showers. Jakes hovered in the back until everyone had found a place to sit before he took his own place opposite Angie.

He frowned as he studied the group before he glanced at Angie briefly. He almost immediately returned his gaze to Chris, who for once had joined them. Chris looked uncomfortable and didn't make eye contact with Jakes.

What was going on? Why did Jakes glare at Chris like that?

Angie didn't get a chance to think about it, as the group had finished their first beers and Jesse had signalled for their waiter. Everyone shouted an order. When the waiter left, Angie realised Chris was not there. He might only have gone to the bathroom, but when he didn't reappear half an hour later, Angie knew he wasn't coming back.

Her phone flashed to indicate that she had a message. It was from Chris, as Angie suspected. At least he apologized this time because usually he just disappeared. Why couldn't he tell her in person that he wasn't feeling well and had gone home? Jesse, who sat next to Angie, looked at her questioningly when she put the phone back on the table. "It was Chris," she mumbled and relayed Chris' message.

Jesse gave Jakes a knowing glance which in turn looked thunderous as he stared at Chris' empty seat. The atmosphere felt strained, and it had something to do with Chris.

As it was their last game of the year before their break for the Holidays, the players decided to celebrate. Thanks to Jakes, they had a good win and wanted to celebrate. The idea met with an enthusiastic response and soon the group broke up to leave to visit a local nightclub.

Angie was never fond of nightclubs, and tonight she was not in the mood to celebrate. She had hoped to speak to Chris tonight.

She came in earlier with Clara, but now she didn't want to wait for Clara to finish her shift. Angie would take a cab and go home but might have to wait a while. When most of the group had left, she put her jacket on and picked up her bag. She would order a cab outside.

She had just stepped out of the clubhouse when Angie heard her name. She turned in surprise when she realised it was Jakes. She thought he went with Jesse. When he stopped next to her, he frowned. He took her arm and, with a concerned expression, peered into her face, "What's wrong, Angel?"

Angel? Did he realise what he had called her?

Angie suddenly felt emotional. She had to bite her bottom lip, or she would've burst into tears. Was it because of Chris? No, she doubted it.

She knew, however, that she was sick and tired of Chris and the way he treated her, but it wasn't Jakes" problem, even though he thought Chris was stupid. She shook her head but didn't reply. She had to leave before she succumbed to these silly emotions. She turned and mumbled, "I'll see you on Monday."

Jakes didn't give in so easily. His hand slid from her arm and captured her fingers. Angie stopped, her eyes flitting up to meet his when the heat emanating from his skin, shot through her. His voice was soft, almost sympathetic, when he urged, "I told you Chris was stupid, and I stand by it, but I don't want to talk about him. Have dinner with me?"

She pulled her shoulders back. She didn't need Jakes' pity. "Why? Do you feel sorry for me?"

His mouth curled up in the corner as he answered, "No, I may feel sorrier for myself than for you. I'm hungry and I want to celebrate. I don't enjoy doing it alone..." His voice trailed off and uncertainty flitted over his face. He dropped her hand and muttered, "I'm sorry. It was a stupid idea."

He turned to walk away, and Angie decided quickly. Going to dinner with Jakes might not be such a bad idea. It would take her mind off Chris and what she had to do. It was her turn to take his hand to stop him. "I would like that. Where do you want to go?"

Angie's heart fluttered when he gave her a lopsided grin, "Your town. Your choice."

Angie thought for a moment, "There's an Italian restaurant close to the square. We could have dinner there. I don't think you have to book."

Jakes pulled his face in mock astonishment, and Angie stared at him, amazed as it was the first time he did something so outrageous. "Why are you only telling me now? I love Italian food!"

Angie laughed, "You should've told me. I thought you loved the food at The Whistleblower."

"I do, but if I want to eat pasta, I need to indulge now. During the season I can't eat too many carbs."

They had walked towards the square. Angie glanced at him before she asked, confused, "Don't you eat a lot of carbs to refuel?"

"We used to," Jakes admitted, "But we now have a nutritionist who monitors our eating plans. We are allowed to refuel after a heavy workout, but that's at lunch, not at night. Chloe is this tall," he showed with his hand below his chest. "but she already rules us with an iron fist."

Angie laughed at his indignation, but he kept on talking, "I don't mind as much. I got used to it at the Sevens, but some guys still complain about it. At least we have a cheat day once a week when I take my chance to indulge."

"You have a strict regime," Angie noted.

"Yes, but it wasn't always like that. Like most rugby clubs, we liked our food and beer, but we are now one of the smallest but most successful franchises in South Africa. Next year we will compete in a new international club competition and everything changed. To compete with the Kiwi and European teams, in particular, we needed to change our game plan. There are things in the pipeline, such as a high-altitude centre. Management first brought in Chloe after we lost in the Interprovincial Cup. They are working on changing our image and want us to become more professional. We now have a Code of Conduct and..."

He stopped abruptly, but as they reached the restaurant, Angie didn't push him to continue.

The restaurant was cosy, and they were lucky to get a table close to one of the open hearths. Since neither had to drive, they shared a bottle of red wine. This again surprised Angie. Chris, and most of their friends, refused to touch the stuff.

The waiter brought their wine and after he filled their glasses, he took the orders. Only then Jakes noted, "I don't want to upset you again, but you look unhappy."

Angie nodded, "I was... I am, but I don't want to talk about it tonight. As you said, we've something to celebrate. You are back on the pitch and you've won. And you had a good game."

Jakes flushed but didn't reply immediately. Angie, therefore, monopolised the conversation, but in the two hours or more it took to finish their dinner, they both relaxed. Jakes had already learned that he only needed to ask Angie a question, then she would talk non-stop, but she never felt uncomfortable doing that with Jakes, unlike she had with Chris. Jakes listened so attentively that she sometimes forgot that she was doing that.

After Jakes settled the bill, they again braved the cold to walk towards the rank of taxis on the other side of the square. The festive lights brightening the streets reminded Angie of Christmas and she asked nosily, "What type of Christmas tree do you have at home? Is it a real tree or an artificial one?"

"It depends on where we are," Jakes replied.

"What do you mean?"

Angie looked up at him and noticed his smile when he explained, "If we are at our house, we have a traditional tree, but unfortunately it is artificial. When we visit my grandfather's farm in the northern province of South Africa, we decorate a small thorn tree. And if we are at our beach house, we sometimes use a piece of driftwood."

"And this year having a White Christmas would be another new experience, wouldn't it?"

"Definitely," he agreed.

At the first cab with an available sign, Jakes stopped. He bent down to open the door for Angie, at the same time she was turning to thank him. Jakes' face was close to hers, and their eyes locked. Was he aware of her as she was of him? He might be, as his head lowered in slow motion. Angie's heartrate picked up while she waited for their lips to meet.

The kiss never happened. Jakes drew in his breath and jerked away.

In the low light cast by the streetlamp, she could see that his face was flushed. Hers might look the same.

Angie slid into the seat and gave the driver her address. She thanked Jakes for the evening and closed the door before he could reply. She kept herself occupied with her seatbelt and waved at him, not making eye contact.

What was going on with her? For goodness sake, she couldn't be disappointed that he came to his senses?

But she was. She realised it again as she reflected on the evening. She couldn't remember when last she'd had as much fun on a date.

But it wasn't a date. Not really. They were only two friends sharing a meal or maybe not even that. It didn't matter if it was only a temporary arrangement, it was only dinner with her boss.

But it still felt like a date. And that she'd wanted him to kiss her.

CHAPTER EIGHT

J akes stared at the leaving cab in shock before he walked back to the apartment, still in a daze. He needed the exercise and the cold to bring him back to reality.

Geez, he had been so close to kissing Angie, even though he knew he shouldn't do it. He almost hurt Chris twice for cheating on her and then he was close to doing the same. It didn't matter whether Chris was a cheater. He was still Angie's fiancé.

He was getting too close to Angie. He might be a masochist because since he caught Chris, he wondered about Angie and Chris' relationship. It had nothing to do with him, but he just couldn't understand their relationship. They were engaged but were never together and when they were, it looked as if they didn't like each other much. They didn't even talk to each other!

The other day, while he and Angie visited Washington Park, Jakes was nosy and tried to find out more, but she was reluctant to talk about it. He couldn't really blame her. He changed the subject but then chose the most brilliant of topics. Love! For goodness sake, what did he know about love? And what did he ask? "How long do you think it takes to fall in love?"

Jakes should've known he was in trouble. He didn't speak to women about love. He didn't talk to women. Period. But Angie? How did she manage it? She broke through all his defences. Not only did she managed to get him to talk, but she had him share more personal stuff with her than with many of his friends, except André.

That moment, when she answered with a dreamy smile, Jakes would never forget. Her answer even less.

"Oh, I don't think it takes that long," she answered. "Sometimes, all it takes is a moment, a touch, or a smile."

He knew then that she was right.

If circumstances were different, he might've given in to this attraction, but he couldn't do anything about it now. This was not his choice. He still had integrity, but he had to admit: he was close to giving in.

Later, when he got ready for bed, Jakes sat on the bed. What must he do? He accepted Jesse's invitation to spend Christmas with his family. He even changed his flights so he could go, but maybe he should go home.

But then, Angie would spend Christmas with Chris' family up in Colorado Springs. Jakes didn't have to see her. He was anyway friends with Jesse and Rayno too. Would it matter so much if he spent the holidays with the rest of the family? As Jesse and Angie said: it might be his only opportunity to experience a white Christmas.

He might need to distance himself from Angie until she leaves with Chris.

Chris. That was his second problem. How should he deal with the knowledge of Chris' cheating? Jakes had already confronted the man twice, but he didn't realise Chris was such a coward.

Should he tell Angie?

Jakes immediately refuted that idea. He couldn't do it. He might also be a coward, but he didn't want to see Angie hurting. He didn't think he could handle it.

His other option was to speak to Jesse. Her twin brother might know how to deal with it. It might not be as easy, as Jakes understood that the two men had been friends since University. Although recently Jakes doubted that friendship. There was definitely tension between them.

No, he didn't have a choice. It was either Jesse or Angie and Jake's choice would rather be Jesse. He had to do it for Angie's sake.

Before he could change his mind, Jakes picked up his phone and sent a message to Jesse. Jakes didn't expect a reply soon as they might still be at the nightclub. It surprised him to receive a response from Jesse five minutes later. They agreed to meet at a diner at nine the following morning.

When Jakes switched off the light a few minutes later, he still worried if he was doing the right thing.

THIS WAS IT. After last night, Angie had enough. She didn't want to be an afterthought in Chris' life any longer. She always used his friendship with Jess as an excuse but no more. Today was the day she was going to make an end to this farce of engagement, whether it would affect that friendship or not.

Early this morning she had already texted Chris to meet at their house this afternoon. His answer was short, "That's fine" but nothing else. Maybe he suspected what was coming.

It didn't matter how determined she was, she was still nervous. She wiped her palms on her dress before she knocked. In the past, she would've just walked in, but today it wasn't a usual visit.

Chris might've waited for her, because he opened the door almost immediately, a weird expression on his face. He didn't even greet her! He only stood aside for Angie to enter. Angie suppressed her irritation as she walked to the lounge. She didn't sit as she waited for Chris to join her. As soon as he did, he demanded, "You wanted to talk."

Angie took a deep breath. This was her chance, but Chris didn't allow her to respond. He lashed out, "I should've known. He couldn't wait to tell you."

Not that he allowed her to react before he accused, "I should've known. He couldn't wait to tell you."

Angie frowned. What was he talking about?

At least Chris looked uncomfortable when he continued, "I know I should've done it before, but I didn't want to hurt you. Things are not working with us anymore, Angie."

Angie wanted to laugh but now wasn't a good time. Her legs felt numb. She still wasn't keen to have this conversation and had to steel herself when she looked Chris in the eyes. "I'm sorry to disappoint you, but you already hurt me. Every day you didn't phone me or even sent a message, I hurt. I hurt every time you didn't touch me or caressed me. I hurt every time you couldn't look me in the eyes as you do now."

While she was busy, she might as well continue. "All I wanted to know is why? What did I do wrong? Is there something wrong with me?"

"Geez, Angie. I'm sorry. There's nothing wrong with you. It's just ..."

"Then why..." Angie took a deep breath before she could continue, but she wanted to know. "Why then did you not kiss me anymore? Why have you never made love to me? We've been together for almost six years. Don't tell me you've never felt the need...?"

Chris' sudden flush confirmed her suspicions. "No, you didn't have to answer that. I know you cheated on me.?"

Chris snapped, "I should've known. He already told you."

"Who? Told me what?" Angie asked, confused. "Jesse?"

Chris shook his head, "No, Jakes."

Angie sank to the couch, her legs weak as his words penetrated. She didn't expect that. She had to swallow the bile before she could ask, "What was Jakes supposed to have told me? That you were cheating on me? How did he know?"

Chris smirked, "I thought the big guy couldn't wait to tell you, but it hadn't been him, it seems that he keeps his own secrets."

Angie hissed, "How did Jakes know?"

Chris looked uncomfortable when he realised it hadn't been Jakes who told Angie about his cheating. He admitted with a flush, "That night he cooked dinner here, he arrived earlier and almost caught me."

"What? That was more than two weeks ago," Angie exclaimed shocked.

"Yeah, he threatened me then to tell you if I didn't do it, and I promised I would," Chris admitted.

"And like all your other promises, you couldn't keep that one either."

He shrugged in a careless gesture.

Angie shook her head as she studied him. Right now, she didn't even like him. How could she have thought he was the man of her dreams? Had she ever loved him? It didn't feel like it now.

"When was the first time you cheated on me?"

"Geez, Angie, do you need to know?"

"Yes, I do," Angie insisted.

He didn't even look apologetic when he admitted, "Since you moved to Boulder. It was nothing serious. Just ..."

"Leave it, Chris. I heard enough. Just tell me one thing: Did Jesse know?"

"Jakes told him this morning. I promised to tell you when Jakes caught me again yesterday before the game. When I didn't, he contacted Jesse. Jesse had already confronted me when you phoned."

"Why didn't you tell me? Are you such a coward?"

Chris shrugged, "Probably. I didn't want to hurt you."

She shook her head with regret while she got up, "Well, you did. I wish you'd told me long ago. I'm upset you cheated on me. I've suspected for a while. It doesn't matter, though because I've realised that I don't love you, Chris. I don't know if I ever did. At first, I thought there was something wrong with me. I know now it isn't me. You never made me feel..."

Angie took the ring off her finger and flung it to him. "Sorry to disappoint you. There was a time when you had hurt me, but I'm over it already. I am unhappy that you cheated on me. I suspected it for a while, but just like you, I've also been a coward. I should've ended this farce before now. I came to the conclusion that I don't love you and maybe I never had. Maybe I just loved the idea of being in love. I do, however, deserve to be happy. I deserve to know that there is someone who cares about me and support my dreams. I thought there was something wrong with me, but I know now that it wasn't me. You don't make me feel like ..."

She shook her head, "Forget it."

When she turned to walk away, Chris was still talking, "There's something else I want to tell you. I'm busy packing. I'm going to..."

Angie kept on walking and answered him over her shoulder, "I'm not interested anymore."

Angie exhaled the moment she closed the front door behind her. She suddenly felt tired. Deflated. She worked herself up for nothing. She didn't have to worry about Chris' feelings. He didn't have any.

Why then did she feel so disappointed?

Then it hit her like a sledgehammer. She wasn't disappointed or sad that six years of her life ended just like that. She was disappointed that Jakes knew that Chris cheated on her and didn't tell her. Was that what last night was all about? Did he take her out to dinner because he felt for her? Or maybe he felt guilty?

It might not be the most logical reason, but then, she never claimed to be the most rational person on earth. She was a person who 'feels'. And now she only felt hurt and disappointed.

Angie drove to her parent's home as if on auto-pilot. They were away for the weekend, so she could hide in her studio and lick her wounds. Art was the only way Angie knew how to deal with her broken engagement and everything going with it.

Before she even entered the studio, she sent messages to both Clara and Jesse to tell them not to worry about her. She knew they would anyway but as long as they knew where she was, they would understand that she needed time on her own to deal with everything. She didn't even wait for their replies before she switched her phone off.

MAYBE ANGIE SHOULD'VE SPOKEN to someone. If she had, she might not have worked herself up so much. She might not have stormed into the gym where Jakes was training, to confront him early on Monday morning. Someone would've warned her that it was a bad idea.

At least she didn't have an audience to witness her tirade as Jakes was alone. He was standing in front of the mirror with a dumbbell in each hand when she stormed in. "Why didn't you tell me? You knew for two weeks, Jakes. I thought we were friends."

He dropped the dumbbells to the floor and turned to face her. Angie carried on her tirade without giving Jakes a chance to respond.

When she ran out of words and accusations and had to take a deep breath to continue, Angie really looked at Jakes. He was tense, his jaw clenched and his eyes wary.

When he lifted his hand to wipe sweat from his face, Angie's brain made sense of what was in front of her.

Jakes wasn't wearing a shirt.

Droplets of sweat ran down his temple, over his cheek and disappeared into the thick muscles of his neck. Fascinated, Angie followed the droplet. Her mouth almost dropped open. He didn't have any hair on his chest!

But wow, all that that incongruous fact did was to accentuate his well-formed pecs. The drops travelled further down over his six-pack and down...

Angie inhaled when she realised she was drooling over Jakes' body. It wouldn't surprise her if it was already running down her chin.

Her eyes flew up to meet Jakes' eyes again, noticing the vulnerability in them. She didn't want to see that.

She turned and rushed out of the gym faster than she had arrived. She only stopped when she reached her car. She was so out of breath that she needed to lean against her car to get oxygen back in her lungs.

That was the moment she realised what she did. She covered her flushed cheeks with her hands and groaned. What got into her?

If it hadn't been bad enough that she ranted to Jakes, but then she went into a state about his body. Just thinking about it made her shiver.

Angie had never felt like this before, and although it surprised her, it shocked her even more. She had to think rationally. For goodness sake, it's Jakes! It didn't matter what feelings he evoked, nothing could come of it.

Better yet, nothing *should* come of it. This was not the best time to think about another man. She would be far better off to focus on herself now, and not on men or relationships.

With that decision still freshly in her mind, she got into her car and drove back home. The whole time she made plans on how to get her life back into order.

First, she needed to avoid Jakes. She didn't need the job anymore. Clara had finished her internship at the company where she was going to work. She would earn an excellent salary. She had no excuse to go sightseeing with Jakes anymore.

Before she even got out of the car, she sent him a message to cancel the trips for the week. There would be no more excursions planned for the following week.

Angie could now focus on her own job and her art. That was all. Not on a certain green-eyed man who made her feel things no other man had managed before.

JAKES STARED at the door through which Angie disappeared. Although he wanted to, he realised it was best not to follow her now. Jakes expected her to be angry because he didn't tell her about Chris, but not like this.

He thought about his conversation with Jesse yesterday. Jesse had suspected something was going on with Chris, but he didn't know what. He was furious, of course. It took a while for Jesse to calm enough to have a rational conversation. And his first words were, "Now I understand why you were angry with Chris in the locker room. I would have reacted the same, but I don't understand. Why didn't you tell Angie yourself?

Feeling uncomfortable, Jakes flushed. "I had hoped Chris would do the right thing and tell her himself. And, if I have to be honest...I didn't know how to tell her. I know how it feels to find out your partner is cheating on you, and I know how much it hurts. I couldn't bear to see how she hurts... Anyway, I thought you knew her better. You would be better able to deal with it."

Jesse was quiet for a long time before he nodded. Jakes felt as if Jesse saw more in his unwillingness than Jakes would've liked. They had said little and parted soon afterwards.

From Angie's tirade just now, Jakes gathered she knew the truth. He wasn't sure if Jesse told her or if Chris had found the courage and told her, but it didn't matter. She blamed him anyway for withholding the information from her. If she was angry with him, she might not want to see him, and if he didn't see her, he might not feel as if he wanted more.

THAT DECISION CAME TOO LATE. Angie accepted it as she stood in her studio two hours later, studying the painting in front of her.

How did this happen?

When she painted yesterday, she painted without thought, working through the disappointment, hurt, and anger. The first two or three paintings were rubbish but this one...

Her fingers trailed over the canvas, following the sharp lines of his cheekbone, the full lips curling up in one corner, over the crooked nose to the bright green of the eyes.

"For the mouth speaks what the heart is full of."

Angie swung around to find Clara, studying the painting with interest.

Angie gasped, "Clara! Don't creep up on me."

"I didn't. I called you three or four times, but you were

oblivious to the world, and now I understand why but in this case it wasn't the mouth but the paintbrush," Clara protested.

Angie turned back to the painting and studied it. "I didn't plan it. Yesterday I painted without thought. It had never happened before."

Clara hugged her from behind and laughed, "Because you were never in love like this before."

Angie's heart skipped a beat, "I..."

She turned towards Clara in shock, "I'm not in love with ..."

Her voice trailed off, and she stared at Clara, shocked. "I can't be. I mean, I only met him a month ago. He... I..."

"Love doesn't have a time frame, Angie. It happens when it happens."

Angie took a deep breath and muttered, "No. I'm not in love with him. It's ... I'm upset about Chris, and it's because I spent so much time with Jakes over the last few weeks."

Clara raised her eyebrows, but Angie ignored her. There was no way she could be in love with Jakes. She hardly knew the man. She glared at the painting one more time before she took it off the easel and put it on the floor facing the wall. She didn't want to see it now.

Angie's gaze flitted over her studio. Since she was busy...

She took an empty box left in the corner and threw every little thing reminding her of Chris into it.

Clara watched her with a thoughtful expression. When Angie closed the box, Clara grinned. "Feeling better?"

When Angie shook her head, Clara laughed, "then this calls for a double chocolate chip ice cream with caramel sauce."

Angie stared at her friend and then burst out laughing. At least some things would never change, and she was now grateful for it. She hooked her arm through Clara's and walked to the kitchen to raid her mother's secret stash in the freezer. Her mother had tried to hide her secret indulgence but, Angie and Clara, and sometimes Amy, always found it. Her mother confessed when they were teenagers. Although she liked the flavour, she bought it for the girls. She only pretended to hide it from them because they enjoyed the search.

Over a bowl of ice cream, Angie poured her heart out about Chris' deceit and Jakes' knowledge about it. Angie admitted confronting Jakes. She was so angry with him because he hadn't told her about catching Chris.

Clara put her chin on her hand, studying Angie. "You sound more upset about Jakes not telling you than you are about Chris' cheating," she deducted.

"I am. I suspected Chris was cheating on me, and I already decided I don't want to carry on with our relationship. I think... I thought Jakes was a friend... I'm disappointed."

"You know it's not his fault, don't you? You can't blame Jakes. If you do, blame me too."

Angie frowned, "Why?"

"Because I knew too. Okay, I haven't caught him with someone else, but I've seen how he flirted with other women."

Angie thought about it. Clara was right. She should be angry with her, but she wasn't. In Clara's defence, Angie might add that Clara had urged her to speak to Chris since her return to Denver."

Clara put her hand on Angie's arm and urged, "Why don't you enjoy the time you and Jakes still have together? One day you may regret the time you wasted."

Angie understood Clara's feelings but shook her head, "I don't think it's a good idea. Anyway, I already cancelled our outings. It's better if I avoid him as much as possible. Or at least until I learned how to deal with it."

．　．　．

IT DIDN'T MATTER how many times he used that argument, Jakes still felt disappointed when he read Angie's message after his shower. He had suspected that she was going to cancel their excursions.

She blamed him for keeping the information from her, and maybe it was better that way. If she were angry with him, she might not want to see him. And if he didn't see her, he wouldn't be tempted.

There were no training sessions with the club. They would only resume their programme in the New Year. Jakes had seen none of the group of friends he'd made during the last few weeks. They still talked to him, though, even if it was only through text messages. Jesse was busy at school with a Christmas pantomime. Rayno had an active social life with year-end functions and other end-of-year responsibilities.

It was only the Thursday before they were to leave for the cabin that Jakes received a text from Jesse, confirming that Angie and Chris had broken up. Chris had moved out of the house he shared with Jesse and Rayno. In fact, he had left Denver altogether. From Jesse's messages, Jakes deducted that that friendship didn't end on a friendly note.

Jakes didn't sleep well that night. The dark circles under his eyes emphasized that. He also lost his appetite. The last proper meal he had was the one he had with Angie. He looked rough and he felt it too. He could, therefore, understand Michael's concerned looks throughout Friday. It was Jakes' last day of therapy at the centre, which was another indication that his time in Denver was coming to an end.

Late afternoon, after Jakes said goodbye to everyone, Michael waited for him outside the centre. Michael asked without preamble, "You have any plans tonight?"

When Jakes shook his head, Michael decided, "Then we're going out."

Jakes wanted to argue, but he knew Michael was right. He needed to get out of his own head. Jakes knew where he might end up if he would be alone. He followed Michael without argument. They were silent on the walk to the pub. As soon as they sat and ordered a beer, Michael spoke up, "So, what's up? You look like crap as if you've not slept. What's eating you?"

Jakes took a deep swallow of his beer then put it down on the table in front of him. He dropped his eyes to his hands where his fingers automatically had searched for the rubber band. He took a deep breath as he tugged on the elastic before he admitted, "Angie and Chris broke off their engagement. Chris had been cheating on her. I caught him and told Jesse, and things went from there. Angie is now angry with me because I didn't tell her. She doesn't speak to me."

"So, why are you miserable? Don't you now have a chance with Angie?"

Jakes took a deep breath. "I can't, Michael. You know my schedule. You know about the pledge. No, it wouldn't be fair to Angie. It can't work."

"How does Angie feel about you or a relationship?" Michael probed.

Jakes looked at him, irritated, "I don't know! I'm relieved she's angry with me and doesn't want to see me. But now Jesse told me last night she is also going to Keystone. I don't know what to do. Maybe I should take the first flight home. But then... Maybe I should take a chance? I think about her. I think about the pact. It's driving me crazy."

"You know what your problem is?"

When Jakes shook his head, Michael continued, "You're overthinking it. Sometimes you must let your heart take over, my friend."

"I'm scared. I did it before, and it didn't work. I promised myself if I ever have another relationship again, I'll decide with my mind, not my heart."

"I suspected, and I think you do too, it may already be too late. Jakes..."

Michael said his name so urgently Jakes lifted his head to look at him. "Don't waste time. Take the chance. Do something before it's too late. You may never get that chance again."

Jakes studied Michael. He knew Michael's history and that his advice came from personal experience. He took a deep breath before he answered, "I'll go to Keystone, but I can't go back on my pledge. Michael. I can't let the team down."

Michael sighed, "That's your decision. I'll be in California if you need me."

"At least you'll get sunshine. I'll freeze my butt off in the mountains," Jakes grumbled.

Jakes almost heard the envy in Michael's voice when he said, "But you will spend time with a special woman. Time is precious, Jakes."

Jakes looked up to argue, but his eyes caught Angie. She was talking to Clara but had been watching him, and he couldn't look away.

Maybe Michael was right.

CHAPTER NINE

Angie sat at the end of the bar, where she could have a chat with Clara between her duties. She didn't fancy being on her own tonight.

It wasn't long since she and Chris broke up, but every day Angie was more relieved it was over. She still hurt because Chris cheated on her, and she was still angry with him, but she had dealt with Chris and their relationship.

Her problem lay with Jakes.

When Jesse told her last night that Jakes thought Chris had to fix his own mess, Angie still felt betrayed. She took most of the night before she admitted she hadn't been fair to Jakes. She couldn't blame him for Chris's unfaithfulness or cowardice.

Clara came to stand next to her and asked, "What's going on with Jakes?"

"I don't know. I hadn't seen Jakes or spoken to him again," Angie admitted with a flush.

Clara shook her head, "I mean, what's going on with him tonight? He looks down, and miserable," she said, indicating with her head towards the far corner of the pub. Angie looked up and saw Jakes with Michael.

Clara was right. Jakes looked terrible. His hair was messy from the way he pushed his hand through it. There were dark circles under his eyes as if he hadn't slept well. She could see his tension in the way he tugged at the rubber band.

He spoke to Michael, but every time he had to take a deep breath first. Neither of the two men smiled, which made it evident that the conversation was serious.

Clara studied her, then remarked, "You look as miserable as he does. You should talk to him."

Angie returned her gaze to Clara and saw her friend's concern. She looked back at Jakes. They were leaving for the cabin tomorrow. If they had to spend time together, it would be best if they could talk things through. It could otherwise be awkward for everyone. She exhaled and nodded. "You're right."

Jakes suddenly looked up, straight into her eyes. Neither of them glanced away, but it was as if his eyes spoke to her. Angie got up and walked towards their table. He still hadn't looked away from her when she stopped. Michael looked up when she mumbled Jakes' name.

Jakes clenched his jaw and mumbled her name. Only her name, but it felt so much more. Angie didn't notice Michael until he got up and threw a few notes on the table.

Angie broke eye contact when Michael got up. He first looked at Jakes and then to her as he almost gave them an order, "You need to talk. I'll see you tomorrow, Jakes."

Angie had barely taken her seat opposite Jakes when he took a deep breath and muttered, "I'm sorry I didn't tell you earlier."

Angie flushed, "I'm sorry I took it out on you. I hope you're not angry with me."

Jakes shook his head, but his eyes didn't leave her face. He sounded earnest, "No, I'm not. I'm... I wish..." He took a deep breath before he tried again. "I want..."

He closed his eyes and Angie could see how much he struggled to talk. Before she could stop herself, she put her hand over his on the table. "Don't worry, Jakes. You don't have to say anything now."

Her heart stuttered when he turned his hand and threaded his fingers through hers, holding her hand tight. Even when he loosened his grip, he still didn't let go. He opened his eyes and stared at their linked hands with fascination. When he looked up at her, his face was calmer, and even his voice sounded less anguished. "Thank you."

"What for?" she asked, confused.

Jakes flushed and looked away. When he looked back at her, he said, "For grounding me. I can't explain now, but one day I will."

Angie nodded, "That's fine. I thought it would be better if we talk it out before we join everyone tomorrow."

Jakes nodded. "I agree."

They sat in silence for a while. Angie guessed she should leave now they'd cleared the air. She got up and mumbled, "Okay, if we're fine then, I'll leave you."

Jakes held her hand tighter. "Do you have to?"

When Angie shook her head, Jakes pleaded, "Please stay then. Have something to drink with me?"

Angie didn't have to go. For the first time since she knew Jakes, she was free and single. She smiled and accepted without having to feel guilty, "I'd like to."

When his mouth curled up in a smile, Angie knew: they would be okay.

. . .

THEY HAD NOT ONLY HAD one drink. They followed it up with another round and something to eat. When they left much later, Jakes took her hand to pull her out of the way of a large group of people entering the pub. One man smirked at Jakes, "Dude, aren't you going to kiss her?" indicating the mistletoe above their heads.

They both looked up and then at each other. When the group was inside, Jakes still hadn't let go of her hand. Angie looked up to thank him, only to find that he was not looking at her. His eyes stayed fixed on her mouth. Angie knew then he wanted to kiss her as much as she wanted him to kiss her.

He slowly pulled his eyes away from her mouth to meet her eyes.

Jakes moved closer as if in slow motion, his eyes still holding hers. She felt the heat of his palm slide over her cheek, then under her hair to cup her neck. He bent his head so slowly that it felt like an eternity before his lips touched hers. It was so tender, and gentle, Angie almost thought she imagined it. He lifted his head, their lips almost touching, and Angie opened her eyes to stare at him in a daze.

With a soft groan, Jakes bent his head and kissed her again, but this time his lips touched hers with more urgency. How long it lasted, she didn't know, because Angie succumbed to the sensations his mouth evoked.

Kissing Chris had never felt like this. It was so sweet and tender, yet so full of the promise of what it could be between them.

When Jakes lifted his head again, his mouth curled up in that lopsided grin, "I like your Christmas traditions."

Angie grinned. She loved the heat in his gaze. She loved the gentle stroke of his thumb over her bottom lip. More than that, she loved the gruffness in his voice when he whispered her name, his eyes serious. "Angie, I..."

Angie might now never know what Jakes would've said as the door opened behind them and Jakes stood aside to let another couple step around them.

No matter how much he tried, he couldn't forget the kiss. If it was a different time, a year or even six months from now, he might've taken a chance. If he did it now, he would hurt her and other people. That was the last thing Jakes wanted to do.

He had to keep it platonic between them, but it's more than ten days. He didn't know if he could manage that, especially now.

If he could tell Angie why he couldn't have a relationship with her now, she might understand, but he couldn't break his teammates' confidence. On the way home, he created a mantra and repeat it over and over.

Remember your focus. Remember your team. Remember the glory.

Jakes forgot his mantra the following day. He was alone as Michael had left for the airport earlier to spend Christmas with his younger brother.

It wasn't Jesse or Rayno who stood in front of him when he opened the door. When Angie smiled, Jakes accepted that he was in a lot of trouble, but now it was too late to cancel.

Angie studied his suitcase and duffel bag and asked, "Do you have enough warm clothes?"

Jakes shrugged, "I packed everything I have here. I hope it is enough."

Angie laughed, "You'll be fine. It's warm indoors, and there are loads of things to keep us busy. It's fair to warn you, though. My family like to play games, and they are competitive, especially Jonathan. He thinks he's the oldest and should win."

Jakes' mouth turned up. "It sounds like my family, but I've not played board games for ages."

Angie pulled her face. "Ooh, I'm sorry for you. They will rip you apart."

Jakes shook his head at Angie's expression. She was still chattering when they walked to the car but didn't speak much on the way to Jesse. Jakes already learned that Angie preferred silence when she was driving as she concentrated so hard on her driving.

Jesse and Rayno were waiting for them, and it didn't take them long to transfer Jakes' luggage to Jesse's car, and they could leave.

Jakes woke up with a headache that morning, and it got worse as the day progressed. He tried to hide his discomfort from his companions, but he didn't miss Angie's sidelong glances as he became quieter and quieter. It didn't help much that traffic was heavy, resulting in them only arriving at the cabin late afternoon.

From the discussions on the way to the cabin, Jakes understood that he was going to share the loft room with Jesse and Rayno, but Mary Summers only gave Jakes one look and vetoed it. After the introductions, Mary muttered, "Jakes can't sleep in the loft. He is way too big to fit a single bed and would bump his head against the low ceiling the whole time. No," she turned to Jakes, "You can have the bedroom next to Jonathan and Claire."

Jakes' head was pounding by then, so he didn't argue. He was grateful to escape to his room after they had coffee, so he could be alone for a few minutes. Even though he hated doing that, he drank two of the prescribed headache tablets, but he was convinced he wouldn't survive the evening without them.

He barely finished unpacking before there was a knock on

the door. It had to be Angie as she had volunteered to show him the house before they joined the rest of the family in the family room.

When Jakes saw the loft room, he appreciated Mary's thoughtfulness. He would have slept there if there hadn't been another choice, but he had to agree with Mary that it would have been uncomfortable. Angie smiled when Jakes had to bend his head to walk out of the room, "My mom was right. You would've struggled to sleep here. How on earth did Jesse think you would've managed?"

Jakes shook his head, "He's used to it, I guess."

The size of the cabin amazed him. Angie hadn't lied. There was enough to keep them busy indoors. It even had a gymnasium, hot tub and a library. Jakes' favourite room though was the warm and cosy family room where the rest of the family was waiting for them. Several comfortable couches and chairs were arranged around the fireplace. There was also a television and a pool table.

Jakes was quiet throughout the evening and only listened to the conversations around him. He answered when someone asked him a question, but otherwise, he only listened. He was aware though that Dr Summers observed him throughout the evening. The dark circles under his eyes hadn't disappeared, and Jakes knew he looked like crap. Jakes blamed it on another sleepless night and the pounding headache. If he still had a headache in the morning, he would speak to Doc in the morning. Now, however, he couldn't wait to have an early night.

At least the others had the same idea, and not long after dinner, they all disappeared to their rooms. Jakes took another couple of painkillers and crept into bed.

.   .   .

JAKES DIDN'T COME DOWN for breakfast. When there was no sign of him at ten o'clock, Angie went to knock on his door. She didn't have to be a doctor to immediately know that he was sick when he opened. His eyes were red, and his skin flushed. He held onto the door with one hand, and the other held his head. His voice sounded husky when he mumbled, "Sorry, I'll be there soon."

Angie shook her head firmly, "There's no way. Come on, let me help you back to bed, then I will call my Dad."

Angie didn't even notice his magnificent body only dressed in sleeping shorts. She was too concerned about the heat radiating from him. He had a fever and didn't look well at all. He had to feel really ill as he leaned heavily on her as she helped him back to the bed. When he fell on the mattress and curled up, she covered him with the blanket, but she hadn't even reached the door before he had kicked it off.

She hurried to the room where the rest of the family had gathered and called from the door, "Dad, Jakes is sick."

Angie didn't wait for him and rushed back to Jakes' room. She stood aside when her father entered with his medical bag, so he could examine Jakes. When he finished, he told Jakes, "You have flu. You know the drill. Take lots of fluids and stay in bed for at least a day or two. You can take the prescribed flu medication, painkillers and vitamins. If you're not better tomorrow, we'll start with antibiotics."

Jakes sank back against the cushions while Dr Summers took the medication out of his bag and told Angie, "It's no use telling him what to do. Make sure he takes these, every eight hours for the next forty-eight hours. Jonathan and Claire will be here soon, then we'll take turns to check on him, but he should be okay in a day or two. If you want to, you can give him a sponge bath with lukewarm water to see if we can break his fever quicker."

Angie nodded. "I'll get the orange juice, and then I'll be back."

She rushed to the kitchen to get the juice, a glass, a bowl for the water and a cloth. She briefly stopped at her room to pick up her tablet. There was no way she would leave Jakes alone until his fever broke. Back in his room, her father waited until Jakes took the medication, then left Angie alone with Jakes.

Angie went to the bathroom to fill the bowl with water as her father instructed. Back in the room, she wiped Jakes' face, neck and shoulders. When she rubbed his chest and stomach, Jakes grabbed her hand and mumbled, "I may be sick, but I'm not dead."

Angie flushed when she got his drift. Her eyes drifted down to his flat stomach where her hand was still resting. Jakes smiled faintly, "It's okay to look, though."

If it was possible in any way, Angie's face turned an even brighter red then. Thank goodness Jakes had closed his eyes and didn't notice her embarrassment. She mumbled, "It's good to know you're not that sick," but wasn't sure Jakes heard.

He clutched her hand tighter when she wanted to stand back and pleaded, "Please, stay with me."

Only when Angie reassured him, "I'm not going anywhere. I want to get my tablet," did he let her hand go. She went to pick up her tablet from the dresser, and when she returned, she pulled the chair closer to the bed. She took Jakes' hand and waited until he fell asleep.

Angie didn't know how long she sat there, just watching him. Her thoughts lingered on the last few weeks since she'd met him until his mumbling pulled her out of her reverie. He was restless and soaking wet. He only calmed again when Angie sponged him off for a second time. Angie again sat back in the chair to study him.

His skin still had a flush typical of fever, and a sheen of sweat had already formed again. He hadn't shaved, and the dark stubble of his beard covered his face. That was what he looked like when they first met. Angie was disappointed when he shaved it off. Maybe she should convince him to keep it this time.

Her eyes drifted to his chest, the skin surprisingly hairless and tanned. He had kicked off the blanket again to expose his long, muscled legs that reached the foot of the bed. Angie could swear his calves were bigger than her upper thighs.

Even his feet looked muscular and tanned. Angie wouldn't be surprised if he wore a size twelve shoes or even larger. Was it true what they say about the link between the size of a man's feet and his...?

She jumped when Claire whispered next to her, "Wow, it's a shame to hide that magnificence under layers of clothing." Claire almost swooned, and Angie didn't blame her, but she still reprimanded, "Claire, you're a married woman."

"Tsk, Angie! I'm only giving my professional opinion. This... Uhm... This perfection is what my patients should to aspire to look like."

Angie snorted, "Yeah, right. Your patients are babies."

Claire didn't even look embarrassed as she grinned and handed Angie a cup of coffee. "When I heard one of our guests is sick, I volunteered to bring you coffee and check his fever."

Claire studied Jakes again and grinned at Angie, "Now I'm glad I had the chance to inspect."

Angie shook her head. She knew Claire well, but her sister-in-law still amazed her when she became professional as soon as she took out her stethoscope. She listened to Jakes' heartbeat and took his fever then muttered, "His fever is still too high. Did he have anything to drink since Dad saw him?"

Angie shook her head, "No, not since he took his medicine. Although he was restless, he had been sleeping the whole time."

Claire was decisive. "We need to get him to sit up for a moment, so I can listen to his lungs. You could also give him something to drink."

Angie wasn't sure what to do. She poured orange juice into a glass and waited for Claire's instruction. Claire studied Jakes before she instructed, "He'll be heavy. Maybe you should try to wake him up."

Angie nodded. She bent over Jakes and without even thinking about it, she stroke Jakes' cheek, "Jakes? Do you think you can sit up for a moment?"

His eyes fluttered open, but his eyes looked dazed and unfocused. He mumbled something in his mother tongue, but Angie didn't understand any of it. He tried to sit up, though. Angie sank down on the bed next to him, slipped her arm around his shoulders to support him and lifted the glass to his lips. He leaned heavily on her while he drank. Claire grabbed the glass from Angie when he finished and put it on the table. Angie supported his body while Claire listened to his lungs. When they let Jakes down on the pillows, his eyes had closed already.

"The good news is his lungs are clear."

Angie sighed relieved, "Well, that's good news."

"He was lucky to have a doctor on hand and could get immediate medical attention. Most macho men wait and then try to sweat it out. By then it might already have gravitated towards pneumonia or bronchitis. It's also a good thing Dad was here. I've never treated a professional athlete before. Dad explained that they could only use a specific medication and the effect of antibiotics. I never knew there were so many things to consider when you're a professional athlete," Claire chatted.

Angie wet the cloth again and sponged Jakes' face, arms, and chest. She only sat back in her chair and picked up the coffee Claire brought when she noticed he was fast asleep to agree with Claire, "I didn't know there are so many things that can influence their game. I admire how hard they train, and how tough they must be, both physically and mentally, to be successful."

Angie put down her cup and sat up to stroke Jakes' hair back from his face. He was still too hot for her liking, and she watched his face, concerned.

He mumbled something, and she took his hand, and soon he was quiet again. His breathing became regular, and Angie sat back, still holding his hand in hers.

When she looked up, Claire had left. She picked up her tablet with the other hand and opened the book on her tablet she started the day before.

Angie spent most of the day taking care of Jakes. One of the other family members relieved her for periods, but Angie never stayed away too long.

Jonathan came to check in the early hours of the morning. He helped her to give Jakes his medication and fluids before he left them. Angie could feel herself drooping. When she finished sponging Jakes down, she went to the bathroom. When she came back, she stretched out next to Jakes. She only wanted to lie down as her body was getting stiff from sitting in the chair the whole day.

Jakes mumbled in his sleep again. Angie strained to hear what he said, but he spoke in what she now knew was Afrikaans. She could only make out her name. Angie retook his hand, threading their fingers. Minutes later, Jakes fell asleep again, and it wasn't long before Angie also succumbed. She was out cold and didn t even know when her mother and Jonathan came into the room later to check on Jakes. She also didn't see them smile when they saw how Angie and Jakes were sleeping, their hands entangled. Her mother took a blanket out of the cupboard and covered her before they left them alone.

It was a while later Angie opened her eyes and looked straight into Jakes' eyes. At first, neither of them said anything.

CHAPTER TEN

J akes woke up when the light filtered through the curtains. He blinked into the soft glow of the morning light, not knowing where he was and then realised his headache was gone. His brain still felt fuzzy, and his body ached, but at least he was more awake than he was the previous day.

The second thing he became aware of was that he was not alone, as someone held his hand.

Jakes turned his head slightly to that side. His breath hitched when he realised it was Angie. He rolled onto his side to watch her.

His gaze drifted up to her face. Even in sleep, she was beautiful.

Her lashes fluttered and her eyes opened.

"Good morning," Jakes managed.

Angie smiled, "Good morning."

For long moments they just lay there, looking at each other before she raised the hand that didn't hold his. She stroke it gently over his cheek and forehead and then smiled relieved. "Your fever broke. How do you feel?"

Jakes thought for a moment. "Much better, thanks. At least the headache is gone. I'll get up in a minute."

Angie shook her head firmly. "Oh no, you won't. You may feel better, but Dad gave strict instructions that you must stay in bed today."

Jakes could feel the blushing creeping up his cheeks when he explained, "I need to go to the bathroom."

He knew she was teasing him, as he could see the amusement lurking in her eyes. "Do you need any help?"

Was she serious? He couldn't even answer her because her mischievous remark called up a whole new trail of thoughts. He had to turn away from her to hide his sudden reaction to that image. He moved to stand up but immediately sank back on the bed.

In a flash, Angie was around the bed and at his side. "Are you okay?"

"I suddenly felt dizzy," Jakes admitted.

"You would be."

Jakes looked up when he heard a different voice coming from the doorway. It could only be Jonathan, as he had the same blue eyes as Jesse, Angie and their father. Jakes watched him warily. Jonathan came to stand in front of him and studied him with a stern expression. "What do you think you're doing? You're not allowed up yet."

Jakes' shoulders dropped. "Sorry, but I really need the bathroom."

You could see that Jonathan and Angie were siblings. The same humour flashed over Jonathan's face before he replied with a sage nod, "Then I'll help you. You can freshen up, but I'll leave the bathroom door open in case you pass out on me."

Jakes grimaced gratefully. "Thank you."

Jonathan turned to Angie and chided. "And you can go freshen up and get something to eat and drink. When you come back, you can bring something for Jakes. Ask Mom or Claire. They'll know what to give him."

Jakes was back in bed when Angie returned with the tray her mother prepared. Under Jonathan's supervision, Jakes drank the juice and ate the scrambled eggs, fruit and yoghurt. Jonathan nodded when Jakes put his cutlery down and drank his medication. Jonathan picked up the tray and said to Jakes, a smile lurking at his mouth, "You're well trained."

To Angie's surprise, Jakes' mouth also turned up. "Years of experience of knowing not to argue with the doctor. You never know when they will bring out needles."

Jonathan laughed and left Angie and Jakes alone.

WHEN ANGIE SAT on the chair next to the bed, Jakes reached for her hand. "Jonathan mentioned that you took care of me," and then admitted, "Nobody, except my mom, has ever done that for me. Thank you."

Angie squeezed his hand. "Anyone would have done it. I'm just glad you feel better."

Jakes snorted and shook his head. "No, trust me, not everyone would have done that." Realising that he might reveal too much, he mumbled, "I'm sorry I messed up your plans."

Her laugh was revitalising. It kept Jakes captivated, as usual, so much so that he almost didn't hear what she said. "What plans? I did what I planned to do. I went through my photos, I read, and relaxed. I only did it with you, although you won't remember much."

"I may not remember much, but I knew when you were here," he admitted.

She looked proud of herself. Jakes realised how much it must have taken for her to sit here so quietly with him for such a long period. He wished he could've told her how much it meant to him, but he felt so sleepy that he might say something that he shouldn't. He shifted into a more comfortable position and asked, "Tell me about the book you are reading."

Angie started telling him, but Jakes must have drifted off to sleep. When he woke up, she wasn't there and hadn't come back, but there was always someone with him. Only later that evening when he woke up again, she was there. "You're back," Jakes muttered relieved.

Angie looked up and smiled, "Yes, I got instructions to go out. I went shopping and painted for a while."

"That's good. I felt guilty about keeping you here the whole time."

She put her hand over his and reassured him quickly, "I wanted to do it, Jakes."

Jakes had to swallow hard to control his emotions. Luckily Angie jumped up with the announcement, "I'm going to get you something to eat."

As soon as she left the room, Jakes got up to go to the bathroom. At least he didn't feel as dizzy as he had this morning. He was already back in bed when Angie returned with her father. Jakes waited patiently for Dr Summers to examine him. When he stood back, Dr Summers told Jakes, "You have the strength of an ox. You can get up tomorrow, but I still want you to take it easy, and when you're tired, rest."

"Thank you, Doc. I'm sorry for the inconvenience."

"You couldn't help it, Jakes and anyway, Angie took the brunt of your care."

Jakes nodded, still feeling uncomfortable. When her father left, Angie put the tray on his lap. She waited patiently while he ate and drank his medication before she took the plate away while Jakes got comfortable. It wasn't long before he drifted off again with Angie's hand still in his own.

. . .

WHEN HE WOKE the following morning, Jakes felt far better than he had the past two days. He got up, still cautious, and when he felt no dizziness, he went to shower.

After dressing in a pair of jeans and a long-sleeve T-shirt, he made the bed. He cleaned up the bathroom as best he could before he went to find the rest of the household.

They were all in the kitchen, gathered around the table in the middle of the room. His eyes immediately fell onto Angie, where she sat between her two brothers. Jakes wanted to smile when he saw the paint streaks on her face, which was the subject of her brother's teasing. She had clearly painted already.

Jakes' gaze drifted to greet the other occupants, and he stiffened immediately. Next to Rayno, on the opposite side of the table, sat a beautiful woman.

A woman with red curls.

Jakes forced himself to look again and then noticed her impish smile and the way she looked at Jonathan. The panic that was building up disappeared when he studied the woman further. Maybe it was her natural smile or that naughty glimpse in her eyes which reassured him, and he could relax.

Dr Summers sat at the one end of the table, drinking his coffee and listening to his children's good-natured arguments. Mary stood at the counter and was the first to look up when she saw Jakes hovering in the doorway. She motioned with her head that he should enter and smiled friendly.

When he did as she asked and murmured a greeting, she handed him a mug. "Here, help yourself. There's always coffee on the go. Milk and sugar are on the table, or here on the counter."

"Thank you," Jakes muttered and helped himself to the coffee. When he finished preparing it to his liking, he turned to the room to find a place to sit. His heart sank in his shoes when he noticed the only empty seat was between Rayno and the redhead he suspected was Claire. He hesitated, but when he looked at Claire again, Jakes realised that there was no sign of his usual panic. He didn't even want to analyse it now, just grateful that it was not there, and approached the table.

He put his mug on the table before he took his seat. It was just as well he was already sitting before he looked up and straight into Angie's eyes. His heart rate accelerated when she smiled. Jakes couldn't even return the gesture because he couldn't breathe.

Even with that paint on her cheek, she was still the most beautiful woman Jakes had ever seen.

Vaguely he heard a dramatic cough. He pulled his eyes away from Angie when Claire bumped his arm and announced, "I'm Claire."

Jakes flushed as he turned to Claire and held out his hand. He hadn't been wrong. It looked like Claire had a wicked sense of humour as the mischief was still lurking in her eyes when he replied, "I'm Jakes. I remember you vaguely from that first day I was sick."

Jakes was still surprised by the lack of panic when Claire shook his hand. "That's right. I had the privilege to monitor your... condition," as she sneaked a gaze to Angie.

Jakes heard Angie's shocked inhale before she muttered, "Claire," before she jumped up and disappeared through the door. There was definitely something more behind Claire's remark as Jonathan spluttered when Jakes stared surprised at the door through which Angie went.

Angie didn't come back for the rest of the morning. Jakes suspected she was painting again, but he didn't want to ask anyone where. It might be best that he didn't know where her studio was. Who said he might not give in to the temptation and went looking for her?

He didn't even want to think about it. He would've joined

Angie. He would've spent more time with her even though he knew he shouldn't. He, therefore, didn't ask and played cards with Jesse, Rayno, Jonathan, and Claire, until Claire gave up and went to help Mary in the kitchen. Jakes sucked at the game and wished he could have joined them. He was a far better cook than he was a card player. It didn't help that his attention wasn't with the game today. He just couldn't concentrate.

ANGIE LOOKED tired when she re-appeared at lunch after Claire went to haul her out of the studio. She still had the paint smear over her cheek and Jakes itched to rub it off.

After lunch, when everyone disappeared, Jakes also took the opportunity to rest. He still didn't feel a hundred percent. He hardly read a chapter before he fell asleep with the book in his hands. It was close to six when he woke up with a start. He got up quickly and hurriedly changed into a pair of dark jeans. He was still busy putting on his shirt when there was a knock on the door. He immediately apologised when he opened the door to Angie, "I'm sorry, I overslept."

He concentrated on buttoning the white shirt he had chosen when he realised that Angie hadn't answered him. When he looked up, he noticed that her eyes were fixed on his hands. Heat suddenly rushed through him when she slowly raised her eyes to meet his.

The knowledge hit him like a sledgehammer, but it shouldn't have come as a surprise. That kiss had changed everything. He wanted to hold her and kiss her until neither of them knew where they were.

But he didn't do it. He didn't dare to because Jakes knew if he was going to kiss her one more time it was over. If he had to hold her one more time... No, he didn't want to think about it.

He tore his gaze away from her and finished buttoning his shirt with trembling fingers.

When he stepped into his loafers, Angie was still watching him in silence. The old insecurities rushed to the fore, forcing him to ask uncomfortably, "Is this okay?"

Angie angled her head sideways and took in his appearance. Jakes again felt the heat when her gaze drifted slowly from his face down and then took her time to follow the same route back to meet his eyes. And then she smiled, "Perfect. I love the white shirt with your skin tone."

Jakes swallowed when he realised: Angie hadn't criticized him. Quite the opposite, in fact. He was convinced that he had read admiration in her eyes, the same he had that day in the gymnasium. That emphasized the knowledge: When was he going to trust his own judgement again? He knew why he asked her if his outfit looked okay, but the reason behind it, he could not share with Angie.

"Come," she ordered. "The others are waiting."

Jakes followed her to the lounge in silence. She stopped so suddenly in the doorway that Jakes almost bumped into her. It didn't help much to lessen this sudden awareness of her. Neither did it help when Jonathan spotted them and shouted, "Kiss, kiss.

Everyone turned to the door and echoed Jonathan's words, "Kiss, kiss."

Oh no! Jakes glanced down at Angie, remembering their first kiss. How the hell could he kiss her in front of everyone? Jakes remembered how he felt then. And it wasn't as if he didn't want to kiss her. He wanted to, desperately. It was all he could think of since Friday night.

Angie turned. Her eyes shone mischievously as she whispered, "You may kiss me, you know."

Jakes whispered back, "With an audience watching?"

She laughed, and before Jakes realised what was happening, she took the decision out of his hands. She stood on her tiptoes and kissed him. It hadn't even been a long kiss. It wasn't remotely like Friday night's kiss, but geez, the woman stole his breath. And then she nonchalantly stood back, smiled at him before she turned and walked into the room as if she hadn't just turned his world onto its head.

Jakes stared at her, too shocked to follow. His heart was beating way too fast and he couldn't move a muscle. He abruptly returned to reality when someone bumped his arm. Jakes tore his gaze away from Angie, where she was now sitting on the couch, talking to her father. Jesse held a bottle of beer out to Jakes with a similarly amused grin as Angie's. Jakes didn't blame Jesse. He probably looked as dazed as he felt.

He blushed and took the bottle. He took an appreciative sip of the cold brew before he followed Jesse into the room to join the other men. Throughout the evening, his eyes often strayed to Angie. He didn't even have to speculate why he felt this magnetic pull towards her. He had spent enough time over the last two weeks thinking about it. She was so different than...

No, he shouldn't even think about it. Angie was Angie. Unique. One in a million. She was one of those people whose beauty wasn't only on the outside. Her heart was soft and beautiful, and she had so much empathy with people that it softened his own heart.

Her love for her friends and family was evident. Just look at her now when she leaned against her father while they spoke quietly. The otherwise strict doctor seemed so different when he looked at his daughter. Jakes didn't blame him, especially when she smiled and her face lit up.

Jakes swallowed hard. This might have been a mistake. He was barely hanging onto his last bit of resistance and didn't know how much longer he would manage.

Sometimes you could feel someone was looking at you. Jakes tore his gaze away from Angie, just to look straight into her mother's eyes. Mary, in turn, was studying Jakes with a thoughtful expression. Jakes could feel his ears getting warm. Mary had to have seen the way he looked at Angie like a lovesick teenager. He undoubtedly had given away the secret he had tried so hard to keep.

THAT RESISTANCE he thought earlier he still had? That crumbled faster than Jakes could even imagine when he followed Angie into the kitchen after dinner. She had decided he needed a lesson to make proper hot cacao.

Jakes followed her quietly. That's when he saw it, and he accepted, he could forget about staying away from Angie. The mistletoe hung above the door of the pantry. Jakes didn't even think twice. Maybe he should have, but he reacted instinctively.

When Angie came out of the pantry, he blocked her away. When she stared at him in surprise, Jakes muttered, "I want a do-over."

Angie frowned at him, "A do-over? Of what?" she asked, confused.

The corner of Jakes' mouth curled up. He held her eyes for a moment before he looked up. Angie followed his eyes, her mouth almost dropping open when she noticed the mistletoe. When she looked back to Jakes to meet his eyes, her eyes shone with mischief. He didn't give her a chance to say anything before he closed the distance and murmured, "This time, we don't have an audience."

Jakes cupped her face and seconds later he claimed her lips. It was like that kiss on Friday night, but also not. It might be as soft and gentle as Friday's kiss, but yet it felt more intense. Jakes wouldn't have minded if it lasted forever.

It might have if Jesse hadn't shouted Angie's name at full volume from the doorway, and they jumped apart. Angie dropped the chocolate and marshmallows on the floor. When Jesse came closer and asked, "How far are you with the hot chocolate?", she knelt to pick it up. Angie kept herself busy, so she didn't have to look at Jesse. Jakes didn't have that luxury. He didn't know where to look. When Jesse laughed and remarked, "I see Jonathan was busy again," while giving both Jakes and Angie knowing looks, Jakes knew that Jesse came to the right conclusion.

With a smirk in Jakes' direction, Jesse walked over to the cupboard and took out the mugs and a pot. Angie had managed to pick up the ingredients and put them on the table. She retraced her footsteps to fetch milk and cream from the fridge. Back at the hob, Angie measured a cup of milk for each of them and added it to the pot. Over her shoulder, she told Jakes, "One secret of our cocoa is that you only use pure ingredients. Use whole milk, and pure cocoa powder," and summarily added almost a cup of cocoa and sugar to the milk. She laughed at Jakes' shocked face when she added a pinch of salt. "Is that the other secret ingredient?"

Angie shook her head with a laugh but didn't answer. Jakes anyway wouldn't have heard it, as Jesse stirred the cream with an electric mixer. With the sugar and cocoa dissolved and the milk heated, Angie took the pot off the stove. She broke a bar of milk chocolate into the liquid and added a dash of vanilla. She then poured the mixture into the mugs, and Jesse finished it off with cream and mini-marshmallows.

Angie handed a mug to Jakes. "Try that."

Jakes took a tentative sip, and when the taste hit his tongue, his eyes widened. "Whoa, that's good," he said before he took another sip. "I wouldn't be able to drink too many of these—this is serious sugar overload."

"You're right. This is our special Christmas cocoa. The rest of the time we're not this decadent."

"What is your other secret ingredient then?" Jakes asked, suspicious after another sip.

Angie looked up at him to answer, but Jesse beat her to it. He picked up the tray, and just before he walked out of the door, his gaze flitted between Angie and Jakes. He wiggled his eyebrows and smirked, "The other secret ingredient? It's love."

IT TOOK Jakes several minutes before he could assimilate Jesse's cryptic remark and gesture and recovered enough to join the others.

The big room was now a hive of activity. Someone had brought in the Christmas tree which had still been standing on the veranda that morning, and it took the place of honour in the one corner. Claire was busy unpacking boxes with Christmas decorations. Jakes joined them, Claire exclaimed, "Now we can decorate."

Soon Angie gave orders to everyone, including to Jakes and Rayno, in such a way that Coach would've been proud of her. They started with the lights, which were followed by the mismatched decorations, none of which followed a cohesive theme. Some were clearly homemade, most likely when the kids were small, while others were store-bought. Mary had a story to tell about each decoration, reminding Jakes of home and his own family. For the first year in a long time, Jakes couldn't spend Christmas with his family, but surprisingly enough, he didn't feel sad.

Angie brought out one more box of decorations and handed it first to each one in her family to take one of the decorations. Even Rayno got his turn before she held out the box to Jakes and explained, "Each year we get these at the chocolate shop in the village. Everyone chooses their own decoration, but as you were sick, I took the liberty to choose one for you."

There were only two decorations left in the box. One was a little bird and the other an angel. "Which one is mine?" Jakes asked.

Angie laughed, "It doesn't matter. You can choose."

Jakes realised everyone was busy hanging their decorations. He stepped closer to Angie and whispered, "My choice? Are you sure?"

Angie nodded, now just as solemn as Jakes. Why he did it, Jakes would never know, but he held her eyes as he whispered, "Then you don't have to ask. I choose the angel."

Did she grasp the meaning behind his words? Words he should not have said, but had escaped before he could stop them? Maybe she had, as a subtle flush spread over her cheeks. Her hands shook as she took out the angel and handed it to Jakes and then took out the bird. They turned in unison to hang the two decorations.

Angie's embarrassment at least didn't last long. The tree still needed one decoration, and that was the star meant for the top of the tree. Jakes guessed it was a family tradition that Angie put the star on top because she took it out and turned around to add it, then groaned in dismay, "Why did you get such a big tree? I'll never reach the top."

She turned to her father and asked, "Did you get a new ladder? You remembered what happened to the old one, Dad?"

Embarrassed, doc Summers shook his head. Everyone stared in consternation to Angie and the star she still clutched in her hand.

Jakes realised that he should be more careful with this family. Jesse got a similar mischievous glint in his eyes as Angie often had, and Jakes noticed Jonathan also exhibited a couple of times. Jesse bumped Rayno's arm, and then he proposed, albeit with a mischievous expression as he gestured to Jakes, "He can help you. He's tall enough, and he's anyway used to lifting men heavier than you."

If looks could kill, the looks both Jakes and Angie shot at Jesse, might have done the trick. The whole family now turned expectantly to Jakes. Jonathan and Claire looked just as amused as Jesse about the proposal, but Jakes couldn't refuse now. He turned to Angie and gestured "Come on. Let's get the star on the tree."

Angie stood closer to him, her face still full of doubt. With the star in one hand, she pointed the other to him and warned, "Okay, big guy, let's do this. But if you drop me, no more hot chocolate for you."

She looked so cute that Jakes smiled, completely oblivious that the rest of the family was watching them. Before Angie could add anything, he bent and without any warning, slid his hands around the top of her legs and lifted her up. Angie shrieked and grabbed his head. He stood up and pushed Angie higher, "Okay, if you straighten too, you should be able to reach."

When Angie balanced the star, everyone cheered. They then turned to start cleaning up the room, unaware that Jakes was still standing there with Angie in his hands. Jakes only looked up when she put her hand on his head. Jakes slid her down slowly, close against his body and not once did they break eye contact.

There was not even a hint of a smile, possibly because of the intensity of the contact between them.

CHAPTER ELEVEN

Angie couldn't sleep. She relived that moment between her and Jakes after she put the star on the tree. Even before then, she had a feeling that she might not be the only one who suddenly had to deal with feelings they didn't know what to do with. That kiss in the kitchen? No, it had been amazing, but it wasn't that. Maybe there was something when he chose that angel decoration but never, not even at the beginning of their relationship when everything was new, had Chris made her feel like Jakes had tonight. It was as if Jakes awoke feelings Angie never knew existed.

After she turned over for the umpteenth time, Angie flung the blanket off in irritation and jumped up. She might as well do something constructive if she couldn't sleep.

She opened her door and peered outside. Except for the lights that usually stayed on throughout the night, only silence and darkness greeted her. She smiled. She might as well put her presents under the tree. She already knew she was not going to be the first. Her parents always beat her to it, no matter how hard she tried to be first.

She switched on her bedside lamp and pulled her suitcase from under her bed. With her arms loaded, she tiptoed to the family room. There was enough light in the hallway to find her way, but she knew the house so well that she didn't even have to look where she was going.

SHE MIGHT HAVE MISJUDGED it because the next moment she bumped into a hard object. When that hard object stretched out hands to keep her from falling, Angie didn't have to guess who it was. She recognised Jakes' now-familiar deodorant even before she lifted her head.

Keeping silent, he dropped his hands from her arms, then turned slightly so that Angie could push past him to reach the tree. Angie's heart was beating fast and her hands shaking when she knelt next to the tree to put down her gifts. She took her time, more to calm her tumultuous emotions. It didn't help much. When she got up and turned, he was there, so close that she could feel his heat.

He lifted his hand to brush the hair away from her face. The light touch of his fingertips stroking her skin felt like butterfly wings. Angie looked up her heart in her throat.

The lights of the Christmas tree turned the room into an intimate cocoon, but Angie could still recognise Jakes' features in the soft light, even the scar where the remnants of an old injury left a white mark and contrasted against his suntanned skin. It was his eyes that drew her in as usual.

She knew he was going to kiss her even before he lowered his head. His lips were soft as it whispered over hers. He lifted his head slightly, but then he groaned her name before he took her mouth with more urgency. All rational thoughts flew out of the window. Angie was only aware of his hand, which had sculpted around her neck and the sensations caused by his mouth.

She wanted to protest when he lifted his mouth. She didn't want him to stop. He was breathing hard as he rested his forehead against hers. At last, he lifted his head to look at her, "I wanted to do that since I saw you the first time."

No wonder the man had rattled her so much that first night they met. He already then evoked feelings in her. Surprised when she realised that, Angie whispered, "I might shock you, but I wouldn't have minded."

The left side of his mouth curled up before he whispered back, "I want to do it again."

"Sounds like a good idea," she replied with a smile.

Both sides of his mouth curled up, and he mumbled on a resigned sigh, "Then that's what we'll do."

There was, however, nothing resigned about the kiss. Angie's smile hadn't disappeared when he captured her mouth again, but it did when he followed up his words with a kiss even more intense than the previous one.

She hoped it wasn't the last time.

JAKES ONLY HALF-LISTENED to the conversation at the breakfast table the following morning. He suddenly realised that it was unusually quiet. When he looked up, all eyes were on him. When he looked around, it looked like they all waited for him to say something. Jakes flushed, and mumbled, "Sorry, I..."

Jesse grinned, "We don't even have to ask. If a man could sit and daydream like that, his thoughts are on only one thing, and that is a girl."

Jesse was so close to the truth that it wasn't even funny. Jakes flushed, but he didn't answer. He also didn't dare to look at Angie because he knew by now what would happen. At least

Jesse didn't carry on about it and asked, "We wanted to know if you want to go ski with us?"

Jakes shook his head and said, "No, I never learned, and I don't want to take any chances."

Dr Summers agreed with Jakes when he grumbled, "I'm glad that you're sensible. I would anyway have advised you not to do it."

"You're excused then. Do you mind if we go? That's Jonathan, Rayno and I," Jesse asked.

Jakes didn't want to spoil their fun and shook his head, "No, not at all."

"That's fine then. You can keep my dad and the women company. My mom is planning a full-scale meal for tonight, and they want to cook."

"I'll help," Jakes volunteered. He looked hopefully at Mary, "I love cooking."

Jesse, Rayno, and Angie confirmed his statement enthusiastically, "He *can* cook. He made a delicious chicken curry with all the trimmings and even a dessert!" Angie exclaimed wide-eyed.

Mary smiled at Jakes, "You're more than welcome. It would be nice if you can inspire Angie in the kitchen."

Angie snorted indignantly, "I can cook—if I have to...," she admitted unwillingly.

The whole family laughed when Jonathan teased, "Yes, if you remember." He said to Jakes, "Angie invited us to dinner one night when she lived in Boulder. There was only one problem. She started painting and forgot we were coming. When we arrived at her apartment, we surprised her and had to get pizza in the end."

When Angie blushed, Jakes stepped in to save her from further embarrassment. "I told you. You're the same as my mother."

He explained to the rest of the family, "My mum's a sculptor. When she gets involved with a project, she forgets everything around her. I was still small when my grandmother came to live with us and took over the household. After she died, I didn't have much choice. I had to learn to cook if we didn't want to starve. My dad is as helpless as my mum."

Mary laughed, "Then we should remember not to put your mum and Angie in charge of the kitchen."

Jakes could only imagine that scenario and smiled at Mary, "No, rather not, but I think they'll get along like a house on fire."

He turned to Angie and said, without thinking, "It wouldn't be long before you would be in her studio."

The words had barely left his mouth when he realised what he said. He would've loved to introduce Angie to his mother. He was convinced that they would get along, not like...

His shoulders dropped as he admonished himself to stop hoping and dreaming. That might never happen.

When he looked up a long time later, he found Jonathan's thoughtful gaze on him. Jakes shifted uncomfortably and dropped his head again.

JAKES STOOD AT THE WINDOW, looking in wonder at the scene outside. He'd seen snow before. It often snowed during winter in the Lesotho Mountains and the passes near Harrismith. That, however, was nothing compared to the scene in front of him.

He didn't have to look to know that Angie had joined him. He breathed deep, inhaling the subtle smell of her perfume as he had done the whole morning in the kitchen. It only proved how low his resistance was.

He almost snorted. Resistance? No, that had disappeared

already. He just had to count the number of times he had already kissed her. And he didn't want to stop. Every look, every touch, only confirmed his already growing attraction.

Jakes glanced down at her when she sighed dreamily, "It's so beautiful. I love the mountains in winter, but I love it even more in spring and summer. The hills are green then, and there are wildflowers everywhere."

"Do you like spring flowers?"

When Angie nodded, Jakes walked across to the coffee table where he left his phone and picked it up. He sat on the couch and opened his photo book. Without hesitating, Angie joined him and Jakes made the mistake of looking at him. Her mouth looked way too inviting when she smiled at him in anticipation. He shifted uncomfortably and quickly turned back to his phone to continue his search. When he finally found what he was looking for, he held the phone out to her to show her the photos. Instead of taking the phone, she leaned closer. Jakes felt the sensations where their arms and legs touched. He had to breathe deep before he could explain, "I've taken these on our farm in the Eastern Free State. It's at the foot of the Maluti Mountains, between Fouriesburg and Clarens. Between April and May, but sometimes as early as February, the Eastern Free State is at its most beautiful. Then the cosmos flowers everywhere on the side of the roads and in the fields."

ANGIE LOOKED in amazement at the photos on Jakes' phone. She asked him to stop at one picture and studied it in detail. She would have loved painting it. "Will you send this one to me?"

Did he know what she wanted to do? Possibly because he sent it to her without asking for another explanation, a smile curling around the one corner of his mouth.

He showed her a few more photos then there was a picture

of a group of people. Jakes stared at the photo for a while, but when he wanted to put his phone away, Angie stopped him and asked nosily, "Is that your family?"

Jakes hesitated before he showed her the photo. "We took this at my sister's wedding two years ago. This is my sister." He pointed out each one of his family members. Apart from his sister and brother-in-law, there was also two younger brothers, his parents and an older couple who could be his father's parents. Angie quizzed him on his family. At first, he looked uncomfortable, but he still answered. It was only much later that they realized that they were alone. Voices lead them to the kitchen where Mary and Claire relaxed with a cup of coffee each. "Is there something we can do?"

Mary shook her head, "No, everything is ready. Why don't you go for a walk? You don't know if you'll get another chance as they predict more snow for later today."

Jakes turned to Angie with an eager expression, "That will be nice, even if it is only for a short while."

Angie nodded, "Just dress warmly. I don't want trouble from my Dad if you get sick again. I'll meet you at the front door."

Angie was still putting on her jacket when Jakes joined her. He already had his coat on. Angie zipped her jacket up, then reached to open the door, but Jakes stopped her with his hand on her arm. Surprised, she looked at him, but she didn't have to wonder for long why he stopped her. He lifted both hands to thread his fingers through her hair. He held her eyes for a moment, and then he leaned forward, his mouth touching her in a soft kiss. When he pulled back, his eyes twinkled as he pointed upwards, "Mistletoe."

Angie laughed and shook her head. "You caught on quickly, didn't you?"

The smile tugged at the one corner of his mouth. "I like Jonathan's way of thinking."

Angie liked this Jakes, the one who smiled and teased, even if it was just a small smile, more, if possible. Unfortunately, he didn't give her a chance to appreciate him more because his smile disappeared and he turned in a hurry. He zipped up his parka because he opened the door and walked out.

The first part of their walk was in silence. What happened? Why was he suddenly so tense?

Angie had learned quickly to leave Jakes when he was like that. Today, however, she wasn't in the mood to talk. Her mind was in turmoil, and nothing made sense. And then, suddenly, she felt his hand touching hers and soon after he threaded his fingers through hers. Neither of them said anything. Angie couldn't talk as her heart was beating at a hundred beats per minute.

On their way back to the house, Angie asked, "Have you ever made snow angels?"

Jakes shook his head. He looked wary when Angie pulled him to a flat stretch of ground outside the house. She pointed to the snow. "To make a perfect snow angel, you need fresh snow that's deep enough so you couldn't see the ground underneath it. The top should be soft, like such as a powder. Watch me first, and then you can make yours."

ANGIE SUMMARILY SANK down on her haunches and dropped onto her bum in the soft snow. She stretched out on her back and spread her arms straight out. With her arms still straight, she moved them through the soft snow. She first stretched them almost to the top of her head then straight back to her side.

She did it a few times and then did the same with her legs,

but not a full stretch as she had with her arms. Angie was so busy with her demonstration she didn't see Jakes take out his camera to snap a few pictures of her. She finally lay still, grinning up at Jakes, and he took one last photo.

She sat up and held out her hand to Jake, "Pull me up but do it carefully. I don't want to hurt my angel."

He stretched out and grabbed her hand to pull her up as she instructed. He stepped back and pulled her up against him. Angie grinned and turned sideways to look at her angel.

"Don't you think it's a beautiful angel?" she asked Jakes excitedly.

He said, "Beautiful," but Jakes wasn't looking at her angel. He kept looking at her.

Angie grinned, "We need a picture of my snow angel, and then you can make yours."

Jakes pulled his eyes away from her to take the photo before he handed the camera to Angie. He still was a bit sceptical about the whole thing. "You realise snow is frozen water?" he asked her.

Angie looked at him, amusement lurking in her eyes, "Yes, and?"

"Then you know I will get wet and cold."

Angie shook her head at him and teased, "Jakes, Jakes, Jakes. Really? You're not scared of a little cold water. Come on, I know you can do it."

Jakes lifted his chin and glared at her, "I'm not a wimp. I'll show you."

Angie laughed at him. Now, determined to prove her wrong, Jakes followed her example and running instructions. He was aware that she was taking photos of him while he made his snow angel but didn't argue as he was concentrating too hard. When he reckoned he was finished, he used the strength of his upper thighs to stand up without causing too much damage to his angel.

He studied his angel and, even if he had to say so himself, he didn't do a lousy job. Satisfied, he turned to Angie and muttered, "See, I did it. I'm not a wimp."

ANGIE'S HEART SKIPPED A BEAT. There was definitely another meaning behind those words. She smiled, but she hoped he knew she was not laughing at him when she reassured him, "I never thought you were."

He stared at her, then, something like wonder, or relief flitted over his face.

And then he smiled.

It was not one of those smiles when his mouth always curled up on one or both sides. No, this was a proper smile, showing off his straight white teeth. Tiny lines formed around his eyes, and Angie could only stare.

Wow! That smile was potent.

She took a deep breath to hide the effect his smile had on her and turned to admire his angel. She studied it for a second or two just so she could find her equilibrium again. When she felt ready, she slapped him on his arm and agreed, "Not bad for the first time."

Jakes looked so proud when Angie took another picture of him with his snow angel. He was smiling the whole time, even when he insisted that they took a selfie. When he was satisfied with the result, he put the camera in his pocket, and they fell into step to return to the house.

Angie couldn't stifle the urge. No trip to the mountains in winter would be complete without a snowball fight. She, however, had to think strategically and fast. She turned in a circle while she formed a plan. When she stopped, she turned and pointed in the direction they came from, "Look there."

Jakes turned the way she pointed, but she was well aware he was not going to see anything. He narrowed his eyes in concentration and frowned, "Where?"

He still wanted to turn to look at her, but he was too late. Angie had by then managed to gather a handful of snow. The ball hit him between the shoulder blades. Jakes turned to Angie, shocked. "You didn't just do that."

Angie laughed and turned to run away as fast as she can when she saw Jakes bend to pick up a ball of snow.

When his snowball hit her in the back, she laughed even harder. She turned around to see where he was and stopped, watching in fascination.

It was almost happening in slow motion. At first, only the left corner of his mouth turned up, ever so slightly, then the other. That was fine. Angie was almost used to that. The same beautiful smile from earlier flitted over his face again, but that wasn't all. His laugh started, slow like a murmur of a stream until it burst out in full force.

Angie stared at him, transfixed. His laughter was so beautiful.

She was drawn back to reality when she realised he was advancing towards her with a handful of snow. Rattled, she bent to pick up another ball of snow, but before she gathered enough to make an impact, Jakes already reached her. She lifted her arm to throw it, but he slid his arm around her and pulled her tight against his body. With his other hand, he pressed the bunch of snow against her cheek.

Angie shrieked, "You're not playing fair."

Jakes grinned, "I'm not in the game to play fair, Angel. I play a game to win."

Angie laughed, squirming to get away from him and his

handful of snow. She asked between giggles "What's the prize if you win?"

Jakes dropped the snow, and before she knew what he planned, he had swung her around and lowered his head.

"This," he mumbled against her cold lips. When he lifted his mouth a while later, Angie smiled. "I guess we're both winners then," before she slid her arms around his back and pulled him closer.

"Hmm," was all he managed, before his mouth swallowed all the words, laughter, and thoughts from Angie's mind. It was a long time later when Jakes lifted his head and stared at Angie as if in a daze. Angie smiled as she stroked his cheek. "You laughed."

Jakes stared at her as if he only realised it then and said surprised, "I did."

It seemed that he only realised it then. He looked surprised as he agreed, "I did."

Angie didn't have a chance to think about it and the reasons why he never laughed, as his hands cupped her face. He angled her head while he slanted his lips over hers. It wasn't as hot and passionate as the previous kiss, but to Angie, it felt so much more because with that kiss he took that last piece of her heart for himself.

JAKES BECAME aware of something else, other than Angie, and how she felt in his arms and against him and the feelings she evoked.

When someone cleared his throat rather loudly, Jakes returned to reality. For several seconds after he had managed to pull his mouth from hers, he could only stare at her, as if his brain still hadn't realised what had just happened. A second cough, followed by a snort, made him realise that since it wasn't Angie, they were not alone anymore.

He dropped his hands from her face, although he didn't move away from her. He just kept on staring at her. When she broke eye contact and shifted, so she could peer around him, Jakes knew it hadn't been his imagination. Her face had turned a bright red. He also knew that he couldn't let her suffer alone. He turned meekly so he could face the persons behind him.

The three men who went skiing this morning watched Jakes and Angie with their arms folded across their chests. Neither of the brothers looked angry. Quite the contrary, in fact. They seemed amused, but even then, Jakes knew that Angie's brothers were not going to leave it there. They would confront him in the future to find out what his intentions were with their sister.

He knew what he would've liked to answer but that he couldn't do.

Jakes wasn't in a hurry when he followed the others to the house. When he got rid of his boots and jacket, he entered the kitchen just in time to see how Jonathan greeted Claire with a smacking kiss. She stood back, laughing, "Not that I'm complaining, but what was that for?"

Jonathan grinned, "I don't know. I think it's contagious. Must be the fresh mountain air."

When Jesse and Rayno laughed, Claire probably realised that Jonathan had implied something more. She looked around her and snickered.

Jakes dared to look at Angie quickly. He didn't doubt that his face was as red as Angie's, confirming that they were the reason for Jonathan's remark.

Jakes fled to his room in a hurry with the excuse that he wanted to get rid of his wet pants. He didn't dare to look, but he knew that Angie was right on his heels. A short while later he joined the rest of the family for lunch. Like most mothers, Mary asked about their excursions that morning during lunch. After Jonathan and Jesse elaborated about their ski escapades, Mary asked Angie, "How was your walk?"

Angie peered at Jakes only briefly before she answered, "We didn't walk far but Jakes could make his first snow angel, and he also had his first snow fight."

"And I won."

Everyone turned to Jakes when he made that announcement, but Angie argued, "You didn't. I won."

Jakes shook his head, "I won. I told you: I only play to win."

Jesse pretended to be serious when he asked, "And if I may ask: what was the prize for the winner?"

Both Jakes and Angie blushed again. This time Angie's brothers and Rayno didn't hold back. They burst out laughing about their embarrassed faces. They would because they had seen the result with their own eyes.

CHAPTER TWELVE

J akes sat on the steps in front of the house with a mug of coffee in his hands. He enjoyed watching the antics of the two women.

Angie had insisted they make a snowman after breakfast. She told Jakes he couldn't leave Colorado without building at least one snowman. Jakes didn't want to think about going home yet and fell in with her plans. It was two days before Christmas, and his time was running out fast.

He and Jonathan, therefore, helped to build the snowman under instructions from Jesse and Rayno, who did it from the safety of the veranda. The women were adding the final touches on the snowman while Jakes and Jonathan went to get coffee, which the two women declined.

Jakes put his mug down and took out his phone. He took a few pictures of the snowman and the laughing women. He zoomed in on Angie's face as she looked up at him, a smile tugging at her lips. Her beauty and the brightness of her eyes struck him again. He took the photo and swallowed hard when he lowered the phone.

He studied the last photo for a long time before he put the phone back in his pocket with a sigh. When Jakes picked up his mug, his eyes immediately returned to Angie.

"You're in love with Angie."

Shocked, Jakes turned to Jonathan, who was now sitting next to him with his own mug in his hand. Jonathan didn't look at Jakes but at the two women.

It wasn't a question, but a statement, as if Jonathan already figured it out for himself.

Jakes' heart beat faster, and his chest felt tight as if he couldn't breathe. He closed his eyes, feeling the shock echo through his whole body.

Jonathan was right. Jakes couldn't even argue about it.

He was in love with Angie.

Why did he not realise it earlier? These feelings were not only an attraction as he suspected before. It was way more than the friendship he allowed himself to have with Angie.

He loved her.

Jakes took a deep breath and let it out again. "I am," he admitted warily.

J0nathan studied him with a frown, "You don't look happy about it."

"I... It doesn't matter how I feel, there is nothing I can do about it."

"Why not?"

Jakes put the mug down again. His fingers automatically searched for the rubber band around his wrist as his eyes followed Angie. With a sigh, he admitted, "Apart from the fact I'm not good relationship material?" He pointed to Angie. "Look at her. She's everything I'm not. She's beautiful, sociable, loving... I can go on and on, but the bottom line is, I'm not like Angie. I'm an introvert, not someone Angie needs in her life. I also can't have a relationship for at least the next six months."

"Why not? You can tell me? I promise what you tell me will stay between us."

Jakes felt instinctive that he could trust Jonathan. Jonathan had the same quiet confidence as André, his best friend and confidante, but this wasn't only his story, though. He can't share it with Jonathan or anyone else. He shook his head, "I know I can trust you, but I can't. But you can believe me when I tell you I'm not good for Angie. I wish I were."

His fingers rubbed rhythmically over the rubber band as he admitted, "I didn't even realise I was falling in love with her. I was attracted to her from the start, but I promised myself that I will not get involved with her. Now, look at what happened. How Angie got through all the barriers I've put up around me, I don't understand. I thought we could be friends at most. I never thought I would fall in love. Geez, Jonathan, I know myself. I don't do social. I get regular panic attacks but with Angie..."

"Does Angie know about this, your panic attacks?" Jonathan asked.

Jakes nodded. "She helped me through a couple, but she doesn't know why I get them."

"When do you get them?"

Jakes sighed again. "Most of the time, it's when I'm in awkward social situations or with strangers. I have a phobia about aggressive or ginger women. I try to avoid those situations as much as possible."

"But you haven't had a panic attack with Claire, and she's ginger, or with Angie? Or have you?" Jonathan frowned.

"I know it was strange. I can't explain it to you.

"And Angie?"

"Only once but not again. Angie talked me through one of the worst ones I had in a year. It's weird how she manages to calm me. I'm not as tense with Angie. I can talk to her." He swallowed before he almost said to himself, still surprised about it, "Angie taught me to laugh again."

For a while, they sat in silence, watching the women. Jakes didn't know where it came from, but he suddenly asked, "How do you know it's love and not lust or attraction?"

Jonathan laughed. "It's different for everyone but believe me: you know it when you know it."

That statement didn't make much sense, but Jakes still understood. Was that what happened to him?

Jonathan took a sip of his coffee with his eyes still on his wife. He folded his hands around his mug and smiled. It almost looked as if he had forgotten about Jakes until he spoke again. "You know it's love when you want to be with that person twenty-four seven. Even though you know it isn't possible, you still hope and dream about it. You can't wait to be with her again. The anticipation while you wait to see her again, but when you do? That's the best part of your day. That moment when you see her face and her smile, you know, it was worth the wait. She's the first person you think about when you wake up in the morning and the last person before you fall asleep."

Jakes stared at Jonathan in awe, but the other man scarcely noticed him. Jonathan took a sip of his coffee and carried on, a sappy grin on his face. "When you walk into a room, and you look for her straightaway, and when your eyes meet, it feels as if you're coming home. It's not to say she's perfect, but you love her anyway. You want to be a better person for her, not because she asked you to, but because you want to be so for her. If you're lucky enough, she's your best friend. She's the one you can laugh with and be yourself with. The one you can share your deepest thoughts and secrets with, and you're not scared she'll laugh at you."

"Wow, you're good," Jakes said with admiration. "I would

never have been able to put it like that, but it's how I feel about Angie."

Jonathan grinned, "I guessed. You must remember. I have a lot more experience loving the right woman, and I've had a lot of time to think about it. You also pick things up over the years. Claire has been the love of my life since the moment we met. I often wonder why it's working for us, but it does. But it doesn't mean because it's working you have to stop showing her you care. You must make it fun to be with each other. You shouldn't be scared to show you care it doesn't matter where you are. Never stop the romance, as my Dad told me."

Jakes' mouth lifted in the corner, "So that's where the mistletoe comes in?"

Jonathan grinned. "Exactly."

When Angie and Claire joined them, Claire commented, "You two look so serious. What are you talking about?"

Jonathan chuckled and said, "Mistletoe."

ANGIE DIDN'T EVEN WANT to think about mistletoe. Every time she did, she remembered all too well the kisses she shared with Jakes under the mistletoe and then blushed again. She hoped nobody noticed it. To draw their attention away from her blushing face, Angie pressed her cold hand against Jakes' cheek, "Feel here."

Jakes pulled back, shocked and chastised her, "Geez, Angel. Your hands are freezing. Where are your gloves?"

The next moment he jumped up, grabbing her hands in his. He summarily started rubbing them and then, while he still held them, he pulled their hands underneath his woolly jumper. Angie's eyes flew up to his when the heat flowed from his body to her hands. Embarrassed, she tried to pull her hands out, but Jakes didn't allow her. The warmth spread to the rest of her body. Did he know what he was doing? And that right in front of Jonathan and Claire? And no, it wasn't only his touch causing these feelings, but Jakes' expression. There are worry, tenderness and something she couldn't define. She barely heard when he asked, "Better?"

Angie couldn't get a word out and only nodded.

Still embarrassed, she glanced at Jonathan and Claire, but those two were missing. When she looked back at Jakes, she knew he came to the same conclusion. There was more than tenderness in his expression when he framed her face with his big hands. "Silly girl," he whispered against her lips and kissed her almost silly.

Angie forgot about the cold. She slipped her hands around his back underneath his jumper and kissed him back. Breathing hard, he pulled his mouth away from hers, and Angie opened her eyes. His eyes were twinkling when he mumbled, "You don't know what you are doing to me, Angel, but one thing I do know is that I sure like kissing you."

Angie grinned back. "The feeling is mutual."

Jakes narrowed his eyes. "Yeah?" he asked, his face serious. Angie nodded, even though she suspected that he asked more than just about the kisses.

"COME, let us get you coffee, then you can get warm inside," Jakes uttered the words, but he didn't let her go. His excuse was that he had good intentions and that he only wanted to kiss her on the forehead. It didn't happen. As soon as his lips trailed over her forehead, Angie closed her eyes. She looked so soft he couldn't resist. His lips followed a trail over her eyelids, then her cheek to breathe in her smell. He reached her lips at last. He started at the corner of her mouth and followed the seam of her lips to the other corner.

Jakes lifted his head a little and saw she hadn't opened her eyes. When he lowered his mouth again. When Angie opened her mouth with a sigh, Jakes was lost. He hadn't planned to take the kiss this far, but instinct took over. He slid his tongue into her mouth, touching the edges of her lips with the tip of his tongue. When Angie didn't pull away, he pushed his tongue in further to investigate past her lips.

Jakes almost lost control when Angie's tongue met his. With a groan, his hand tangled in her hair and with the other arm pulled her closer. Angie's hands stroked his back, and her tongue duelled with his. Her smell, her taste almost overwhelmed him. It felt as if he couldn't get enough, but he had to stop because he had to breathe. He pulled away, far enough to breathe, but he couldn't move away yet. He still needed to taste. He still needed her touch.

Through shallow breaths, his mouth and tongue still hovered against her lips. His teeth nibbled at her bottom lip, and his hand slid over her back, but shallow breaths were not enough. He needed more air to his brain and his lungs. It felt as if both were not functioning as it should be, and Jakes pulled away.

Angie hadn't opened her eyes yet. Her breathing was as laboured as his, and she looked even more beautiful.

He untangled his hand from her hair to brush his thumb over her swollen bottom lip. When his breathing returned to almost normal, Jakes said, "Angie..."

Later on, Jakes felt relieved that they had been interrupted, but at that moment, he was not. Who knew what he would've said if Jesse hadn't protested rather loudly behind him? "Geez Rayno, we need to get out of here. Jonathan was right. This kissing thing seems to be contagious. First, we caught my parents, then Jonathan and Claire, and now these two."

At Jesse's voice, Jakes opened her eyes but didn't release

Angie. He still looked down at Angie when she opened her eyes. Jakes was very close to kissing her again. He would've if they didn't have an audience.

"MAY I USE THE GYMNASIUM?"

Jesse and Rayno stared at Jakes in astonishment. They had just returned from Keystone where they attended a chocolate tasting.

Jesse grumbled, "You know you've now made us feel guilty. We're now obliged to join you."

Jakes shrugged. If they wanted to train with him, it was their choice. He glanced at Angie. "Do you want to join us?"

She laughed, shaking her head. "No, big guy. I'll leave the exercising to you. I've something else I want to do and need to change."

Jakes was relieved but didn't want to show it.

Jesse sighed at Angie's remark, "You're going to paint. We have to pull you out of the studio again?"

Angie grinned. "You may have to."

She thought for a moment then corrected herself. "No, you definitely have to."

Jesse sighed over-dramatically as he and Rayno left to get changed. Angie's eyes widened when Jakes asked with an exaggerated sigh, similar to Jesse's, "How long a warning do you need?"

She grinned. "An hour should be enough."

Jakes put his hand on her back to push her forward, saying, "Okay then. Off you go."

Angie grinned over her shoulder at him and disappeared into her room to change. Jakes stared at the closed door for a few moments before he walked to his own. His chocolate-indulgence was just an excuse, but he needed the endorphins from the exercise to clean his head. Too many things had happened today.

ANGIE STOOD in front of her easel, but she hadn't started painting yet. Music played in the background, and the smell of paint and turpentine permeated the air.

She surveyed her surroundings and nodded happily. Even though there were things to improve, it still was her happy place. For now, she had only brought enough to keep her busy while they were here.

She removed the cloth covering the canvas she started yesterday and studied it carefully before she opened the first tube and dabbed some of her chosen colours on the palette. For this painting, she had chosen acrylic because it dried so much quicker. She didn't have a lot of time to finish it, but she missed the smell of the oils. Jesse had teased her about it in the past. He said the smell was so pungent it could put you on a trip. He didn't understand it when she said it relaxes her.

While she got everything ready, her thoughts drifted to Jakes and his promise to call her when it was time to get ready for dinner. It still surprised her how fast and without effort he'd accepted her absent-mindedness. Even more surprising was that he never complained about it. She could get absorbed in her work, but Jakes didn't judge her. Maybe the phrase 'judge' was a bit harsh, but sometimes it felt that that was precisely what Chris did. She even got the impression sometimes that Chris resented her art. He made a big deal when she was late for a date and had never shown interest in her work.

Jakes did. She was now used to it, but in the beginning, it felt weird when he questioned her about her art. She then suspected he asked her all the questions because he knew she would chatter non-stop whenever she got a chance. Even that did not bother him. He never looked irritated when she was such a chatterbox and not once had he told her to keep quiet.

How many times had Chris done that? If she thought about it now, Angie still couldn't understand why she stayed with him for so long? Why did she allow him to treat her like that?

She shook her head. Chris was in the past, and that is where he was going to stay.

Angie pulled back her shoulders and unlocked her tablet, where she stored the photo before she chose a brush. Before long, she lost sense of time and reality.

JAKES ENJOYED THE WORKOUT. The easy banter between the three of them hadn't bothered him, even though he would've preferred to be alone. He still had enough time to think about Angie.

He hadn't lied earlier. He loved kissing Angie, and when he did, it was as if he couldn't get enough. That, however, wasn't fair to her. It had already developed much further than it should've and now... Jakes didn't know what to do.

His talks with Michael, Jonathan and André, didn't bring him closer to an answer. All three urged him to give whatever this between him and Angie was a chance, but only André knew all the reasons preventing Jakes from taking it further. That was what surprised Jakes. André knew about the oath and his past and everything that came with it. André hadn't even met Angie, but he still encouraged Jakes to go for it.

He wanted to so badly. There were times he wanted to say, 'to hell with the oath', and tell Angie but then... He couldn't. There were too much at stake here. So many people's lives could be affected. He couldn't drop them now. His conscience wouldn't allow it.

Angie's door was open when Jakes went to shower, so she might still be painting. After his shower, he changed into a comfortable tracksuit before he headed to the kitchen in search of coffee. Mary sat at the table, drinking a cup of coffee when he came in. "Can I help with anything?" Jakes asked hopefully, but Mary waved him off. "No, everything's ready. Angie will come and set the table." Angie is painting. I'm not sure if she will remember."

Mary shook her head with an indulgent smile. "Tsk, that child. I don't know what we'll do with her."

He should've censored his thoughts, but before he could stop himself, Jakes murmured, "Still love her anyway?"

The moment the words left his mouth, Jakes realised what he had just admitted. He blushed when he noticed that Mary was studying him carefully before she nodded. She laughed, "Yes, you're right. I'll ask Claire to set the table."

Jakes took a mug from the cupboard and hoped he appeared nonchalant when he asked, "Where is Angie's studio?"

Mary waved her hand towards the garage, "If you walk through the garage, you'll find another door. It was an old storeroom we converted into a studio for her."

"Should I take her coffee?" Jakes offered hesitantly.

Mary nodded, "I'm sure she'd like that."

Jakes took out another mug, poured the coffee, and prepared Angie's coffee the way she liked it with milk and one sugar. When he turned with the mugs in his hand, he realised that Mary had been watching him the whole time. His cheeks turned red again when Mary said, "Thank you, Jakes."

He turned to her, confused. "What for?"

"Because you care and understand her."

Jakes had been right. Mary hadn't missed his admission earlier. Geez, twice already today he admitted his feelings to two of Angie's family members. If he carried on like this, he might as well told Angie how he felt.

It wouldn't help to fret about it now as it was too late. He just needed to be more careful.

Jakes nodded, and before he could doubt again whether he was doing the right thing, he turned towards the door leading to the garage.

JAKES STOPPED IN THE DOORWAY. His heart rate accelerated when he saw Angie standing in front of her easel. She hadn't seen him as she was studying the painting in front of her. Her body swayed to the music in the background. When she stepped back from the easel, she nodded as if she liked the result.

Watching Angie, Jakes ached to follow his heart and build a relationship with her. He was still hesitant, though. There were more obstacles than only his fears and insecurities.

Jakes pushed those thoughts to the back of his mind and called, "Knock, knock. May I come in?"

Angie looked up in surprise and smiled, "Yes, but wait there."

She covered the canvass before she called, "Now you can come in."

She accepted the mug he held out to her and took a grateful sip before she beamed up at him. "Thank you, I needed this. I didn't want to stop while the light was good."

There was a table in one corner with two bar chairs underneath. Jakes pulled one out. Sitting down, he apologised, "I hope I'm not bothering you."

Angie shook her head. "No, I'm done for the day."

She put her cup next to his and went to clean her hands and the brushes. Jakes watched her while she was busy. She looked comfortable and relaxed here between the paints and a couple of half-finished canvases. For an artist, the place was neat and organised, but Jakes was sure it might not always look like this.

It was bigger than he expected. Shelves lined one wall, but it was empty. The only other furniture was the counter-high table and the barstools, and her easel. On the table were a sketchbook and pencils, a container with brushes and paints, Angie's tablet and the radio playing in the background.

He would add a couch against the other wall. He could read there or study while Angie painted...

Before his imagination ran away with him, he asked, "May I see?"

She shook her head. "No, not yet. If it comes out the way I planned, I'll show it to you."

It sounded familiar. Jakes shrugged, "Okay," and took a sip of his coffee.

Angie gaped at him, "You're not even upset I don't want to show you?"

Jakes shook his head, "No, why should I be? You'll show me when you're ready. If you don't show me, I know you didn't like it, and might've painted over it already."

"How did you know?"

"My mum, remember?"

Angie's smile disappeared. She looked emotional when she whispered, "Thank you."

It was the second time that afternoon that someone thanked Jakes and he didn't know why. For the second time, he asked, "What for?"

"For not laughing at me."

Jakes knew he shouldn't, but he still put his mug on the table and got up. When he stood in front of her, he did the same with her mug. Angie didn't look at him, her face downcast. She looked close to tears, and he couldn't understand why.

Jakes suddenly had this overwhelming urge to protect her. Geez, he knew she didn't need it. She might even be a stronger person than he was, so he didn't know where that feeling came from. Why did she look so emotional and insecure?

Okay, maybe he didn't have to ask. After he had the dubious pleasure of meeting Chris, he had an idea.

Jakes didn't even think twice about it. He pulled her in his arms. Heat rushed through him when she lay her head against his chest, and her arms slipped around his waist. He stroked her hair, his chin resting on top of her head, trying to give her the comfort she craved.

They embraced for a long time, without talking. When Angie exhaled and her arms relaxed, Jakes did the same. He stood back to see her face, but Angie didn't look at him. Jakes slid his hand under her chin and lifted her face, so her eyes could meet his.

For a moment he thought she needed another hug but then she smiled, and Jakes knew she was okay.

When he dropped his arms and stood back, he didn't know if he should feel relieved or disappointed. Jakes just knew if he held her for a second longer, he might kiss her again. It wouldn't be fair on her.

He couldn't tell her how he felt. Anyway, not now. And before he didn't figure out his own head and heart, he couldn't string Angie along.

He therefore turned and picked his mug up from the table before he looked at her and mumbled, "Okay, then. You probably need to get ready for dinner."

CHAPTER THIRTEEN

She thought Jakes was going to kiss her again this afternoon. She had to admit that she was close to taking the initiative, but she didn't.

He didn't give her any less attention than usual, and neither did he stop looking at her. When he walked into the room earlier, he looked around, and when Jakes saw her, he gave her a sweet, shy smile that made her insides melt.

Although they hadn't been alone much, Jakes gave her more attention than Chris had in the past year. He made sure Angie had a glass of wine. He pulled out her chair and waited for her to sit before he sat next to her. The rest of the time, she could feel that intense gaze resting on her.

Angie had always envied her parents' and Jonathan's relationships. That was the kind of relationship she wanted but thought that it was not for her. It hadn't been with Chris, but Jakes gave her hope that she still might have that in future. Look at that moment he stepped in when her brothers teased her again. The next moment she felt Jakes' hand folding over hers where it was resting in her lap. When she looked at him, he first looked as if he wanted reassurance that she was okay and then he smiled. Of course, she smiled back, without even thinking about it.

That was what she wanted. That feeling that there was someone else on your side. That feeling of intimacy and secrecy, of a look that says we are sharing a secret that is ours. She never felt it with Chris. It scared her to think about it. She only knew Jakes for a short while, but her heart told her that he was the man who could be that person for her.

Later, when they decided to walk down to the pub in the village, Jakes gave her so much attention that her brothers couldn't miss it.

The pub was full, and the only place where they could find seats was one of those high tables and three bar stools. Claire, with her long legs, had no problem getting on her chair but Angie was dubious how she was going to manage it gracefully. The next moment Angie shrieked when Jakes put his hands on her hips to lift her and depositing her on the chair without ceremony.

When she looked up at him, she was surprised to see that he was laughing with the others. Angie thought her heart would stop. She barely got used to that smile, and now, for the second time in two days, his laughter left her breathless.

And, as Jonathan did with Claire, Jakes stood close to Angie, probably to make sure that she didn't fall off the chair. That was a real possibility, considering how wobbly her legs still felt.

As the evening progressed, the gap between them evaporated and his light touches less subtle. That moment when he was still in deep conversation with Jonathan and Claire, put his arm around her waist and pulled her against his chest, Angie wondered if he realised he was doing it. It felt so natural as if they did it before.

Angie realised then that it was something else that Chris never did. He also never spoke to her brothers as Jakes did then. Yes, Chris and Jesse spoke, but not about the kind of things that Jakes and her brothers were discussing now. And Jakes spoke comfortably and openly as if they all knew each other for a long time. A couple of times he hesitated after he made a comment, looking unsure, but he relaxed more and more.

When he pulled her tighter against him, and she looked up at him, he smiled at her. That smile felt special and just for her, and Angie fell a little bit more in love with him.

She knew she shouldn't dream. It wouldn't last forever. Jakes was leaving soon, going back to South Africa, but for one night, Angie held onto the magic and her dreams and the happiness Jakes brought her.

IT WAS AN HOUR BEFORE TWELVE, the night before Christmas. Jakes glanced at the people around him. They were all relaxed, looking peaceful. Was he the only one who didn't feel the spirit of the season?

He felt festive earlier, but his insecurities returned shortly after dinner. His surroundings and his comfort with Angie lulled him into a dream where everything would work out, and everyone would be happy. He now knew it could not happen.

Jakes wished he had ignored his phone. If he had, he could've held on to this dream for a short while longer. He kept his phone on, and now it was a stark reminder of what couldn't be.

He had friends and family scattered all over the globe tonight. He wanted an opportunity to wish them all Merry Christmas, the same as they tried to do. He got quite a few messages already, and several were in his team's chat group. Those messages reminded him again of the spirit in the squad.

It was that spirit and camaraderie that saved him last year. Could he be selfish and ignore that?

Jakes stared into the fire seeing nothing. He would need to work hard in the next few days. He had to make sure the romantic atmosphere that surrounded him would not influence him. He could make the wrong choices.

Never having experienced a white Christmas before, everything was romantic. It lulled you into this dreamy picture of cuddling in front of the fireplace, and moonlight sleigh rides like they did tonight. Jakes always thought those were things you only found in storybooks. Now he knew it was real.

To prove his point, Jakes felt Angie's head on his shoulder. When he glanced down at her, he noticed she was fast asleep where she sat between him and Jesse on one of the big couches.

He lifted his arm and shifted position. He pulled Angie against him so she could cuddle against his chest. Jakes breathed deep, inhaling the smell of her hair.

Geez, that wasn't his best idea. He was in big trouble., way bigger than he thought. He had now, as he had last night when he lifted her onto the bar stool in the pub and later pulled her against his chest, did it without thought. It felt so natural as if he'd done it many times in his life.

Jakes knew he never had. Moira wasn't that type of person.

He closed his eyes and sighed against her hair, unaware of the glances resting on them.

Tomorrow was Christmas Day. The family would spend most of the time together, and he wouldn't have any choice but to join in. The day after Christmas he needed to put distance between him and Angie. It wasn't as if he would hurt any less when he touched her or not because, for him, the outcome would always be the same.

He didn't want to hurt Angie, so it was better if he stayed away from her now.

He hoped it wasn't too late.

ANGIE KNOCKED ON JAKES' door early on Christmas morning. She grinned at Jakes when he opened the door, still half asleep. "Wake up, sleepyhead. We want to open the presents soon. No need to dress up..."

Her gaze flitted over his bare chest, and she laughed embarrassedly, "Okay, maybe a shirt." She wouldn't be able to stop drooling if she had that in her eyesight the whole morning. And Angie did *not* want to hear Claire's comments.

Jakes rubbed the sleep from his eyes and apologised, "Sorry. I overslept."

Angie shook her head. "You didn't. It's my job to wake everyone up."

Jakes frowned. "What time is it?"

Angie grinned. "Seven. Come on, I made coffee."

Angie turned, but then halfway she turned back to Jakes and stepped closer to him. She leaned up and whispered against his mouth, "Merry Christmas."

At first, it looked like he was not going to respond, but then he groaned. His arms slipped around Angie, and he pulled her close to him. That was the end of her initiative. Jakes then took charge and kissed her like she had never been kissed before. When he finally pulled away, they were both out of breath. They stared at each other, but then his expression changed suddenly.

He stepped back, looking rattled as he mumbled, "I'm sorry. I shouldn't have. I promised myself I won't, but..."

Angie swallowed her disappointed because his attitude had changed so suddenly. "Geez, Jakes, relax." Remember, I kissed you first."

The look he gave her almost broke her heart. He looked so

unsure and suspicious when he admitted, "I know, but I still shouldn't have... It is just so difficult to keep my hands off you."

He pushed his hands through his already messy hair and mumbled, "I need to leave soon..."

Angie was suddenly angry because he carried on about it. "We kissed. It's not a crime. We're both single and just for the record: I like kissing you. Just leave it."

She turned in a hurry but instead of waking the others as she had planned to do, she rushed to her room, aware of Jakes' eyes following her. She needed time on her own.

JAKES POURED himself a cup of coffee before he followed the rest of the family to the big room. When he arrived, everyone had taken their seats, except Angie. Jakes waited for her to sit, but she gestured for him to take his place, "I'm the youngest, so I hand out the presents."

Jesse snorted, "Only by two minutes. You only remind me you're the youngest when it suits you."

"But I'm the only girl. It makes sense," Angie argued.

Jesse pulled a face, causing Angie to laugh harder. When she calmed enough to speak, her gaze drifted over the room as she asked, "Okay, everyone ready?"

Was it his imagination, or did she avoid eye contact with him? Not that he would blame her. But, typically Angie, he often found her concerned gaze on him while she handed out the presents.

It surprised Jakes that his pile was almost the same size as the rest of the family's. He was now grateful he had Angie's help in choosing presents for everyone. He regarded his pile and carefully selected the gifts he wanted to open first and last, as he did since he was a child. He recognised Angie's handwriting and kept hers for last.

The first present he opened was from Jesse and Rayno. Jakes smiled when he pulled out a Bears' rugby jersey with his name and number on it. "Thank you, guys, this is special."

Jesse admitted, "It wasn't easy to get the right size. The one you wore during the game was a bit tight, but we managed to get one at the last minute. We just had to find a way to thank you for the advice you gave us on and off the pitch. To be honest: we hoped to convince you to come and wear that jersey for real one day."

Jakes' eyes flitted to Angie. Could he...? No, he couldn't think about it. Not yet, anyway.

He concentrated on opening the rest of the presents. From Jonathan and Claire, he received his favourite aftershave and from Mary and Dr Summers a leather-bound organiser. Then it was only Angie's gift left. His fingers rubbed over the paper before he lifted the tape carefully. He had to swallow his emotions when he saw what it was. At last, he looked up at Angie, who was watching him warily.

"I don't know how to say thank you. Where did you get it?"

Gone was that dirty look he got earlier when she smiled, "At a bookshop in Denver, specialising in rare editions. They only had one left of those illustrated sets you were looking for."

Jakes dragged Angie to every little bookshop he could find, searching for this box set with specially illustrated editions of all Dan Brown's books. He might have missed this shop. That Angie remembered and bought it for him, made it even more special... He cleared his throat before he could mutter, "I appreciate it. You went through a lot of trouble."

The rest of the family laughed. "Angie is like a child over Christmas. She loves shopping for presents and searched high and low until she finds the right present for someone."

"But it's nice," Angie argued, as she opened Jakes' present

Jakes knew what she meant when she folded the tissue

paper away and pulled out the carved, wooden jewellery box. Her expression when she hugged it against her chest, tug at his heartstrings. "You remembered."

Jakes had, just like Angie, went to a lot of trouble to buy Angie's present. She admired it in a craft shop one day. He first thought it was too personal because she had been engaged to Chris at the time, but now he was glad he got it.

HE SHOULD'VE SAID no when Mary asked him to take coffee to Angie. Or he should've brought it and left immediately, but Jakes didn't. His argument was that this would be the last time he could spend time alone with Angie, and he had taken the same seat at the table as he did the previous time. He waited for Angie to cover the painting and cleaned her brushes, sipping his coffee.

When she finished cleaning and putting away her brushes, she turned. Jakes' heartrate accelerated when their eyes met. His heart wanted to escape from his chest as she approached him, her eyes not leaving his. Jakes knew what was coming. His hands shook when he returned the mug to the table.

Angie stopped in front of him, then shifted his leg so she could stand between his legs. She lifted her hands, sliding them over his arms, his shoulders then fold them around his neck. Jakes couldn't breathe. He didn't know how it happened, but he suddenly became aware that his hands were on her hips and he involuntarily pulled her closer.

She put pressure on his neck and whispered, "I haven't thanked you properly for my present yet."

Jakes whispered back, too scared that if he was loud, it would shatter that tender moment, "And I didn't thank you."

She smiled, pulling his head down towards her and then she

kissed him. Jakes couldn't move. She kissed him this morning, but this kiss!

He was still stunned when she lifted her mouth to study his face. When he didn't have the same reaction as this morning, she became more daring. She leaned forward again. Her breath whispered over his skin. Heat rushed through him when she traced the outline of his mouth with her tongue.

Jakes didn't know how much longer he would be able to resist. His voice sounded husky when he groaned her name, "Angie." His hands clenched on her hips.

Angie smiled against his mouth and then her tongue slid between his lips.

That was all it took. Jakes closed his eyes and gave in to the sweet demand of her kiss. Their tongues met, duelled with each other, and Jakes couldn't hold back anymore. His hands slid to her back and pulled her flush against him. Her breasts pressed against his chest, burning his skin even through the layers of clothing between them.

Her one hand tangled in his hair, the other stroking the bare skin on his nape not covered by his T-shirt.

That small touch made him more aware of what was going on, pulling him back from the sensations she evoked. He had to stop. He had to focus, and he couldn't concentrate when he was this close to Angie. He needed space, distance, and a lot of willpower.

Jakes managed to pull his mouth away, taking gulps of air. Angie had the same problem. He dropped his forehead against Angie's and gasped, "Jeez, Angie. You'll be the death of me. That was amazing."

Angie opened her eyes, and a slow grin spread across her face. She seemed proud of herself when she said, "Absolutely."

Jakes groaned. "You're full of surprises."

Even though Jakes knew he had to get more distance

between them, he didn't do it. It was as if he couldn't stop touching her. He should, especially after that kiss.

Angie hesitated before she admitted, "I haven't done that before."

Stunned, Jakes leaned back to stare at her. "You never kissed Chris like that?"

Jakes didn't know if he should be shocked or pleased. How was that possible? They had been together for how many years. And if she hadn't kissed Chris like that, did they...? He had no right, but he still asked, "If you hadn't kissed like that, had you...? I mean..."

Angie shook her head, now embarrassed, "I'm still a virgin."

Her words and the knowledge that came with it, hit him like a sledgehammer, confirming his opinion that he was the wrong man for Angie. She deserved so much more. She was pure, innocent and untouched, and he was a mess with too many demons and baggage. He couldn't do it to her. It would be easy to destroy her in the process. No, he couldn't do that.

Jakes dropped his hands and pushed his chair back. "I'm sorry... It is... I'm so sorry."

Jakes stepped around Angie to get space, aware that she was watching him concerned. He should leave, but he couldn't. It felt as if all his muscles had ceased working. He desperately turned to the window.

Please, not now.

It was too late. Jakes tried to find a fixed point to focus on, but all he saw was snow. He closed his eyes and breathed, in and out, in and out.

Where did this come from? He thought he was okay. He was, but now...

The rubber band snapped under his fingers, and he came back to reality. He didn't even realise he'd taken hold of it. The pieces fell from his numb fingers when he dropped his head to the cold glass of the window. His breathing became more regular, but he couldn't look at Angie.

"Jakes, please. Talk to me."

Angie's voice penetrated through the haze. Jakes swallowed hard and turned towards her. She looked so concerned, but he couldn't talk to her. Not now. Maybe never.

He shook his head. "I can't."

He didn't wait for her answer but left, unaware Angie had seen the torment in his eyes.

ANGIE ONLY SAW Jakes again when they met for dinner. He had stayed in his room. She heard his voice and guessed he was on the phone.

He didn't make eye contact with her when he arrived, as he did the other evenings. He reminded her of the man she first met. She was not the only one who noticed it, because both Rayno and Jesse looked at him concerned. He answered only when someone asked him a question, but it was the same short replies he had given in the beginning. His smile had also disappeared.

Angie had picked up the pieces of the rubber band when he stormed out of the studio earlier.

What went wrong? Did she do something wrong? Was she too aggressive or something? Maybe it had something to do with the fact that she was still a virgin. It looked to her that men didn't like virgins. Look at Chris. He never wanted her, so why would Jakes?

She sat there for a long time, wondering what she did wrong. Maybe she came on too strong, she thought. Maybe Jakes felt pressured when she told him she was a virgin. Maybe there was something wrong with her?

Angie got frustrated with all the maybes and what-ifs

running through her head. At last, she came to a conclusion: there was nothing wrong with her. Chris had his own agenda, but Angie knew in her heart that it wasn't the same with Jakes. Something happened in his past, which made him the man he was these days. There were signs of the man he could've been before, and in the last week she got glimpses of him, but she might have lost him today.

He might feel that she was watching him because he looked up, straight at her. His skin pulled tight against his jaw, but then he dropped his eyes again. Maybe she should help him rather than feeling upset. She rolled the rubber band in her hand so she could hold it with her fingertips and pressed it against Jakes' hand. His head shot up, but then his hand opened, and she dropped the band in his palm. From the movement of his arms, she surmised that he was sliding the band over his wrist. Relief shot through him when he briefly closed his eyes, breathed deeply and then exhaled.

HIS PHONE BEEPED, and Jakes pulled it out of his pocket. He stared at the screen for a long time. Angie noticed how his jaw clenched even before he opened the message to read it. His body language changed immediately. His shoulders dropped, and he sighed as he switched off his phone.

Angie whispered so only Jakes could hear, "Is everything okay? Did you get bad news?"

He opened his eyes and turned his head towards her. Her heart clenched when she noticed the defeated look in his eyes. He took a while to answer. "It was our team captain, reminding us of something important. Even though I remembered, I almost..."

He shook his head and turned away. He closed his eyes again and took deep breaths. He only opened his eyes again when the others said goodnight. He mumbled good night, but he didn't get up. It surprised Angie. She thought he would take the opportunity to escape.

The room was eerily quiet. Angie started to feel uncomfortable, unsure whether she should leave first. He didn't look like he wanted to talk to her anyway.

Several times she felt his eyes on her, but whenever she looked up, he looked away. He couldn't even meet her eyes! No, she couldn't stay here any longer. She had to leave before she burst into tears. As she was about to get up, Jakes mumbled, "I'm sorry. I know I am confusing you."

He stayed quiet for a couple of seconds before he added, "I shouldn't have kissed you."

She knew it! He didn't want her, and now he regretted it.

She wanted to dive underneath the pillow to hide. How must she look Jakes in the eyes again? No, she couldn't. She got up and was just about to walk away when he muttered something in Afrikaans. When she looked at him, she surmised that it was an expletive if she had to judge his expression. The next moment he stood in front of her. He grabbed her hand in a tight grip and pleaded, "It might be true that I shouldn't have kissed you, but hell, I like kissing you. I want to kiss you and..."

He sighed, "It's not fair to you, Angie. I'll be leaving soon, but the fact is that I can't start a relationship with you, nor anyone else. Not now, or at least for the next six months."

So many emotions flitted over his face but one she could read clearly: frustration. There was another one, she could only describe as pain, but that wasn't all. It was clear that something was bothering him.

And then his whole demeanour changed. His eyes lost that glittery intensity and softened to a green moss. His fingers around hers relaxed. When his eyes roamed over her face again, Angie heard, and felt, the sigh escaping his lips.

.   .   .

JAKES SHOULD HAVE KNOWN he would lose the battle not to touch her. He slid his gaze over her face as if trying to memorise every part of her face then lifted his hand and let his fingers trail over her skin, discovering it as a blind man would. There were sadness and confusion in her eyes, and Jakes knew he caused it. That was why he shouldn't kiss her or touch her again.

He thought about it the whole afternoon since he left her in her studio. His long discussion with André was enough to calm him that he confessed his feelings. André knew his situation, but his friend still advised him to follow his heart.

It wasn't as if he didn't want to. He desperately wanted to. After that first call, he thought about it again and tried to figure it out. A second call convinced him to follow André's advice. He would tell Angie how he felt. He would be honest and tell her that he couldn't start a relationship now, and ask her if she would wait, or give him a chance.

It was a risk, and he hoped she would agree.

Then he received Daniel's message. Jakes knew his team captain was only doing his job, reminding them about their pledge. The uncertainty returned immediately, and Jakes saw it as a sign. He couldn't fail now. It would affect not only him but also his friends and the team.

He couldn't tell Angie how he felt.

Why then was he still here, touching her like this? Why did he even want to kiss her when he knew he should stay away?

Gratitude, because she understood? Yes, he appreciated the rubber band she dropped into his hand during dinner. He was thankful for how she calmed him, but he didn't want to kiss her out of gratitude.

He didn't even have the excuse of the mistletoe, but he

didn't stop. It could only happen one more time. He would kiss Angie once more, but it had to be the last time.

His fingers fluttered over her lips. He felt her breath tingling his fingertips when her lips opened. Jakes couldn't resist it any longer and bent his head, trailing his lips feather-soft over hers, then over the top of her nose, and eyebrows, and cheek. He continued his exploration over her jaw and met her lips again. Her mouth opened underneath his as Angie returned his kisses with the same passion as she had that afternoon.

Jakes drew his mouth away, breathing raggedly, and pulled Angie close to him. He buried his face in her hair, breathing in the soft, clean smell of her shampoo. His arms tightened around her, already dreading the moment they had to say goodbye.

This was it, he realised. The last time he should hold Angie like this.

Not trusting himself to not kiss her again, or look into her eyes, he dropped a kiss on top of her head. He then turned without a backward glance at Angie. He couldn't say goodnight.

Not with a throat so choked up, he couldn't swallow.

CHAPTER FOURTEEN

I t was as if he had already said goodbye last night. He was there, but also not. The worst thing was that he *was* here, so close she could see him and touch him and hear him, but she couldn't react to it.

Why he still brought her coffee, was anybody's guess. He put the mug on the table and immediately turned back to the door. He only gave two steps and stopped, but he didn't turn around. She now would never know if he would've turned or spoke to her because Jesse called his name. Jesse was already walking into the studio before Jakes could reply.

He put her coffee on the table and stood with his own mug at the window without making eye contact. Apart from thanking him for the coffee, neither had said a word before Jesse came in.

Jesse addressed them both, but he looked at Jakes when he asked, "We want to go snow tubing. Do you fancy going?" He looked at Jakes when he added, "My Dad says it is fine if you want to go."

Jakes looked uncomfortable. There was no way she could

spend time in his company today, so Angie shook her head, "No, thank you. I want to finish this, but you should go."

Angie didn't miss Jakes' relief that she wasn't going. Her throat ached as she swallowed her disappointment. He shouldn't look so relieved not to spend time in her company!

She turned away and kept herself busy rearranging her brushes. It was unnecessary, but she didn't want them to see her hurt. They spoke about the arrangements, but Angie didn't listen. She heard footsteps and wanted to sigh with relief, but then she heard Jakes asked, "Do you need anything before we go?"

Angie didn't understand it. Why was he still so attentive? Couldn't he just leave her alone?

She didn't look at him and replied abruptly, "No, thank you."

His sigh echoed through the room, but then she heard his footsteps fading away. She had to swallow the tears. She was not going to cry and wallow in pain and self-pity.

The silence that followed was getting too much, and Angie turned to switch on the radio. The station she usually listened to were playing slightly melancholic Christmas songs, and she wasn't in the mood for that today. She searched for another one until she found a station playing loud and hard music which could deafen the voices in her head.

She only then removed the cloth she used to hastily cover the painting when Jakes walked in. She studied it for a while. Should she finish it? Did she want to finish it?

She sighed. She liked the painting, and it would be a shame not to finish it. What she wasn't sure of was whether she was still going to give it to Jakes, but time would tell.

. . .

It didn't take Angie long to get engrossed in her work and the music. When it was suddenly quiet, she looked up in a daze. Her mother shook her head, "How can you work with such a deafening noise?

Angie laughed, "It's not a noise, but sorry if it was too loud."

Her mum studied her quietly, and Angie suddenly had the uncomfortable feeling that Mary could see right through her. She wouldn't be surprised, but luckily, Mary merely asked, "May I see what you're working on?"

Angie studied the painting before she nodded. She needed a second opinion, and it had reached such a stage that her mum would have an idea where she was going with it. It would be best to do it now before she continued.

Angie only then noticed the tray Mary brought when she put it on the table before she joined Angie in front of the easel. Angie got nervous when Mary studied it for a long time before commenting. Several minutes passed before she breathed, "This is beautiful, Angie. I think this might be your best work yet."

Angie had thought so too, but she was glad that Mary agreed.

Mary turned back to the table and ordered, "Jakes said you had barely anything to eat this morning so come on. I brought sandwiches and coffee."

When she joined Mary at the table, the rich aroma of the coffee hit her nostrils, and she realised only then how hungry she really was. Jakes was right. She couldn't eat with Jakes watching her from across the table. No, she came to find refuge in her studio instead.

"It is only you and me at home for lunch, so I hope you didn't mind that I invited myself."

Angie shook her head, "No, I'm glad you are here, but this is nice. I'm getting spoiled today."

"Thank Jakes. He asked me to make sure that you eat and take a break."

Angie asked, surprised, "Why?"

Mary sounded matter of fact when she replied, "Because he cares."

Angie snorted but didn't reply. She probably didn't have to because her expression might have reflected her thoughts as Mary asked, "Why do you look so sceptical? Because I said he cared?"

Angie took one of the sandwiches while she tried to formulate her thoughts. Before last night she might have believed Mary that Jakes cared. She saw it in his eyes when he looked at her. She could feel it when he touched her or kissed her.

Now? No, that dream she buried deep last night. Jakes made it clear he didn't want a relationship. There was no way she would wait for a man again, not even Jakes du Plessis.

"Why do you say that, Mom?" Angie asked as she gestured to the sandwiches. "This doesn't prove anything."

Mary took a sip of her coffee before she answered, "Apart from the fact that he let it slip? Angie, the signs are all there. When Jakes walks into a room, he first looks to see where you are. When he finds you... I wish you can see his expression. His whole face softens. It's as if he knows where you are the whole time. He is aware of your needs, whether it is to refill your wine glass or pull out your chair or make your coffee just the way you like it. That man can't keep his eyes off you. Can't you see it? Don't you feel it?"

Angie couldn't stop the tears any longer. Irritated, she wiped it away, but then she looked up at Mary to admit, "I thought so too. I felt it, but not anymore. Jakes told me last night that he is not interested in a relationship with me."

Mary looked gutted. "I don't understand. Why?"

Angie shrugged. "I don't know. Het mentioned an oath, but I didn't take everything in. And then he kissed me and just walked away. He couldn't even look me in the eyes today!"

Mary pondered a while before she said thoughtfully, "Maybe it is because he has to go home soon. Maybe he feels it is too soon? I anyway heard when he told Jesse and Rayno how busy his schedule is going to be in the next six months. That might be the reason."

"Well, I won't know because he didn't give us a chance."

"What if he wanted to. If I'm correct, he might not be able to come back to Denver soon. Would you have waited for him?" Mary asked.

Angie had thought about it. A lot, to be honest, and she could answer immediately, "I could've visited him."

"Would you have done that?"

When Angie nodded, Mary asked gently, "Why? Are you in love with him?"

Angie again nodded, "I am, Mum. I didn't know you can fall in love with someone so quickly, but I had."

"You had been engaged to Chris until fairly recently and, even though you never told me what happened," Mary accused, "Jesse told us what happened. How do you know that what you feel for Jakes is love and not just a knee-jerk reaction to your failed relationship?"

Angie first felt irritated, but then she realised her mother was right to ask that question. She tried to explain, "My whole life, I had an example of what a relationship should be like when two people are in love. You and Dad had it and Jonathan and Claire too. I envied you, especially the last year. I also want a relationship like that, but I never had it with Chris. In the beginning, I thought I was different, and it bothered me that much, but... I know everyone thought Chris and I had a sexual relationship, but we never had. Chris didn't want to be with me. He barely held my hand or kissed me in the last few months."

Mary shook her head, "You and Chris were together for so long. I always thought you slept together, but as a mother, I didn't want to think about it."

"I now know why, but I also didn't want to be with him. I never felt that need that I wanted to have sex with Chris, but with Jakes..."

"Don't you think it is only because you are now ready for a sexual relationship. Jakes is the first man after Chris. Wouldn't you have felt the same with any other man?"

Angie shook her head firmly, "Yes, Jakes make me feel things and wants I had never done before, but it isn't just the physical aspects that are different. It is the way he can make me smile and laugh. It is the way he listens to me and supports me. I don't know how to put it, Mom, but when Jakes looks at me, he makes me feel as if I'm the most important person in his world."

She sighed, "Well, he had."

"Angie?" Mary pleaded, "Don't give up on Jakes too quickly. I've watched you in the last few days. Everyone can see that you belong together. You complete each other, and I can see how you are when you are together. It looks like the man is fighting a difficult battle. Give him a chance."

JAKES STOPPED when he heard Angie and Claire's voices. He shouldn't eavesdrop. You never hear something good, but he stood at the doorway of the library as if rooted to the floor. Angie's voice filtered out to him, "I don't know how I managed. I missed the family and home terribly."

"And how is it going with the jobhunting?"

Jakes heard Angie sighed before she answered Claire's

question. "It's not easy. There are not many positions available for art therapists. I had a temporary position for a few weeks, but I need a fulltime job if I ever want to obtain my certification."

Her words were like a punch in the gut. When he decided to stay away from her, he only thought about himself and his team. He didn't even consider how a relationship would affect Angie. If she struggled to find such a position in the US, how much would she struggle to get one in South Africa?

And if she missed her family while in a neighbouring city, how much would she miss them if she had to move to the other side of the world?

Jakes had to admit. He thought about it. He hoped and dreamed that she could go to South Africa.

He couldn't move. He couldn't hear what they were talking about then, but he stood there as if he was planted. That was until Angie said much louder, probably to get her message across, "There is no way I'm going to wait for a man again."

That was all Jakes needed to finally convince him that he had no right to hope for a future with Angie. So, that was it.

He turned, disappointed, and returned to his room without the books.

ANGIE FLED to her room as soon as they cleaned up the kitchen after dinner. Later, when she went to get something to drink, she realised that the house was unnaturally quiet. Her parents had mentioned they were going to their neighbours to play bridge and Jonathan and Claire went out to dinner, but she doesn't know where the other three were. They never mentioned any plans.

Alone, Angie had enough time to reflect on the last six weeks. She had enough time to realise she had again fallen in love with a man who didn't reciprocate her feelings. This time she wouldn't be so daft to waste another year of her life on a man who didn't want her even when she loved him more than she ever loved Chris.

She knew Jakes didn't feel the same, so she was prepared. All she had to do was to avoid him as far as possible. There could be no more hugging or kissing or holding hands. And she should remember: don't look Jakes in the eyes. That was her downfall every time.

She wished she had this conversation with herself before she had fallen in love with Jakes. She should never have dreamed of a future with him. And she should never have allowed him to get close.

JAKES HAD EAGERLY ACCEPTED the suggestion that the men should go to the pub, and this time, Jonathan joined them. The guys might've guessed he needed it because for the second night in a row, they kept the beers flowing. Jakes, always a lightweight with drinking, had more than his share.

The following morning, he felt terrible, of course. Not even the water he drank before he went to bed, prevented the hangover he suffered. Jakes did what he always did when he experienced it in the past. He exercised to sweat the toxins out of his body. He pushed himself hard, but he still had time to think, but he didn't have an answer yet. Every time his brain paused, it was at a different place.

Exercise and a shower helped to get rid of the toxins but not the heavy feeling in his heart. With the hope coffee would help, Jakes strode to the kitchen.

Jonathan was alone, sitting at the table with a cup of coffee and his laptop open in front of him. When he saw Jakes, he grinned. "The man I was waiting for."

Jakes frowned and poured his coffee. When he sat at the table, opposite Jonathan, he asked cautiously, "Why?"

"I think we should take Claire and Angie out to dinner tonight. It is our second last evening, and tomorrow we have a traditional family dinner in the mountains. And you need all the help you can get."

Jakes rubbed his hand through his hair, "No, not happening. I can't do it."

"Why not? You admitted last night you loved her, even though you might not remember it..."

Jakes could vaguely remember that. If she said that, what else had he spoken about? He hoped he hadn't... He asked hurriedly, "What else did I say? I can't remember much."

Jonathan snorted, "Apart from the fact that we couldn't keep you quiet when you spoke about Angie? It didn't make sense. I could gather that you are crazy about rugby. To be honest, I also can't remember much. Is there something else?"

Jakes shook his head, relieved that he hadn't given anything else away. "Nah, that about covers it."

Jonathan was suddenly serious. "Come on, Jakes. Give yourself a chance. Give you and Angie a chance."

Jakes shook his head, "I want to, but I can't. I need to stay away from her. I should never have kissed her."

Disappointed, Jonathan closed his laptop when he accepted that he wouldn't convince Jakes to fall in with his plans. They drank their coffee in silence until Jesse and Rayno joined them and they made plans for the day. When they met at Jesse's car later, Jakes didn't want to show his relief that Angie hadn't joined them.

JESSE MADE it easier for Angie to keep her resolution to stay away from Jakes since they were again going out for the day.

Even though Claire joined them, Angie declined. She pretended she wanted to paint, but it wasn't the truth. She finished both paintings: the one of the cosmos at Clarens and the one she painted of Jakes.

Earlier she wrapped the cosmos painting even though she was still not convinced whether she should give it to Jakes. In the end, she decided to do it. She would try to find him alone before they go out for dinner, as was their family tradition on the last night in Keystone.

Angie had often spent time alone at the cabin to paint. She was used to the silence, but it felt different today. Today she felt alone.

She kept herself busy cleaning the studio and packing away her supplies. When she finished, she studied the room as if seeing it for the first time. Suddenly excited, she grabbed her sketch pad and started making notes. She hadn't mentioned it to her family yet, but the last few days when she painted again, convinced her that that was what she wanted to do fulltime. She had the studio here. She could stay here, but if she wanted to do that, she needed to make the place warmer and more intimate.

The Young Artist's Gallery sold her last two paintings before Christmas and wanted more. She had a few completed works and would take those to the Gallery as soon as they were back in Denver.

She might have to find a part-time job for a month or two so she could accumulate enough cash to buy more supplies. She could paint on the days she wasn't working. On their twenty-fifth birthday, she and Jesse would receive the trust funds left by them by their grandparents. It wasn't too long a wait until then.

She turned back to the easel with the painting of Jakes. Her heart clenched as she studied it. Her fingers trailed over the image, outlining the full lips that knew how to kiss her senseless.

This painting belonged to her. That, and the few photographs she took of Jakes, would be her most treasured memories.

Disgusted, she rubbed away the sudden tears. Maybe she read too much into Jakes' kisses. Apart from the kisses, Jakes said nothing to give her a sign he felt the same.

It had, therefore been a dream that only came from her side.

THE REST of the family only returned to the house by late afternoon. They all gathered for coffee in the family room. Angie half-heartedly listened to their chatter. Angie knew everyone was going out, but she really didn't think she would have to spend most of the day alone. When lunchtime came with no sign of anyone, she accepted that she shouldn't expect them back soon.

She got irritated when she started feeling sorry for herself while she heated the soup and ate it alone at the kitchen table. She probably had to get used to it if she wanted to live here alone in future. But she wasn't alone now. They were all here, and she still felt alone and excluded as she listened to the fun they had.

Mary suddenly asked Angie, "Have you had anything to eat for lunch? If I'd known you were going to be alone, I would've left something for you."

Claire didn't even allow Angie to reply, as she protested, "Oh no, Angie! I thought Mum and Dad were here. If I had known, I would've come back to fetch you, so you could've had lunch with us. Last night too! I should've invited you to come with me to my friends if I had known the men were going to leave you on your own. Now you were again alone the whole day. It isn't fair. It's supposed to be family time."

Angie wanted to protest, but she couldn't get anything out

as Jakes jumped up. She wished she could analyse his expression. It was something between shock, or mortification or guilt, but before she could think about it, he turned and left, rushing in the direction of the library.

She stared at the open door in a daze before she looked at Claire and shook her head. She didn't want to talk about it now.

JAKES FLED. He had to get out of the room, and he wouldn't make it to his room to find the privacy he desperately needed. The closest room was the library. He stopped in front of the window, but he didn't see anything. His mind was reeling and he couldn't control it.

He felt guilty. When Angie didn't join them in the last two days, he felt relieved. He wanted to avoid her, but he didn't want her to be alone while he had all the fun with her family.

Fun? He snorted. How could you have fun when it feels as if your heart was breaking?

His heart rate accelerated, and Jakes already knew what to expect. He stared out of the window, breathing deep and exhaled. It didn't help today. It was as if he couldn't get enough oxygen into his lungs and to his brain. His jaw clamped shut, and his hands clawed into fists. He needed to focus, to gain control.

When he heard Angie's voice behind him, he tensed even further. He had hoped nobody would find him like this.

It took all his willpower to turn to face her, just in time to see her rushing towards him with concern written all over her face.

. . .

ANGIE WENT SEARCHING for Jakes as soon as she could. She had seen his expression, and she suspected what might happen.

When she entered the library, he was standing in front of the window. Not to frighten him more, she called his name. At first, she thought he might not hear her, or if he did, he was not going to turn, but then he did. Her heart clenched. She hadn't been wrong. Jakes clenched his hands so tight, his knuckles showed white. It looked like he struggled to breathe.

Angie acted instinctively. She dropped the canvas and rushed to him. Putting her hand on his jaw, she said, "What's wrong? Talk to me."

He shook his head, but she could see the panic in his eyes. Without thinking about it, Angie slipped her arms around his waist and held him close and immediately his arms slid around her, and he pressed his face into her hair. He held her so tight it almost hurt, so tight that she could feel and hear him breathe. Angie synchronised her own breathing with his, breathing in and exhaling, in and out until his breathing slowed down. She felt his deep inhale and then exhale on her hair but then his grip lessened.

She pulled back a little, and Jakes lifted his head. His usually calm green eyes were now stormy when he stared at her. Then he brought his mouth down to hers to claim her mouth. It wasn't a sweet kiss. It felt almost desperate.

It might be what they both needed, so Angie kissed him back. He lifted his mouth from hers at last. Then, instead of meeting her eyes, Jakes buried his face in her neck again. He spoke, but Angie couldn't decipher everything he was saying. What she did hear was his apology, "I'm sorry. I shouldn't have kissed you."

It felt as if he had slapped her. She jerked back and stepped away from him. "Stop. I know you don't want to kiss me. Why you are still doing it, is anybody's guess but..."

His head shot up, and he looked at her, shocked. "No, that's not true. I want to. You won't know how much I want to kiss you or hold you and... I wish..." He halted and shook his head, "Please, I can't do it. I..."

He moved away then went to stand at the window. He looked defeated as his shoulders drooped, and he rubbed his hand through his hair, almost desperately.

It would be best if she left him alone. Angie turned to the door, but then she saw the painting she had dropped earlier. She picked it up and returned to Jakes' side. She had to call his name twice before he turned to face her, his expression tense and closed.

Angie held out the canvas to him, "I made this for you. I wanted to give it to you before you leave."

Jakes took the canvas, still hesitant. His hands shook when he struggled to untie the ribbon and opened it. He studied it for a long time before he looked up. His eyes were shining, and his voice sounded husky when he thanked her, "Thank you, Angie. It's beautiful. I'll always treasure it."

He rolled the painting up and stepped closer to her. He brushed his lips over hers. It was so brief Angie thought she imagined it. He then stepped around her and left the room.

Angie turned to watch him go, unaware of the tears running down her cheeks.

CHAPTER FIFTEEN

J akes said goodbye to Jonathan and Claire and withdrew to the couch to allow the others to say their goodbyes. If it had been so difficult to say goodbye to them, how difficult would it be to do it with the rest of the family in two days?

He became aware that it was silent, and when he looked up, he realised that he was alone with Angie. Rattled, he jumped up, but then he looked into her eyes and the thought of fleeing evaporated. Idiot he was, he instead stepped closer to her. He stroked her hair. His hands shook so much that he rather threaded it through her curls.

He looked up to meet her eyes. He had to take a deep breath before he managed, "I wish I can tell you how much these last few weeks with you means to me. You're a wonderful woman, Angie. If circumstances were different, I..."

Jakes struggled to find the right words.

"I wish you were not engaged when I met you. I will never interfere with another person's relationship, but if you were single then... Things could've been different, but I did what I thought was best. Angie, I like... I'm in... You... I..."

Her eyes sparkled with mischief. Jakes saw it. He heard it, but he couldn't help his reaction when she teased. "Oh, you admit you are attracted to me, and you did nothing. Even though it makes you sound old-fashioned and stuffy?"

Jakes didn't even hear the rest. His hand in her hair stilled, and he dropped it to his side. His heart beat faster and harder in his chest, so much that Jakes could feel it. He stepped away from Angie because he knew if he didn't get away from her soon, he might either say or do something he would regret later.

Shock flitted on Angie's face when he stepped away from her. He turned and left without another word.

How had he misjudged it? How had he misjudged Angie? He thought she was different and accepted him as he was. Hell, he knew he might not be the best catch in the world. He was too serious, but that was who he was.

It hurt to hear Angie say it.

Flashes of Moira's taunts rushed through his mind while he stalked to his room. He couldn't do it again. He couldn't go through a relationship that dragged him down and, little by little, ate at his confidence.

He locked the door behind him, leaning back against it. A knock and Angie's soft voice brought him back to reality. Jakes stepped away and stared at the door. He couldn't face Angie now. He took breaths as he walked towards the bed, but he didn't sit on it. He slid to the floor and started the breathing exercises, his fingers plucking at the rubber band.

It was a long time later that he could think properly again.

He dropped his head in his hands. His reaction was most likely irrational to most people. He knew Angie wasn't a mean person. She didn't mean it in the way he took it. She had teased him, but he couldn't help it. That phrase brought back too many bad memories. He thought he was over it. He thought he had made progress over the last few weeks.

Just thinking of facing Angie tomorrow brought the tension back. He couldn't. Panic took over. He needed to get away, back to Denver and then catch the first flight back to South Africa. He had to go, and the sooner, the better.

He didn't even rethink that decision. Jakes jumped up and grabbed his suitcase. He threw his clothes in, not bothering to pack it neatly and precisely as he usually did. He only left out a set of clothes for travelling and his toiletries. Finished packing, he picked up his laptop and retrieved his flight schedule. The only flight he could get was leaving for London the following afternoon. Jakes took it anyway even though the flights from Johannesburg to London were full. His only choice was to travel via Amsterdam and stay one night in a hotel in Schiphol. He could then catch the daytime flight home, but he didn't hesitate to buy the tickets.

Angie knocked a few more times, but Jakes ignored it. He went to the bathroom and took out his phone, avoiding the risk of anyone else hearing him. It didn't matter what time it was in South Africa. André would answer his phone call when Jakes needed him.

André answered the call on the second ring. "Jakes? How's Colorado? Still freezing your butt off?"

Jakes muttered, "Colorado's fine. Still cold. Where are you?"

André must have heard something in his voice as he asked, "Are you coming back? Do you need a ride from the airport?"

Jakes nodded, then realised André wouldn't be able to see. "Yes, please. Thursday on the KLM flight. I'll send you the details."

"Are you okay, Bro'? Do you need to talk?" his friend asked and Jakes had to admit, "No, I'm not. I can't talk now. Talk to me, please. About anything."

André didn't ask questions and did what Jakes asked. He

told Jakes about his holiday, what happened at the Buffaloes' training camp and the progress with the building of his new house.

Calmer, Jakes mumbled, "Thanks, Buddy. I'm okay now. I will finish packing and write a few letters."

"Okay, call me again if you need me," André urged.

"Will do. Thanks again," Jakes said before he disconnected the call.

Jakes hoped Jonathan could give him a lift to Denver. Since he wanted to be ready in that case, he showered quickly.

He felt the tension building up again when he sat at the desk to write his notes.

Jakes finished all the letters apart from the one to Angie. What should he tell her?

He was pacing up and down in his room when his phone rang. Jakes should've known it was André. His friend would be a good psychologist one day. He knew Jakes and his insecurities and probably knew that he wasn't okay. They spoke for a long while, but this time not only as friends. This time André talked to him as his psychologist. He had done that so many times in the past eighteen months.

When Jakes disconnected, he sat down and poured his heart out to Angie in the letter. By the time he finished, it was almost time to get ready. Jakes re-read the letter and shook his head. No, there was no way he could give it to her. He crumpled it, frustrated, and threw it in the wastepaper basket.

Jakes started another one, but it followed the first.

His fourth attempt would have to do, though as he ran out of time. He would never be able to explain to Angie how he felt in a letter. He folded the paper and put it in the envelope, then changed into the set of clothes he kept out. He packed his last things before he went to knock on Jonathan's door. Jonathan looked surprised to see Jakes.

Jakes cleared his throat, "Sorry to bother you. I need to get back to South Africa. Could I please get a lift with you to Denver?"

Jonathan frowned, "Is everything okay? I thought you are flying out on Thursday?"

Jakes shook his head. "Change of plans. I leave this afternoon."

When Jonathan didn't reply immediately, Jakes added, "If you can't give me a lift, I'll make another plan."

Jonathan shook his head. "No, we can give you a lift. We'll be ready to leave in half an hour."

Jakes felt relieved. "Thank you. I'm ready and packed."

"Jakes?" Jonathan called him back.

Although he didn't feel keen to do so, Jakes turned back and watched Jonathan warily.

"Does Angie know you're leaving? Did you say goodbye?"

Jakes clenched his jaw before he answered. "No, she doesn't know. I wrote her a letter to explain."

Jonathan nodded. "I hope you'll at least say goodbye to my parents. They'll be up to say goodbye."

"Yes, of course. I'll take my luggage to the car and say goodbye."

Jakes rushed back to his room. When he finished cleaning the room, he picked up his luggage. Jakes clenched the letters and the jewellery box he wanted to give to Angie, in his other hand. He didn't dare look at Angie's room when he walked past. If he did, he might never leave.

JAKES EXPECTED the goodbyes to be painful, but it was still more difficult than he anticipated. Angie... No, he didn't even want to think about her now. It was already difficult enough to say goodbye to her parents and Jonathan and Claire later at the airport.

Jakes insisted that Jonathan dropped him at the drop-off zone. He didn't want to drag out the goodbyes for too long. For that, he felt way too emotional.

At the airport, Claire and Jonathan both got out. Claire surprised him when she kissed him on the cheek and gave him a hug before she got back in the car. Jonathan had taken out his luggage while Jakes said goodbye to Claire and was watching their goodbyes in silence. Jonathan might have seen how emotional Jakes was as he said, more grave than Jakes had seen him, "I'm convinced that this is not the last time we meet. I still hope things will work out for you and Angie."

Jakes swallowed hard and nodded. His voice was husky as he admitted, "It doesn't matter how much I love her. I can't hope or think about it now."

Jonathan also surprised Jakes when he pulled him into a hug, the same as his father did earlier. When he stepped back, he nodded, "We'll be in touch, Jakes. Have a good trip."

Jakes nodded, feeling too emotional to reply. He picked up his suitcase and rushed into the airport before he embarrassed himself.

THE HOUSE WAS quiet when Angie woke up. It was still early, but she couldn't sleep any longer. Even though she only fell asleep in the early hours of the morning, she was wide awake. She jumped up immediately. She needed to clear this with Jakes, and the sooner, the better. Angie thought about it throughout the night. What had happened?

She showered and got dressed in a hurry and rushed to Jakes' room. She stopped in the doorway. The door was open, the bed tidy, and it looked almost deserted. She hoped she was wrong. She turned and hurried to the kitchen, where she only found her parents. Their pitying glances were enough to confirm her suspicions.

Jakes left, and he hadn't even said goodbye.

Disappointed she sank onto the nearest chair. Her mother tapped her arm in sympathy as she got up to switch on the kettle. Her dad slid an envelope and a jewellery box towards her. "You might suspect it already. Jakes left this morning with Jonathan and Claire, who will take him to the airport. He said that something happened, and he had to leave."

Angie couldn't stop the tears any longer. She thought she had cried enough during the night, but it seemed not.

"Here, drink this. It's good for shock," Mary instructed, handing Angie a cup of sweet tea.

Angie took a sip and shuddered when the sweetness hit before she asked her father, "Did he say anything?"

He shook his head. "No. He might've explained everything in his letter."

Angie glanced at the jewellery box and the letter. She was almost too scared to open it, but she had to. That was her last link to Jakes.

She swallowed the rest of the tea and stood up to pick up the letter and jewellery box. "I'll read it in my room."

A short while later she sat on her bed. Her fingers trembled when she opened the jewellery box. The tears flowed again when she took out the charm bracelet. She recognised it. She had admired the vintage bracelet at the same shop where Jakes bought the jewellery box he gave her for Christmas, but it looked different now. Angie studied it carefully. There were more charms on the bracelet than it had in the shop. Some were odd and modern. Others, like the South African coin, were adapted into miniature art pieces. The rugby ball a few others could've been commissioned.

When did Jakes get this for her, and why did he not give it to her before? He went to so much trouble, after all.

Her hands still trembled when she opened the letter. Her fingers rubbed over the bold, black handwriting on the plain white paper before she read. A short while later she dropped the note in disappointment.

She thought Jakes would explain what went wrong, but the message was cold and stilted. He only thanked her for their hospitality and gifts. There were no promises. She wouldn't be surprised if he wrote the same letter to everyone in the family.

The tears flowed again—and then Jesse was there. He sat next to her on the bed, put his arm around her and pulled her close. "Are you okay?"

Angie shook her head against his chest, but she couldn't stop crying. When her sobs subsided into hiccups, Jesse urged, "What did he say in his letter? Did he explain?"

Angie shook her head and handed him the letter to read. There was nothing in the letter to embarrass her. After reading it, Jesse dropped the note onto the bed and to Angie's irritation, he smiled, "That explained nothing, but this might."

Angie stared wide-eyed at the balls of paper Jesse had dropped onto her bed. Her fingers trembled when she unfolded them. Two of them were one page each, and just the beginning of a letter, but the other one was at least four or five pages. Angie rubbed out the wrinkles, and soon she was oblivious to anything apart from the letter in her hand. The tears still flowed over her cheeks, but this time she didn't feel as despondent as she had before.

MY BEAUTIFUL ANGEL

When you read this letter, I'm on my way back to South

Africa. I don't want to go. I don't want to leave you, Angel but I have no choice.

Before I go any further, I must warn you this letter may not make sense because I wrote how I feel. I may repeat and contradict myself, but please know this letter is from my heart.

From the minute I first saw you, even after all the disasters, I knew you were special, but I knew I should stay away from you. We could only be friends, and not just because you wore another man's ring.

I never thought I would ever have the confidence to talk to a woman as I spoke to you. I can be myself with you. I can laugh and have fun. You made me see that life has so much to offer that there are women who are sweet and beautiful. You gave me so much more than friendship. You gave me confidence. You gave me hope and love.

I love you, Angel. I love you with a fierce intensity I've never experienced before.

I love who you are... pure, selfless, kind, and compassionate. I love how you could draw me out of my shell, how you can make me laugh and how you make me feel. I love you from deep within my soul and know this won't go away. You are my forever love.

From that first kiss under the mistletoe, I couldn't resist you. Kissing you made me forget the rest of the universe... Then it's just you and me.

There were so many times over the last week that I got close in telling you that I love you, but I had no right. Not now, and not soon. I'm sorry. I wish things could be different.

Most of all, I wish I was different.

I have so many scars and insecurities. I thought I dealt with it, but last night proved I was wrong.

Last night, you said something that triggered all the bad memories... I tried, but I'm still too vulnerable. It's not your fault, Angel. It's all on me, and I refuse to pull you down with me. I can't go into a relationship when an innocent word or comment could make me over-react. I still have a lot of work to do before I can go into a relationship.

I overreacted last night, I know. Unfortunately, I couldn't do anything about it.

My insecurities are not the only reason I couldn't tell you how I felt. I made a promise, a pledge... It wouldn't be fair to admit my feelings and leave you with the knowledge nothing could happen between us.

You don't know how many times I almost gave in and asked you to give me a chance to wait for me. I thought of coming back to Denver next year, after the World Cup. If you would have me, that is. I then overheard a conversation you had with Claire. You said you wouldn't wait for a man again.

I bought you the bracelet, and the charms, to show you how much I love you. I remember you admired the bracelet in that shop in Cherry Village. I added more pieces to the bracelet, hoping they would be reminders of the fun we had together. I think you may understand what I wanted to say with each pendant, as you know me better than most people do.

I dreamed of a life with you, adding more charms, making more memories. It would always be my dream, even though I know it can only stay a dream. Maybe one day...

Please forgive me if I hurt you, Angel. I never wanted to do that.

I left my contact details with your father. Maybe one day, you will feel it in your heart to forgive me and drop me a line or a note to let me know how you are.

It's going to be a long flight back to South Africa. Every hour on that plane will remind me of the distance between us. I will miss you so much.

I love you, and I know I will always love you, Angel.
Yours

Jakes

ANGIE LOOKED at Jesse and smiled through her tears. "He loves me."

Jesse laughed. "I know."

Angie looked at him in surprise. Did he read the letter? Jesse grinned, "Remember that night we took him to the pub?"

Angie frowned. She remembered it all too well. Jesse laughed again, "I know it upset you, but we did it on purpose. We thought if we could get Jakes drunk, he might tell us why he insisted he couldn't get involved with you."

"And did he?" Angie asked.

"No. Jakes kept on saying he loved you, but he wasn't good for you, and something about a promise. It made little sense. Even Rayno couldn't get it out of him when he spoke to him in Afrikaans. Jakes said it was their secret and looked proud of himself because he kept the secret."

Angie sighed. "He mentioned a promise in this letter. Now he's gone, and he doesn't even know how I feel. I could've told him..."

"Yes?" Jesse asked nosily.

"I could've told him I love him too, and I would have waited."

"What now?"

Angie shook her head. "I don't know, Jesse. He didn't tell me he loved me in person. He said it in a letter I was never supposed to see. He doesn't want to take it forward. I have to respect that."

Jesse scowled. "Are you going to leave it like this?"

Angie fingered the bracelet. "I don't know what else to do. If he doesn't want to let me close, I can't force him."

Jesse took her arm to study the bracelet as Angie did earlier. "He put a lot of thought in these."

Angie nodded.

Jesse sounded brisk when he asked, "Angie, are you sure about your feelings for Jakes? Are you sure he's the man you want to spend the rest of your life with?"

"I've never been so sure of anything in my life."

"So, if Jakes can't come to you, go to him. Take the chance. Show Jakes what love, and commitment is. I think he needs that."

Angie shook her head. "Don't ask me that. He made it clear, even if I would go, he still couldn't have a relationship with me."

"Think about it, okay?" Jesse almost pleaded.

Angie couldn't answer him. She didn't want to think about it, not yet anyway. Hadn't she promised herself not to leave her heart open to a man who didn't want her?

CHAPTER SIXTEEN

.

Arriving back in South Africa, Jakes was exhausted. He slept for almost two days with André keeping a watchful eye on him.

When he felt fit enough to string two sentences together, Jakes told André what happened while he was in Denver, especially about that last night and the reason he fled with his tail between his legs.

Jakes knew what to do even before he had that discussion with André. If he ever wanted to have a healthy relationship with Angie or anyone else, he needed to resume his therapy. Jakes was back at Doc Matthews that first Monday morning. Jakes again had to relay everything he told André. The psychologist was actually impressed with the progress Jakes had made. It was time for the next phase in his therapy.

Jakes followed the psychologist's advice and that afternoon Jakes and André drove to Clarens where Jakes told his family for the first time what really happened with Moira. He hated to upset them, but he also felt relieved. Doc Matthews hadn't been wrong. It was now the time to reveal his secret to those closest to him. It was with a lighter mood they returned to Pretoria early the next morning to be in time for their first training session of the season on Wednesday.

Jakes didn't stop avoiding places where he might run into difficult situations. He wasn't looking for trouble. He still had too many emotions to deal with, which were dominated by regret and sadness.

He thought about Angie. He couldn't help it but just thinking about her made him more determined to go through with his therapy.

That first weekend after they resumed training, Jakes got the ideal opportunity to follow through on Doc Matthews' advice and told his friends. He didn't really have a choice.

Mark Bailey, the Buffaloes' number four lock, invited his close group of friends for a boys' night at his house. Apart from Jakes and André, Mark also asked the captain and vice-captain. Daniel Cooper and Matthew Kemp were Mark's best friends. The rest of the guest list consisted of Rick Walters, the fullback and Richie Campbell. The Scottish winger had joined the team for the new competition. Christopher Brooks, the media officer, was the only non-player in their group.

Late that evening, they were still sitting on the veranda with their last beers of the evening. Jakes was so deep in thought he hadn't heard half of the conversations. He didn't know how they arrived at the topic, but only heard when Richie asked, "What pledge?"

They all stared at Richie, only then realising they hadn't spoken to the newcomers in the squad about it. Daniel didn't hesitate. It was his duty, after all. He exacted a promise from Richie, "Promise what I tell you now will stay with the team and us."

Richie laughed at Daniel, his Glasgow accent very distinct, "You're joking, right?"

Daniel shook his head, "No joke. This is serious."

Richie's face was a picture. His gaze flitted between the friends, but they were all watching him with the same solemn expressions. Richie might have realised that this was serious. He still looked reluctant as he made his promise. They all nodded in satisfaction and turned to Daniel to explain.

"Mark read an article about football players abstaining from sex before the World Cup. Mark said the study claimed that if you don't have sex, it frees a tremendous amount of brain and emotional space that our sex lives often fill. People use that space to plan and re-think and worry about sex. If they don't have to spend that time worrying about that, they can focus on things that will be more beneficial to them. They could thus make their lives more meaningful and productive."

It sounded as if Daniel had memorised the article Mark had read because he could almost quote it word for word.

Daniel laughed, "I have to admit, we had that discussion after we lost the final of the Interprovincial Cup. We moaned because some players were so sluggish that day they might as well not have been on the pitch. We blamed Rick here, didn't we, Rick?"

Rick laughed and shrugged.

"Why?" Richie asked.

Daniel chuckled, "If Rick had less sex, he might focus on his game."

"It might've been the beers talking." Mark added, "I think it was the bears talking, but someone had the bright idea that if we abstain from sex during the new competition, we could win it first," indicating Daniel.

"And another clever person," Daniel pointed at Jakes, "practised his lawyer-skill. He wrote a contract on the back of one of Christopher's press releases. Most of the team had signed the contract by the time we staggered to our rooms that night.

The following day, none of us remembered much about it, except Ryan Foster. He doesn't drink, and without our knowledge, he kept the paper."

"On the Monday after the final, we had to attend our last team meeting as some of us had to report to the Springbok training camp the next day. When Nicholas and the rest of the management team walked in, we knew there was trouble. Nicholas gave us a tongue-lashing of epic proportions. He told us he and the rest of the board were unhappy about the way we lost the final. Nicholas made it clear we as the squad must take responsibility for our destiny. If we wanted to win another trophy, we needed to step up and take charge of our goals. We felt this big," Daniel said, pressing his forefinger and thumb together.

"Then Nicholas dropped another bomb on us. He told us that the Board decided they wanted to change the image of the franchise and rugby. They expected us, as the players, to come up with a plan. We had until the end of that day to come up with ideas of how we would do that. All the senior players gathered in the dining room to figure out how to do that. Ryan produced the pledge we'd made on Saturday night. We reread it, changed and added to it, and by late afternoon we had a useful document. Rachel typed the basic rules which he submitted to the board, but we had another, secret document. She made enough copies of it for everyone to sign."

Richie frowned. "Ye guys did that?"

They all nodded. Daniel said, "It was weird. The more we thought about it, the more we believed in it. It might have been childish, but we not only signed it in ink but also in blood."

Richie shook his head. "You're fucking serious!" and frowned. "What does the pledge say?"

Daniel shook his head. "You must read it for yourself, because we expect you and Ulrich, and all newcomers, also to sign it. The essence of the pledge is that we have to behave like professionals. We had to follow Management's orders, whether or not we like it—and that includes Chloe's rules. We, as players, need to take responsibility for the team. Those of us who are single have to abstain from sex and a new relationship until the final. Those who were in a committed relationship or married are to abstain from sex, at least the day before a match."

Richie swore when he realised it wasn't a joke, but Daniel stopped him, "Sorry Scotsman," which clearly was Richie's allocated nickname, and warned, "swearing is out. We also promised to limit any swearing as part of our new image. We have a swear jar in the locker room, and you have to donate a five rand coin for every swear word," before he admitted with a laugh, "We filled the third jar this week."

Richie stared at them aghast. "Had anyone broken their vow yet?"

When nobody answered, Jakes cleared his throat. He should've known that everyone would turn to him, some more surprised than others, and he asked hesitantly, "Does kissing count?"

It was eerily silent as the group stared at him, but then Daniel asked, "You want to tell us something?"

Jakes glanced at André, who nodded his encouragement. They spoke about it. This was the moment he waited to share his secret with his friends, and that's what he did. He told them everything, from what happened with Moira in his past until he met Angie. They all listened without interrupting him once.

When he finished, it was quiet again until Mark asked, "You're in love with her?", meaning Angie.

Jakes nodded, "I am. I never thought I'll fall in love so quickly. Hell, I never even thought I'll get close to a woman but Angie... I might have broken my pledge if Angie wasn't someone... Angie's not the kind of girl you only flirt with. She's a forever kind of girl."

"Have you told her how you feel?" Mark asked.

Jakes shook his head, "I was going to. I was minutes away from doing so. Then I received Daniel's message reminding us of the pledge."

Matthew sighed, disappointed, "Are you not going to see her again?"

"I don't think so," Jakes admitted. "I still talk to Rayno, but I haven't heard anything from her. I can't keep on hoping."

The rest of the conversation dwelled on relationships, and everyone tried to fish for more information and gave advice. Jakes realised he wasn't the only one in this situation. Everyone had a story. He was lucky that Angie wasn't here to tempt him, where his friends stared temptation in the face daily. If they could do it, so can he.

THE YEAR HADN'T STARTED as Angie hoped it would. It could've been worse so she should be grateful that it wasn't.

It was only the second day since the schools reopened that Angie suddenly felt her heart clenched. Something had happened, and she was convinced it had to do with Jesse. She tried to call him, but he didn't answer. When her mother entered the studio a few minutes later, her face white and tears streaming down her face, Angie knew that her intuition hadn't played parts with her. Something had happened with Jesse

When they walked into the hospital half an hour later, they were relieved to find that Jesse's physical injury wasn't as serious as they first suspected. Jesse struggled more with the emotional effects of what had happened. He couldn't face going back to school and resigned while still in the hospital. Angie had waited for it. Jesse wasn't much different from her. He had already admitted to Angie that his heart wasn't in teaching anymore. The problem was that he didn't know then what he wanted to do with his life.

Rayno couldn't handle Jesse's depression after his release from the hospital anymore. He suggested then that Jesse might need a change of scenery and invited him to go to South Africa with him. Although not keen at first, Jesse got more excited about it later on. He finally agreed, but only if Angie joined them. It felt like emotional blackmail, so Angie wasn't keen at first.

Her parents pleaded. They argued that it might be the best medicine for Jesse, and probably for Angie too. Angie might get closure when she saw Jakes in his natural environment. Her excuses got less, and the last one disappeared when her parents bought the flight tickets as an early birthday present and also gave them an advance from their trust funds for pocket money.

Not that they would need that much because Rayno's family had offered their garden cottage as a base for Angie and Jesse, which the twins accepted.

That was how Angie found herself on a flight to South Africa ten days after Jesse's injury, with Rayno and Jesse next to her.

Angie had prepared herself to see Jakes again. Angie was still sceptical and hoped her family wasn't wrong. She could only hope she was making the right decision.

JAKES WORKED HARD DURING TRAINING. It was hot, and he was sweating, but if he didn't train, he would go crazy.

As the days passed, Jakes was getting more and more frustrated. He didn't want to ask Rayno about Angie. He tried not to think about her, but she slipped into his thoughts at the most inappropriate times.

He didn't really make it easier for himself. His house reminded him of Angie as three of her paintings were now hanging in his home. The one she gave to him as a gift was taking the place of prominence in his lounge. The books she gave him was on his bedside table, next to the photo he took of her that morning when they made the snowman.

Frustrated, he tackled the player in front of him into the ground. André, his unfortunate victim, glared at him, "Calm down, dude. You don't have to kill me."

Jakes realised that the tackle was more aggressive than necessary and he stretched out his hand to pull André back up. "Sorry."

Before he could add to it, Coach Brady called Jakes. Jakes knew what was coming and jogged towards the head coach. He wiped the sweat from his face with his arm as he stopped in front of Tom. The Coach's face was inscrutable when he asked, "How do you feel?"

Jakes shrugged, "Fine, Coach."

"Any pain when you run or scrum?"

Jakes shook his head. "No, Coach. No pain and no stiffness."

Coach Brady looked deep in thought. He nodded, chewing his bottom lip then grunted, "Now what the hell is making you so grumpy? Go see Michael. I want you off my pitch before you kill one of my players."

Jakes flushed. "Sorry Coach."

He felt more frustrated when he jogged to Michael, but he would never argue with Tom. He accepted the bottle of flavoured milk that Michael held out to him and downed it in seconds. When he deposited the empty bottle in the bin, Michael asked, "Why do you look so miserable?"

Jakes shrugged but didn't answer. Michael probed again, "No word from Angie yet?"

Geez, why did Michael mention her now? Jakes clenched his jaw and shook his head. "No, nothing."

A strange expression flitted over Michael's face, but before Jakes could analyse it, Michael changed the topic. "Any niggles? Do you need ice?"

Again, Jakes shook his head. "No, I'm fine."

Michael muttered, "Okay, hit the shower. See you later. You are going to The Final Whistle?""

Jakes nodded and walked to the changing rooms. He glanced at the pitch. The squad now stood in a circle around the coaches. Jakes envied his friends going to Pietersburg tomorrow for the warm-up game. Coach wanted to rest Jakes, but Jakes was convinced there was more behind Tom's decision. There was nothing wrong with him. He wanted to play. If he didn't play, he had too much time to think.

He couldn't even go home this weekend. He was convinced that Sue and Tom collaborated. She arranged a sponsor's function on Friday night and a press interview on Saturday. Not that it mattered. It would still leave too much time alone to brood.

JAKES INHALED SHARPLY. André and Daniel looked worried as they turned to him. The bottle of beer almost fell out of his hand. His heart was beating fast, and his legs felt weak.

He didn't want to believe it... couldn't believe it, but his heart recognised the woman who had appeared in the doorway.

It *was* her. Jakes' eyes drank her in, from her bright, multi-coloured sundress to her dark curls and the brightness of her eyes. She made a stunning picture. If it were not for the two men flanking her, she would've received a few wolf-whistles.

As usual, it wasn't her eyes that drew him, but her smile. It looked bright and cheery, but Jakes could see the uncertainty as she glanced around the crowded room. He knew when she noticed him. Her smile slid a little wider so he could see the small dimple hiding in the corner of her mouth.

Jakes didn't know how he managed to stand up and manoeuvred himself around André's chair, without breaking eye contact with Angie. He was aware of the eyes following his progress. It felt like an eternity before he reached her, but it wouldn't surprise Jakes if he had been running. He needed to make sure she wasn't a figment of his imagination, that she was real.

When he reached her, he noticed the suspicious brightness of her eyes. He picked her up in his arms and pulled her against him in a tight hug. Her eyes slipped around his shoulders when he buried his head in her hair. He closed his eyes and breathed her name.

Angie. *His* Angie. He thought he would never see her again and didn't want to let her go. He held her even tighter.

Until he realised what he was doing.

What *was* he doing? Right in front of his coaches, teammates, and friends! Was he crazy?

He breathed in one more time before he released her. He couldn't look into her eyes when his hands dropped to his sides, and he stepped back.

Jesse saved the moment when he stepped up next to Angie and held out his hand to Jakes. "Bro', it's good to see you." Rayno did the same. And then, all four of them spoke at once until Jakes let the others explained why they were there and how they knew where to find him. Jakes then understand Michael's weird expression and question earlier.

Because Jakes was so painfully aware of Angie, he focused on Jesse and Rayno. He spoke to them when he invited them to join their group. When he turned, he noticed that his friends already made space for the new arrivals. Back at the table, Jakes made the introductions. He knew he could rely on his friends to keep Rayno and Jesse company.

Jakes retreated into his shell, his eyes fixed on Angie. So many emotions rushed through him. He had so many questions, but he couldn't get anything out.

Maybe Angie felt his gaze on her, as she turned her head, and their eyes held. He should've looked away, but he didn't. It was as if the universe faded away and it was just the two of them.

Jakes knew then he was in serious trouble. He worked hard, concentrated on the team, the game, and their end focus, but nothing of that mattered now. Angie was here, and the way she looked at him made his heart race.

Jakes blinked when something blocked his vision. Once, then again, before he realised that it was Daniel's big hand that caused it.

He realised something else. The table was quiet. He turned guiltily to Daniel, who had raised his eyebrow in a typical Daniel gesture. Jakes felt guilty. He let his eyes slide over the rest of the table, seeing his friends' gazes. Their concerned expressions said it all, and he knew what they were all thinking.

Jakes sighed and looked down at his hands.

He couldn't let them down. They already worked hard, and it wouldn't be fair to them.

He scooted further away from Angie. If she didn't sit close to him, if he couldn't smell her tantalising freshness, he might stay away from her.

DISAPPOINTED, Angie's shoulders dropped.

The excitement to see Jakes since their arrival in South Africa that morning evaporated the moment Daniel had waved his hand between her and Jakes.

It had been a mistake. She shouldn't have come.

The anticipation of seeing Jakes again, built while they were on the plane, especially after she read that letter for the hundredth time. She had all these scenarios painted in her head of what Jakes would do when he saw her again. Part of it came true. He looked happy to see her. She saw the emotions in his eyes, and she felt it when he held her. That moment when they looked at each other and almost forgot that the rest of the world existed, Angie felt something tangible. At that moment, she still had hope.

When Daniel broke it up, Jakes withdrew. Not only mentally, but physically too. He moved away from her, removing the heat she felt from him. It felt as if there was now more distance between them than when she was back in Denver.

Angie glanced at Jesse. It might not have been a mistake to come. It had been for her brother's sake. He and Rayno were talking to Jakes' teammates and friends, but Jesse's expression showed something she thought she would never see again. His excitement grew the longer he spoke to the serious-looking man next to him. Unlike most of his friends, this man wore a suit. He also looked more solemn than his friends. It didn't matter. Jesse seemed fascinated and excited by whatever the man was saying to him.

Angie blushed. She didn't come only for Jakes, although she wanted to give him another chance. Angie now just had to accept that he didn't want to take it and learn how to deal with it. She wouldn't make it uncomfortable for Jesse and Rayno.

She refused to let Jakes see how his withdrawal affected her.

CHAPTER SEVENTEEN

Maybe she should follow Jakes' example and ignore him.

Across the table from Angie sat a woman with a short, pixie-haired hairstyle. When she smiled at Angie, Angie returned her smile, although she didn't feel like smiling. It wasn't long before the woman included Angie in their conversation. Angie then realised who she was. Jakes' description of Chloe, their nutritionist, was accurate. The blonde woman who also chatted to her was Melissa, one of the physiotherapists. There were other women too, but they sat further down the table.

When the man on the other side of Chloe drew her attention, Angie had the opportunity to study the other occupants of the table. One man studied her with a curious expression and a smile playing around his full lips. He had Bad Boy written all over him, from the top of his spiky brown hair, down to the tattoos covering his muscled arms and chest. She returned his gaze and took in the grey-blue eyes, and two dimples on either side of his mouth. He most likely thought she admired him as most women did, but he did nothing to her. Angie would've liked to paint him, though. She didn't think he would mind and might even volunteer to pose for a nude.

That painting would definitely not be anything like the one she made of Jakes. His were different, more personal. She sneaked a glance at him, but he didn't even look at her. His face looked like a thunderstorm waiting to happen as he glared at the man who just smiled at her.

Jakes was jealous!

When Jakes turned to her, he tried to mask his reaction quickly, but it was too late.

The knowledge suddenly hit her. If he was jealous, did it mean he cared? Her heart beat faster. Should she test her theory? It was not as if she had anything to lose?

The man sitting next to Jakes had contributed even less to the conversation than Jakes had but, unlike Jakes, he looked relaxed. Angie also recognised him from Jakes' description as Jakes had spoken so many times of his friend, André. She took a deep breath, and she scooted closer to Jakes. She heard his indrawn breath when she leaned over him, her arm brushing against his when she asked the man, "You are André, aren't you?"

André gave her a friendly smile, "Yes, I am."

Angie returned his smile, "I'm glad to meet you. Jakes spoke so much about you."

"Ditto," André grinned when Jakes scowled at him. Angie leaned even closer to Jakes, crowding his space. His muscles tensed when she brushed her arm against his and her hand brushed against his leg. She carried on with what she hoped was a sensible conversation with André, pretending to be oblivious of Jakes.

She might've gone too far when Jakes grabbed her hand when it brushed for the umpteenth time against his leg. He threaded his fingers through hers. Angie stuttered when he stroked his thumb over the pulse point on her wrist. Her eyes flitted up to meet his.

She almost stopped breathing when she read the expression in his eyes. She hadn't been wrong.

She had proved her point, but what now? She hadn't thought that through enough.

She tried to pull her hand away, but it was no use. Jakes held tight, his thumb still making a slow exploration. Angie couldn't think. She couldn't even continue having a sensible conversation.

She had to leave. She dragged her eyes away from Jakes and stared at Jesse. Her twin, attuned to her moods as only twins could be, glanced up. Jesse must have read the desperation in her eyes and winked at her. He spoke to Rayno, and to Angie's relief, they both stood up and said they had to leave.

Jakes didn't let her hand go, though. Rather the opposite, in fact, as he tightened his hold and also got up. With a short, "See you at the car," Jakes pulled Angie up at the same time. He almost dragged her behind him. Angie was aware of the eyes following their progress to a room on the other side of the restaurant.

ANGIE MADE it impossible to control his emotions. He had tried, but a man could only take so much before he lost control. Jakes was very close to it.

Geez, he almost lost control when he caught Rick smiling at her earlier. He could have killed Rick. And when she spoke to André? He had been jealous of André! How sick was that?

Every time she brushed against him or her hand touched his legs, he had to grit his teeth. But he couldn't ignore it any longer. Now that she was here, there was only one thing he wanted to do.

Jakes pulled Angie into the room the players dubbed The Meeting Room of The Final Whistle. He closed the door behind him and immediately pulled Angie against him. Letting go of her hand, Jakes lifted his to frame her face. It could only be seconds before he claimed her mouth, but it felt like an eternity since he last kissed her.

Jakes couldn't get enough. Only the need for air forced him to release Angie's mouth, but even then, Jakes couldn't move away. His hands slid from her face to her back, pulling her against him, breathing in her smell.

She was here. Jakes still couldn't believe it.

But that was the problem. He had known it already in Denver. If he kept Angie close, he wouldn't be able to keep his promise to his teammates. Wasn't that the main reason he left in a hurry?

So, what the hell did he do when he saw her?

He did what he should've avoided.

He had to be stronger. He just had to.

He dropped his hands and stepped away from her so he could get some distance between them. He turned away from her because he didn't want Angie to see the effect she had on him. Jakes couldn't keep the huskiness out of his voice when he asked, "Why did you come, Angie?"

"Why do you think?" she answered him with a question of her. Her voice was soft. That should have been Jakes' clue. Even though he liked detective stories, he would never have made a good one himself. Especially when trying to read women.

He shrugged, "I don't know."

Angie stepped around Jakes, so he had no choice but to meet her eyes as she demanded, "You owe me an explanation, Jakes."

"About what?" he hedged, playing for time.

Angie sounded angry when she said, "Come on, Jakes. Do I have to spell it out? I deserve to know why you left without saying goodbye. What did I do wrong to upset you?"

Jakes couldn't look at her when he muttered, "It wasn't you. I needed to leave."

Angie folded her arms across her chest and stared at him. She didn't believe him and Jakes couldn't blame her. Angie was right. She deserved an answer, but he wasn't sure what to tell her. He couldn't explain all the reasons, or not yet anyway. No, he wasn't He couldn't lose the trust of his friends and teammates too.

"That's none of your business," he mumbled.

Even when he didn't look at her, he could see Angie flinched. He only looked up when she stepped back as if she wanted to get distance from her. His heart clenched as her voice sounded small when she whispered, "Okay then. That's fair enough. I thought we were friends. No, the way you kissed me, I thought.... It doesn't matter anymore."

She stepped around him, and before Jakes knew it, she was at the door. She turned to him, saying quietly, "And to answer your question: You made it clear I mean nothing to you. I'm here because Jesse needed me."

She opened the door and walked out.

Jakes stared at the empty doorway and knew he made the worst decision of his life.

After a long time, he walked back towards their table, where only his friends were waiting. If Jakes thought he felt terrible, the others looked it too.

He took the beer Mark slid over to him and downed it in one go. When he put the empty bottle back on the table, Daniel broke the silence, "So that was Angie."

"Yep," Jakes sighed.

"What will happen now?"

"Nothing. nothing."

"Are you going to let her slip through your fingers? Are you not going to pursue her? She came here to see you," Daniel asked, shocked.

Jakes slumped in his chair, rubbing his hands through his hair. He shook his head. "No, she told me she's here only because Jesse needed her."

"Are you not even going to try and salvage anything?" André insisted.

Jakes threw his hands in the hair. "Come on, guys. You've seen her. There's no way I can resist her. I need to stay away. I can't let you all down now."

Mark's voice was as urgent as André's when he pointed out, "The team's not everything, Jakes."

Did they not understand. Jakes slid his gaze between them and sighed, "It is to me. The team, you guys... You were all I had after Moira. You're the guys who stood by me when I was down. You're the guys who helped me up. You, the team, rugby... That's all I had. It's all I have. I can't let you down. I made a promise. I keep my promises," he managed.

Jakes suddenly felt exhausted. He got up and walked away, leaving his friends staring at his back.

JAKES MET Jesse and Rayno at The Final Whistle about an hour ago and took them on a stadium tour. When Rayno made an excuse to leave, Jakes invited Jesse to lunch and promised to bring Jesse back to the cottage afterwards. It was stupid, but he still suggested they invited Angie. Jesse didn't even ask Angie and shook his head. "Angie won't come."

He should've known Angie won't come. Why he still thought she might, he didn't know, but Jakes couldn't blame her. The less time he spent in her company, the less temptation he had to face. He felt terrible about what he said last night and even worse about the way he said it, but it was too late now.

After lunch, it looked as if Jesse didn't want to go back to their cottage yet. When Jakes invited him to his house for a swim, Jesse almost jumped at the opportunity.

Later that night Jakes reflected on his conversation with Jesse that afternoon. Jesse wasn't the buoyant young man Jakes had met in Denver. He was quieter, more withdrawn than he had been when they met.

Jakes rarely spoke about his panic attacks and the treatment he got for it. Jesse, however, asked Jakes pertinently about it this afternoon. Jakes suspected that there had to be a reason which prompted Jesse's sudden interest, but for once he spoke about it more openly. He had noticed the new scar on Jesse's upper arm when they were swimming, and that might have been the reason behind Jesse's questions and Angie's remark last night that she was here for Jesse. Jakes didn't want to ask. Jesse would talk when he was ready.

ANGIE EXCHANGED numbers with Chloe and Melissa the previous evening, but after what happened, she hadn't expected to see them again. It, therefore, surprised her to get a phone call from Chloe on Thursday afternoon, inviting her to a product launch on Friday night. Angie eagerly accepted. She hadn't looked forward to being alone, and she was convinced that Jesse and Rayno would want to see Jakes.

She was glad she could avoid Jakes, but the party was also an opportunity to dress up. She hadn't had much opportunity recently, and she looked forward to it. Chloe also insisted that Angie joined her, Melissa and Hannah to a pamper session on Friday afternoon at a local spa. When she got into the cab that evening with the three other women, Angie felt confident. The blue cocktail dress accentuating the blue of her eyes and was, according to Chloe, perfect for a cocktail evening.

An hour later, she was glad she took extra care with her appearance when Jakes arrived with a slender, blonde woman on his arm. He looked attractive in dark trousers, a white shirt and a sports blazer, but Angie couldn't admire him as she had enough trouble stifling the sudden flare of jealousy.

Maybe she should leave. Jakes hadn't seen her yet...

She pulled back her shoulders. She was not going to run away. She would ignore him. That shouldn't be too difficult?

Yet it was, as Jakes and his companion walked straight to their table. When he noticed Angie, his eyes widened and it looked like he wanted to turn away, but then he didn't and pulled out a chair for the other woman. Angie struggled to ignore the pain shooting through her chest to see him with someone else. Was that the reason...?

No, she shouldn't even think about it. She was also not going to flee, and she was going to enjoy the evening. She pulled back her shoulders and took a sip of her champagne. She took another one when Jakes introduced the woman as his publicist, Sue. Jakes had mentioned her in the past, but she didn't look anything like Angie imagined her.

It was not easy to ignore Jakes, didn't matter how hard Angie tried. She was too aware of him. She spoke to all her table companions, except Jakes. Why were his publicist and his lawyer here? They were clearly Jakes' guests, but why are they, and Jakes here? Angie's questions were answered when the proceedings started.

The CEO of a company manufacturing a well-known men's body range announced the launch of their new shower gel and that the guests were going to have the opportunity to view the first advertisement. He gestured to the big screen behind him, which previously displayed the company's logo.

Angie's mouth dropped open when she recognised Jakes. A naked Jakes appeared on the screen. It might only be an illusion, but wow! He looked amazing. Angie swallowed the drool. She didn't know where to look when he got in the shower and followed the water droplets as it ran over his smooth, tanned skin. Jakes poured the shower gel in his large hands, lathering his chest and stomach. Angie, completely oblivious that she did it, sighed rather loudly in appreciation.

Angie caught Melissa's echoing sigh. When Melissa caught her eye, Angie waved her hand over her face and mouthed to Melissa, "Hot!"

That's when she heard it again: Jakes' deep laughter she thought she would never hear again. She might not be the only one who was surprised at his sudden chuckle, because everyone gazed at him surprised. Jakes didn't notice as he stared straight at Angie, his eyes still crinkling and the corners of his mouth curled in amusement.

Her heart wanted to soften, but then Angie realised. He had seen that gesture!

Oh my gosh! Let me just die of embarrassment right now!

Angie grabbed her champagne glass and drained the contents, much to the amusement of Melissa and Chloe.

The ad finished, and the guests voiced their appreciation with loud applause. Angie hadn't even seen the end as she was too aware of Jake's intense gaze still fixed on her. For the rest of the evening, she felt it even though she tried to ignore it. Sue and James, his lawyer, had noticed it too. They probably still speculate about Jakes' sudden flash of humour. Angie was convinced that it had surprised them as much as it had surprised her.

The evening finally dragged to a close. When Angie got up

to leave, Jakes stopped her with a restraining hand on her arm, "How are you getting home?"

She looked him straight in the eye without even a glimmer of a smile when she repeated his words of last night, "It's none of your business."

She heard Jakes' sigh but turned to follow the other women out to the waiting cab.

MELISSA RESTED her hand on her chin and mused, "If we had dates, some people's eyes might open."

Chloe scrunched her nose. She sounded sceptical when she shook her head, "I don't think that will work, Melissa."

"How would you know if you don't try it? Have you ever dated since you moved to Pretoria?"

Chloe shook her head, embarrassedly.

Angie suddenly had a bright idea. "What about Jesse and Rayno? I can ask them. It is only for a night, after all."

Melissa grinned. "You're brilliant."

"Do you want me to ask them?"

When both nodded, Angie said, " I'll let you know tomorrow."

"Thank you, Angie," Melissa said. She studied Angie for a moment or two before she added, "But someone else also needs a wake-up call. We need to find you a date."

Chloe almost jumped up in excitement as she exclaimed, "I know who."

Melissa and Angie turned to her surprised, and Chloe grinned, "Rick Walters! I saw Jakes' reaction the night we met when Rick stared at you, Angie. Rick will be perfect!"

Angie frowned, trying to remember which of the men was Rick but then she recalled, "Is Rick the one with the spiky hair and tattoos?"

Chloe nodded, but then Cloe warned, "That's him, but we have to warn you. Rick's a womaniser. Don't take him seriously."

Angie reassured them, "I already got the impression. You don't have to worry that I'll fall for him."

"I'll ask him then," Chloe volunteered. "But what's going on with you and Jakes?"

Angie's shoulders sagged when she shook her head, "I don't know. Jakes mentioned a promise he made. I don't know to whom, but who says it is not to another woman?"

Chloe frowned, "I don't know about that. I've never seen Jakes with a woman, but then, I don't know him well. He's very reserved and only speaks when he has to."

"I also noticed that," Melissa agreed.

Angie shrugged. She didn't know either, and she wouldn't ask again. Jakes had had enough chances to explain.

SHE SHOULD'VE DECLINED when he asked her to dance. She tried to avoid him, but when he came to stand in front of her, she made the mistake of looking into his eyes. The vulnerability in his eyes got to her, and before she could think about it, she had agreed.

He had barely drawn her to the dance floor when he grunted, "What's going on between you and Rick."

"That's none of your business, Jakes."

He clenched her hand tighter when she threw his words back at him again.

"He's a womaniser. He's only interested in one thing."

"So, what about it?" Angie asked nonchalantly. She was taunting him, but she was tired of his contradictory behaviour.

Jakes inhaled sharply and asked, clearly shocked, "You... You had..."

Angie stopped right there, not caring that they were in the middle of the dance floor. She was barely aware of the couples circling around them. She was angry. And hurt.

She took a deep breath and gritted her teeth, "Again, it's none of your business but... I thought you knew me, but if you think I would jump into bed with the first man I meet, you don't know me at all."

Jakes had the decency to look embarrassed when he apologised. "I'm sorry. I guess I'm jealous," he admitted.

"You have no right to be," Angie snapped. "What I do has nothing to do with you. We were only friends. We're not even that anymore. Your choice, remember?"

Angie stepped around Jakes and left him on the dance floor. She couldn't face anyone and made her way to the bathroom. When Angie felt composed enough, she went back to the table, just in time to see Jakes stalking out of the Ballroom, his face as white as chalk with André close on his heels.

Angie didn't stay long after that. Melissa and Chloe seemed to have achieved their purpose and didn't mind that Jesse and Rayno took Angie home. Rick also didn't have a problem. He had found a blonde bimbo to keep him occupied.

HE DIDN'T EXPECT her to agree, but Jesse confirmed that Angie decided to go to Bloemfontein to watch the Buffalces' first game in the competition. He was even more surprised that she had agreed to spend the Saturday night at his family's farm in Clarens. It must be for Jesse's sake because Jakes was sure it wasn't for his.

He hadn't seen Angie since she left him on the dance floor on Saturday night. She and Jesse went to Sun City for two days, and Jakes didn't even have the chance to get information from Jesse.

He hated knowing that she was here, but he couldn't speak to her. He missed the bond they had in Denver, but he could blame nobody but himself.

Instead of trying to fix it, Jakes withdrew into his shell. His friends and teammates were worried about him. According to André, they were scared he would go back to the way he was when he arrived at the Buffaloes, but André knew Jakes well. He hadn't left Jakes alone since Saturday night. He also insisted that Jakes intensified his sessions with Doc Matthews.

It was quiet on the team bus when they left for Bloemfontein. Everything they had worked and sacrificed for was now a reality. This was their first step on the road to glory. Jakes needed to focus. He couldn't let his teammates down.

More importantly, he couldn't let himself down.

CHAPTER EIGHTEEN

A ngie didn't know where to look as there were so many
things to see. Local artists, cheerleaders and mini
cheerleaders were all performing since they arrived.
Some of the young cheerleaders could not be older than twelve.

She'd been to basketball and baseball games in the past.
She'd never been to a rugby match like this. The stadium was
bigger than that of Denver's professional team and filled to
capacity. According to Rayno, the White Rhino Stadium
wasn't even the biggest one in South Africa.

It was a beautiful Friday afternoon in Bloemfontein, and
the anticipation was tangible. The green and black of the home
side's support was predominant. Here and there, Angie could
see patches of dark grey and black jerseys of the Buffaloes.

It had quietened down for a short while. When the music
started again, the whole crowd joined the artist singing the
Rhino team song. According to Rayno, each team had its own
supporters' song too.

The Buffaloes then the Rhinos ran onto the field to the roar
of the crowd. A row of big motorbikes also contributed to the

deafening noise. By the time the referee blew his whistle, Angie was as psyched up as the rest of the spectators.

Angie couldn't see Jakes since they appeared on the pitch. After the kickoff, a player reached high in the air, supported by two of his teammates. He caught the ball with both hands. When he turned, Angie saw Jake's number eight on his back. He was wearing a scrum cap, which was why she hadn't recognised him.

Jakes loved to run with the ball in hand, and for such a big man, he possessed tremendous speed. On top of that, he also exhibited a lot of power. During one movement, things happened so fast that Angie rather watched the action on the big screen. Jakes had received the ball and transferred it to his right hand. She could see the fierce determination on his face. He looked like a bull on a rampage, pushing off opponents before they could tackle him. With the momentum of the centre behind him, Jakes fell over the line for a try. Daniel summarily grabbed Jakes at the back of his jersey and pulled him up. All his teammates were congratulating him by rubbing his head or slapping his back.

They were sitting almost right in front of the commentary boxes. When Jakes scored, the commentator behind Angie got so excited that he spoke even louder. He described the movement in detail and summarily dubbed Jakes the Raging Buffalo. Angie knew then that was how she wanted to make another painting of Jakes.

The commentator behind Angie seemed to love nicknames. After Richie Campbell, the Buffaloes' new signee, scored his second try, the commentator called him The Flying Scotsman, eliciting a giggle from Angie.

.   .   .

ANGIE WAS STILL in two minds whether she should accept Jakes' invitation to dinner. He had invited Jesse and Rayno too, but the two had already accepted Rick's invitation to visit one of Bloemfontein's popular nightclubs in Second Avenue.

If it wasn't for Chloe's pleas for Angie to save her from being the lone woman in the group of men, Angie might've gone to her room and ordered room service.

Angie was nervous while they waited in the restaurant for the group of players to arrive. She hadn't seen Jakes since Saturday night and wasn't sure how to deal with the situation. At least the friends arrived in a group, and she didn't have to confront Jakes on his own. She ignored him, or she tried, but she was still too aware of his every movement and expression. Despite that, she enjoyed the evening more than she expected.

As Angie anticipated, the men spent most of the dinner analysing the game. When Angie mentioned the Buffaloes' determination, Daniel grinned, "Revenge is sweet."

Angie couldn't understand it. After Daniel's cryptic statement, the atmosphere changed. They seemed uncomfortable, shifting in their seats. Dinner also came to an abrupt end, but on the way to their hotel, Mark suggested that they had one last drink in the hotel bar to celebrate their win.

Angie had barely received her glass of wine when a group of women entered. They immediately noticed the players, and it was clear that they were waiting for their chance to get to know them better. Angie wasn't in the mood to deal with her own jealousy. She just finished the wine and put the glass back on the table before she excused herself to go to her room.

Her heart dropped in her shoes when Jakes got up and announced, "I'll go with you."

"That's not necessary," she tried to argue, but he gave her such a compelling look that she swallowed her words.

The quiet between them was uncomfortable. By the time

they reached Angie's room, she already had the key card in her hand. Jakes took her arm before she could swipe it though. Angie could feel the heat burning through her skin. He turned her to face him, but Angie didn't want to look into his eyes. She knew what would happen.

"Angie?"

The pleading note in his voice when he said her name made Angie do what she told herself not to. She lifted her head, and it happened exactly as she thought it would: she got lost in his eyes. With a soft groan, Jakes pulled her closer and lowered his heads. Within seconds his fingers had tangled in her hair, and he kissed her. Angie lifted her hands to push him away but found she was too lost in the kiss.

It was a long time later that reality kicked in. Angie somehow found the willpower to push Jakes away. She turned to the door, shrugging off his hands from her shoulders. Her hands shook when she put the key card in the slot. Angie slipped into her room, closing the door before Jakes could stop her. She ignored his soft knock and sank down on the bed trembling.

This was a mistake. She shouldn't have come.

ANGIE TWISTED her hands in her lap. Jakes had leaned over a few seconds ago to tell Rayno to slow down because they were close to the turnoff to the farm. "It is there, on the left. Look out for two sandstone pillars."

If the tension between her and Jakes were not enough, she felt inexplicably tense to meet his family. Why? It wasn't as if there is something between them. They were barely friends!

She almost jumped when Jakes suddenly put his large hand over hers. He squeezed her hand and whispered, "Relax. My family don't bite."

Angie flushed and took a deep breath as he added, "They'll love you."

Angie glanced at him and her heart twisted when she caught his lopsided grin. He wore a dark green T-shirt today which brought out the colour of his eyes, but it was the intensity which made her insides melt.

The car bumped when Rayno turned off the road, bringing Angie back to reality. Angie looked away and pulled her hand from underneath his. She heard his sigh but ignored it.

Jakes opened the gate with a remote key, and they drove through to follow the gravel road to the house. Angie caught her breath when she first saw the sandstone house on the hill. She recognised it from Jakes' photos, but it was even more beautiful than Angie imagined. The gardens surrounding the house were green with splashes of colour bordering the large lawn. The mountains formed a stunning backdrop to the house.

When Rayno brought the car to a standstill in front of the house, two Labradors came running to meet the guests. They were followed by an older man and two younger versions of Jakes. Jakes had already finished the introductions, but there still was no sign of his mother. As Jakes lifted his eyebrows, his father laughed, "Where do you think?"

Jakes shook his head and laughed, "Then I probably need to try and get her out of there. Angie, do you want to come with me? You can see my mom's studio." He thought for a moment then added, "As long as I won't lose you both in there."

Angie didn't want to think what that rare bout of laughter did to her and how much she missed it. She only replied, "I don't know if I can promise, but I'll promise to try. Is that good enough?"

Jakes chuckled again, "It is if that's the best I can hope for. Come on."

Jakes led her toward another low, sandstone building. When they entered, all Angie could hear was loud rock music from the seventies. Someone muttered a smattering of curse words before a false female voice joined the music. Angie smiled at Jakes who grinned, "Yes, the one, and only Leah du Plessis."

Angie followed him into a large room. A woman, somewhere in her early fifties stood at a counter with a figurine in front of her. From the frown and frustration on the woman's face when she viewed the small sculpture, Angie gathered that she wasn't happy with the result. Before she could see what was wrong with it, Leah slapped her right hand down on it in frustration.

"Oh-oh, it seems we came at the wrong time."

The woman looked up, straight at Angie. She stared for a few moments, blinked at Jakes, giving him a vague smile before she locked her gaze back on Angie. She said nothing but stepped away from the table and walked towards them. Angie thought she would greet Jakes, but she ignored him. She stopped in front of Angie, turning her head in concentration as she studied Angie's face.

Angie knew that look. Leah was studying Angie as if she was a potential model. Jakes coughed, ready to protest, but Angie shook her head.

And then Leah suddenly laughed, "No, you came at the right time." She turned to Angie and explain, as if she knew Angie would understand, "It was the eyes. They didn't look right for an angel, and now I know why."

"Hello, Mum. How are you?" Jakes grinned. He looked so mischievous that Angie's heart almost melted. She was convinced that this is the real Jakes if he could just make more appearances.

Leah looked at him as if she saw him for the first time. Her love and joy to see him were evident when she registered who it was. She threw her arms around him to hug him. "Jakes! How lovely to see you?"

Jakes didn't seem to care that his mother smeared his T-shirt with clay. He lifted Leah in his arms and hugged her until Leah protested with a laugh. Jakes laughed when he put her down. "It's good to see you too, Mum. May I introduce you to Angie now?"

Leah looked back to Angie and to Angie's surprise, she threw her arms around Angie to hug her too. "Angela, angel child. It's lovely to meet you at last. Jakes told me so much about you."

Angie glanced at Jakes, who was blushing profusely. What did he tell his mother? It didn't help to wonder about it though, not now, so she just smiled at Leah, "And he told me so much about you too. I'm pleased to meet you."

Leah noticed how Angie tried to take in more of the studio and smiled, "You can come back again. Jakes won't forgive me if I show you around now. You may never leave. Come, let's have coffee."

When Leah wanted to leave, Jakes smiled at her, "Don't you want to wash your hands first?"

Leah looked at her hands, then at Jakes and Angie, before she smiled, "Oh my goodness. Thanks, Jaky."

When she finished washing her hands and joined Jakes and Angie again, Leah linked her arms with them as they walked back to the house. It amazed Angie. She thought she was a chatterbox, but Leah talked non-stop! Without even stopping or taking breaths in between. She caught Jakes' amused grin when she stared at his mother in such fascination that her mouth almost dropped open.

. . .

LATER, when Jakes showed her the room where she would sleep, he mentioned that look on her face again. "You never thought there could be anyone more scatterbrained and talkative than you are, did you?"

Angie shook her head, "No, I hadn't, but she is exactly like you described her. I like her, Jakes."

"I think the feeling is mutual, Angel," he said while he opened a door for her.

Angie was surprised as she took the room in. It must have been Jakes' room at one stage. Old rugby posters covered the walls, and crime novels filled the shelves.

Jakes grinned, "This was my room. My Mum never got around to re-decorating it, even though I told her she could change it into a guest room. The bed's too small for me now so I use one of the guestrooms. If you don't like it, we can swop."

Angie reassured him. "Oh no, this is fine." She grinned, "I can now snoop around to see what you hide under your bed."

Jakes flushed, but then his mouth turned up in the corner. Angie looked away when he put her suitcase next to the bed. He looked serious as he reached her again. "I'm so sorry, Angie. I messed up. I miss you."

Angie thought her heart was breaking when she saw the expression in his eyes. She took a deep breath and whispered, "I miss you too, Jakes."

It looked like he wanted to say something, but then he stopped first and then tried again, "Friends?"

Angie didn't want to be friends with him. Well, not *only* friends but maybe she could try. Perhaps Jakes would open again.

Jakes anxiously waited for her answer, and when Angie nodded, he grinned. He leaned down, and Angie's breath hitched, but he only brushed his lips over her forehead. He stepped back in a hurry. At the door, he turned back, "When you've freshened up and unpacked, meet us on the front veranda. I would like to show you the cosmos. My Dad said there was already some flowering."

When Angie heard him whistling as he disappeared down the hallway, she exhaled.

She might've just made an enormous mistake letting him in again. Not that it would matter. She wasn't going to be here for long and, knowing Jakes, she wasn't sure how long it would last this time before he put distance between them again.

CHAPTER NINETEEN

I f Jakes could, he would've done a somersault down the hallway. He didn't expect it to be so easy to convince Angie to give him another chance. It wasn't what he wanted, but it was more than he could've hoped for. As long as he didn't mess up again.

When Angie joined them later on the veranda with her camera and sketchbook, he wondered if he shouldn't have waited until after lunch. He had a suspicion they might be late for lunch, and Anna, the cook his father had hired when Jakes went to high school, had warned him not to be late for lunch. He was already salivating just thinking of Anna's cottage pie.

The three men were patient as they waited for Angie to finish, but later on, they were getting restless. Jesse was the only one who had the guts to urge her to hurry up. "Come on, Angie. I'm sure you have enough material already, and we're hungry. If you don't finish now, we will leave you here, and Jakes can come back to fetch you later."

Angie looked reluctant, so Jesse grabbed her book and

walked back to where Jakes had parked the four-wheel-drive. Angie still grumbled when they reached the house.

Anna was upset, as Jakes expected, but Angie managed to change her mood when she smiled and apologised. Jakes had seen it so many times how Angie could change someone's mood with her smile and natural charm. No wonder he had fallen so hard for her.

Jakes saw it again later that evening. Angie charmed their guests without trying. This time he didn't like it though and tried to stifle his jealousy when one of the neighbouring farmers monopolised her company.

Jakes finally gave up the pretence. He stalked to where the two were standing, grabbed Angie's hand and mumbled, "I want to introduce you to someone."

Jakes had no idea who but luckily he caught sight of his primary school coach and led Angie in the direction of the older man. He still held her hand after he made the introductions and they spoke for a while.

It was ridiculous. Friends. They were only friends, but he couldn't help it. It was as if his inner-Neanderthal came to the front when the other men just looked at Angie. He wanted them to know Angie wasn't available even though he had no right.

He only let go of her hand when he poured her a glass of wine and got himself a beer. Angie turned in the direction where Jesse and Rayno sat talking with some of the other younger guests. Jakes had to lean down to hear Angie when she said with a soft smile, "That is the most relaxed I've seen Jesse since..."

When she stopped, Jakes asked, "Since what?"

Angie turned to him. "Didn't he tell you what happened?"

When Jakes shook his head, Angie sighed, "Let's sit somewhere, and I'll tell you."

Jakes lead her to the steps on the side of the house. There they could talk without the fear of someone overhearing but could still keep an eye on the guests. When they sat comfortably, Angie took a sip of her wine, then put it down before she said, "I thought Jesse told you. He mentioned you helped him to deal with everything."

Jakes shook his head, confused, but then remembered how Jesse asked him how he dealt with his panic attacks. "He didn't mention anything, but only asked a lot of questions."

Angie sighed, "I wondered about it. A few days after school re-started, two boys had a fight. They were always fighting, but that day one of them took a knife to school. By the time Jesse had reached them, the one with the knife had stabbed the other one several times. Jesse stepped between them and caught the next jab. The boy dropped the knife and ran away. Jesse's injuries were not serious, but the boy he tried to help had died in his arms while they waited for the ambulance. Since the incident, Jesse suffered from PTSD and resigned from teaching. Rayno suggested that Jesse came to South Africa with him for a holiday in the hope that a new environment would bring Jesse out of his depression."

Jakes could see how her twin brother's situation affected her. Without thinking twice, he put his beer down and pulled Angie against him, "Oh Angel, I'm sorry. It must have been stressful for you. I've noticed how close you two are and it must have been as traumatic for you as it had been for him."

At first, Angie felt tense, but then she relaxed, resting her head on his chest. Jakes stroke her hair until Angie lifted her head to meet his eyes. Jakes took in the blue eyes that now looked dark in the soft light, his hand still on her hair. He couldn't breathe. For a long time they just looked at each other, but then Jakes lowered his mouth to hers. Without touching her lips, without breaking eye contact, he still whispered, "I shouldn't..."

The rest of his words died away, swallowed by the kiss as Angie lifted her hand, and pulled his head down. The distance between them evaporated, and their mouths met with a soft sigh.

Would he ever have the willpower to resist her?

He doubted it. It definitely wouldn't be in this lifetime.

ANGIE BLINKED at Jakes when he woke her up. It looked dark and must be early still. She sat up when Jakes switched on the bedside lamp, checking the alarm clock and then to Jakes, "What is wrong?"

Although Jakes smiled, he looked tense. "Nothing. I want to show you something."

He put the coffee down, and as he left, he mumbled, "Meet me on the veranda."

Angie sipped the coffee he brought and dressed in a hurry. They were now in the four-wheel truck, or bakkie, as they called it here, to goodness knows where. It was still dark, and it felt as if Jakes were driving higher into the mountains. Angie hoped Jakes knew where he was going because she couldn't even make out the road in front of them.

It felt like an eternity before he stopped the truck. He opened his door and told Angie, "Sit still."

He took something from the seat behind him before he came to open the door for her. He handed her a flask with two mugs. Jakes carried a blanket and a flashlight as he led her to an outcrop of rocks. He spread the blanket only halfway open on a flat rock. He sat down, pulling the rest of the blanket up over his shoulders before he invited, "Come, sit."

When she wanted to sit next to him, he shook his head, "No, sit between my legs. You'll be warmer."

This might not be the best idea, when she shivered, Angie did what he asked, but kept a little distance between them. He chuckled softly, "Come on, Angel. Scoot closer. I won't bite."

It wasn't the biting that worried Angie. It concerned her more to be close to him, but she didn't have much choice. She shifted until she felt the heat of his body against her back.

"Hold the flashlight," he requested. Angie took it with shivering fingers and held it while he poured the coffee and put the lid back on the flask. He left the mugs on the flat rock and pulled Angie back against his chest.

Angie almost snorted. So much for keeping her distance.

Jakes pulled the rest of the blanket over their shoulders. When the heat spread over her, Angie relaxed, picking up her coffee to take a sip.

Jakes also picked up his coffee and took a sip. They didn't speak, not while they drank their coffee, nor when the sky changed colour on the horizon and Angie put her empty mug beside her. The whole time, however, Angie felt conscious of Jakes, the heat of his body on her back and his arms encircling her.

She suddenly heard his sigh and felt the soft kiss he dropped on her hair. When he spoke, his voice sounded tense in the quiet of the early morning.

JAKES HAD A SLEEPLESS NIGHT, trying to find a solution. He owed Angie some explanation, even though he couldn't tell her everything. It was only two hours ago he'd formed a plan, and now he couldn't avoid it anymore.

Doc Matthews' last advice on Wednesday morning still resonated through his head. If there was one person who deserved to hear his story, it had to be Angie. If Jakes had any hope of ever having a normal relationship in future, he had to expose his heart and soul to the one person who mattered. Jakes knew Doc was right, but it was going to be even more difficult than when he shared it with his family, and then his friends *because* this was Angie.

He was glad he didn't have to meet Angie's eyes when he finally broke the silence.

"I'm sorry for leaving Keystone without saying goodbye I hope you may understand better if I tell you the reason I over-reacted like I did."

Angie didn't reply, but Jakes knew she was listening. He took a deep breath before he continued, "I guess no man wants to admit he is weak, but I was. Nobody would think I could be, but I now knew that I'm not the only one. We live in this tough, macho environment where nobody wants to show his vulnerable side. I took months of therapy before I could acknowledge that I am vulnerable. I may be physically strong, but emotionally I desperately needed help. I let no one see my vulnerability, the part of me that hurts until it was almost too late."

His chest tightened. He had to take deep breaths before he could continue, "I told you before that I had been engaged. What I haven't told you was that my ex had verbally abused me. It is not something any man wants to admit."

Jakes sighed. "I'm an introvert, as you know. I am only relaxed with a few people, mostly with my family, good friends and my teammates. Under other circumstances, I'm reserved. I don't like the attention on me. It's different when I play rugby. As soon as I run onto that pitch, I forget about everything else. Then, it's about the game, the ball, and my team against the opposition. That's why nobody realised that something was wrong."

He could feel her heat from her hand on his arm and her back resting against his chest. Her touch gave him the strength to talk for a long time. He left nothing out and spoke about twelve years of insecurities, hurt, humiliation, and his ultimate breakdown.

His story didn't start with his recent engagement to Moira. It began when he met Moira as an insecure sixteen-year-old boy. He had tried to fit in with his older teammates and succumbed to Moira when she tried to seduce him, just because so many of his teammates wanted her. He attempted to be something he was not, and he almost lost himself in the process. It didn't end there, unfortunately. Their relationship was tumultuous, to say the least and went up and down, continuing for years. Moira was always the master manipulator and Jakes her slave because he knew no better. That was until Moira got bored with him because he wasn't the party animal she wanted.

"We broke up during my third year at university because, according to her, 'I was stuffy and boring'."

He heard Angie's inhale, but Jakes couldn't stop now. "It didn't matter how much I tried, I couldn't move forward. She had already done so much damage, but I didn't realise it then. When I met her four years later, I still had the same insecurities as I had as a sixteen-year-old. By that time, I was at the height of my Sevens career. Moira liked my new lifestyle and travelling to places such as London, Paris, and Las Vegas and quickly wormed herself back into my life. All my teammates had someone in their lives, but I was alone. It didn't take Moira long to convince me she had changed, and I believed her. Things went well in the beginning. Moira moved in with me. I had a house in Stellenbosch as that was where the Sevens team had its base."

His voice faltered as he explained, "Things got worse when

my contract with the Sevens ended, and I put my house on the market."

Even before Moira came back on the scene, Jakes had signed a contract to return to the Buffaloes. That had been his plan even when he left to Buffaloes to play Sevens. Moira knew it when they got back together, but she thought she could manipulate him to stay with the Sevens to keep that lifestyle. She refused to go with Jakes when he went to look for a house in Pretoria. With André and Daniel's help, Jakes bought the home of the player he would replace at the Buffaloes.

Jakes hated to talk about the things that Moira did in that last year of their relationship, but he had to.

"The meanness might always have been there. I ignored it because I felt insecure in our relationship. Moira would use sarcasm or say something demeaning. When I commented on it, she would tell me she was only teasing, or I'm too sensitive. It started with the way I dressed, or the way I ate or even laughed. Without realising it, I stopped laughing."

Jakes shifted uncomfortably. "That week before my last Sevens tournament in Cape Town, I packed up the house in Stellenbosch. Moira refused to help, and by that time, her behaviour was worse than ever. André had an injury and couldn't train with the Buffaloes. I invited him to come and watch my last tournament. He stayed for a few days afterwards."

Jakes tried to formulate his words before he continued, "I didn't realise before then how jealous Moira had been of my friendship with André. I think she was scared that André saw right through her and didn't make a secret he didn't like her. I only met André at University and introduced him then. I recently found out that none of my friends and family liked her."

He cleared his throat. "There were more of our university

friends in the Cape and André suggested that we get together with them for a barbeque. Moira flirted with the other men that most of them felt awkward. One of them couldn't take it any longer and told her to stop. Of course, Moira got angry. She was rude for the rest of the night and made comments that made everyone uncomfortable."

"The following day, André and I went out for brunch with a few of my Sevens teammates, their wives and girlfriends. Moira still sulked and refused to go. During brunch, André brought up Moira and our relationship. He didn't have to say much, but it was enough for the others to voice their opinions too. Between them, they forced me to face the truth of how toxic our relationship was. It shocked me to hear what Moira had to say about me behind my back. The other women suspected Moira had cheated on me with an Australian Sevens player. I always thought she went out with the women, but they denied it."

Jakes dropped his head on Angie's shoulder and breathed in her smell before he could continue. "I was glad André was there when I confronted Moira later. She didn't even pretend to be joking then. She told me how pathetic I was and how awkward I am in a social situation, and how stuffy I am. Moira admitted to the affair —or rather affairs as there were more than one— and told me the other men were a lot more fun than I am. By the time André got her out of there, I felt like a useless piece of garbage. André rallied my friends, and they arranged for the moving truck to come a week earlier. They all came to help pack up my stuff. Moira didn't come back for two nights. By the time she returned, the moving company was already packing my furniture in the truck.

"Moira went ballistic when she found her belongings packed in boxes, but she changed within seconds. She was so sweet and nice that I almost believed her. She pleaded with me to take her back and was shocked when I didn't comply. If André were not there, I might have. Things got unpleasant, and I was glad to get out of there."

"When I arrived in Pretoria, my new teammates helped me to settle in. I haven't met some of them before, but even then, before the training camp, they were there for me. That spirit of camaraderie had helped me through the first couple of weeks. When I arrived at training camp, however, I couldn't pretend anymore. I had no confidence and hit rock bottom."

If it hadn't been for André, Jakes didn't know what he would've done. André convinced him to speak to the team psychologist. Jakes was sceptical at first, but in the end, he went.

"I realised my lack of confidence filtered through to my game. I kept on hearing Moira's voice telling me I wouldn't make a success of anything without her. I took months of intense therapy to regain my confidence, but sometimes it hits me again. I've not stopped therapy and may always need an escape mechanism to deal with my anxiety."

He suddenly felt breathless. He jumped up and stepped away from Angie.

"I don't know what I would've done without my friends and teammates, in particular, the first four months last year. They were my support, my backup, my anchor, I guess. If it hadn't been for them, the team and rugby, I would've gone off the rails. I owe them so much, and I can't let them down. I can't let the team down. Not now."

From the corner of his eyes, Jakes caught a movement and realised that Angie also got up. He steeled himself, but she surprised him when she laid her hand on his arm and murmured, "I'm sorry, Jakes. I saw how you struggled to talk, and I thought I should relieve the tension. Now I know your story, I realise it was the worst joke I could've made. I promise I wasn't mean."

Jakes cupped her cheek, "I know, Angel. I reacted on instinct, and that was to flee the situation. Since then, I've had enough time to think. I know you're not a mean person. You're the most empathetic and beautiful person I've ever met. You didn't deserve the way I treated you. I wasn't fair, and I'm sorry. I hope you can forgive me."

ANGIE HAD TO SWALLOW HARD. She couldn't bear to think about his pain and hurt, but friendship? She hoped that when he spoke about his past, he would offer her more, but it seemed that he only wanted friendship. Her heart shattered into a thousand tiny pieces.

She looked up in his eyes to ask, "Only friends?"

Pain flashed through his eyes as he too swallowed hard, "I'm sorry. Only friends. That's all I can offer you for now."

Angie had her answer, but she didn't understand. It didn't make sense. She was *not* going to beg, and she wouldn't show him she hurt. If he only wanted friendship, that's what he would get. She now, however, had one chance, and that was to spell out the rules of their friendship. She held his eyes when she admitted, "I must admit that I'm disappointed, but if friendship is all you can offer, I'll accept it. You must, however, understand what you've chosen."

"What is that?" he asked uncertainly."

"Friendship is only that: friendship, and that's how it will be. I'm tired of your mixed signals. You can't hold my hand or kiss me anymore. You can't get angry or upset when I go out with Rick or any other man. You've lost that privilege."

His face was as white as a sheet, and his jaw tightened, "Angel..."

Angie stopped him before he could continue, "Stop calling me Angel. You only have a right to give someone a nickname if she means something to you, something more than friends."

"Can we talk about it, please?"

"What is there to talk about, Jakes? Or is there anything else you want to tell me?"

He swallowed and shook his head. Angie turned, disappointed and went to pick up the blanket, mugs and the flask and returned to the truck with it. Jakes slowly followed her. The drive back to the house was uncomfortable. Before Angie could get out, Jakes mumbled, "I don't want to, but I have no choice. I have to choose my team."

Angie shook her head slowly, "I would never have asked you to choose between me and rugby, Jakes. I know how much it means to you, but I didn't have to ask. You already made a choice without giving me a chance."

"Angie..."

She got out and through the open door told him, "Just leave me alone, Jakes. I need time."

At least she didn't meet anyone on her way to the room. There she couldn't find the comfort she craved. Jakes' memorabilia and belongings reminded her of what could've been, stopped the tears any longer. When she felt calmer a while later, Angie showered and packed her bag before she joined the family for breakfast.

Jakes was even quieter than usual. Angie was also not in the mood to talk and only answered when somebody spoke to her. Angie felt Jesse's concerned glances on her throughout breakfast, but she couldn't look at him. If she did, she might burst into tears again.

She didn't have an appetite and pushed her food around on her plate. She still noticed that Jakes didn't do any better.

Her head shot up when Leah asked suddenly, "What's going on between you two, Jakes, Angie?"

Angie flushed, but when Jakes didn't answer, she muttered, "Nothing."

Leah shook her head. Angie knew she was teasing when she said, "I won't call it nothing. I saw you kissing last night, and this morning you disappeared. I suspect that..."

Angie interrupted. "There's nothing," before Leah could continue.

Jakes met her eyes for a moment but didn't reply. He looked down at his plate, avoiding everyone's eyes. There was an uncomfortable silence at the table, but Angie didn't care anymore.

It could be that uncomfortable atmosphere around the table that prompted Rayno to announce after breakfast that he wanted to leave. Angie was so relieved she could've kissed him. She wanted to be alone, and she couldn't do it here.

When they said goodbye, Leah hugged Angie close and whispered, "I'm sorry. I hoped..."

Angie felt the tears. Leah might feel how much she was hurting. She tried to smile and whispered back, "Me too."

When she arrived at the car, Jesse had joined her in the back, taking the seat Jakes occupied the previous day. When Jakes joined them, Jesse announced through the open window, "I think you'll be more comfortable in front with your long legs."

Jakes shrugged and got in the car. At least the radio was playing in the background, as nobody spoke for the first while. It was only after an ad on the radio that Jesse told Rayno, "We might not have a special girl here, but at least Rick invited us to a club with him otherwise we would be alone on Valentine's Day."

Rayno laughed, "My timing was terrible. I wouldn't have minded being in Denver that day but please don't tell my mum I said that."

Jesse laughed but when Angie asked on impulse, "May I

come too?" his smile faltered, and he frowned, "Yes, sure but I thought ..."

Angie wondered if Jakes even heard any of the conversation. He didn't give any signal that he had as he stared out of the window. She turned away to lean her head against the seat. She must have fallen asleep because she only became aware of her surroundings when the car stopped, and Jakes got out.

Angie was nosy and studied the house while Jakes took out his luggage. She heard that Jesse thanked him for his hospitality, but she didn't look at him. When Rayno reversed out of the driveway, and they drove away, Angie glimpsed him standing there, watching the car leave.

He looked so alone.

CHAPTER TWENTY

He knew it was going to happen at any time, and Jakes had prepared for it, but he struggled to stifle his jealousy when he saw Angie the Saturday evening, after their game against Sicily. She was in Rick's company, and it looked like she was having a great time, as she was talking and laughing as usual.

It could've been me.

That thought flashed through his head, and he sighed. He made his choice.

His friends drifted off one by one to talk to some of their teammates without Jakes even being aware of it. He was so deep in thought that he didn't immediately notice the woman before she took the seat next to him.

It felt as if someone was walking over his grave, and he looked up. He stiffened automatically when he recognised the woman, but that's where his usual reaction stopped. No accelerated heartbeat. No sweaty hand palms or struggling to breathe.

Surprised by his lack of reaction, Jakes studied her.

Was her face always so hard with her mouth pulling downwards? Her eyes were cold slits, reminding him of a reptile. She probably didn't even realise how ridiculous she looked when she pouted and smiled, which she might thought was sexy. Geez, every morone could see that it was false. Even her voice sounded fake and her words insincere when her hand stroke over his arm. Jakes shuddered when he noticed the contrast of her lily-white hand with the bright red nails against his skin.

Suddenly he wanted to laugh, caused more by relief than anything else. For the first time since he was sixteen, Jakes could look Moira Scalebusy in the eyes and felt nothing. Not the infatuation which he thought he felt at sixteen. Not fear. Not angst. Absolutely nothing apart from relief.

"Jakes, I'm so glad to see you. I missed you."

Jakes snorted, "I definitely haven't missed you."

She gave a husky laugh, which he might have thought at one stage was seductive. Now she only sounded ridiculous. "Oh, come on, Jakes, don't lie. You know you still love me."

Jakes pulled his eyes away from her and searched for Angie. For a moment their eyes held. When Angie looked away, Jakes took Moira's hand away from his arm. He returned her gaze and said firmly, "You're wrong. I don't love you, and I doubt I ever had. I met someone else. She made me realise not all women are like you, who feed on insecurities to manipulate other people. I'm not that man anymore. Do yourself a favour and leave. There is nothing left here for you."

Jakes couldn't believe her gall when she sniggered, "You'll crawl back. You're not strong enough without me. I made you what you are."

Moira looked shocked when he laughed. "You're not serious, are you? Well, there might be some truth in that you made me what I am. You almost destroyed me, but I came out of it much stronger than what I've been when we met. I went through hell with you, but I learned from it, and I changed. I'm successful now and have a good future ahead of me. What do you have? Nothing. You're a parasite who lives off other people's weaknesses."

Moira wanted to say something else, but from somewhere across the table, someone clapped hands. Others quickly joined the first person. Jakes looked up to see André, Rick and the rest of his group of friends. Rick surprised Jakes when he too, nodded approvingly. André said, "Well said, mate."

If Jakes hadn't known André so well, he would've been surprised to see how the usually well-mannered man changed in front of his eyes. His eyes flashed at Moira when he said loud and clearly for everyone to hear, "Moira, I suggest you leave and stay away this time. Or you can stay to hear me tell everyone how manipulative you are. You almost sucked Jakes dry and, on top of that, you cheated on him. Your choice."

Moira glared at André then Jakes as she jumped up and grabbed her bag. She hissed at Jakes, "You haven't heard the last from me yet. You owe me."

Jakes couldn't believe her gall nor that he could stay calm as he answered, "I wouldn't mention that if I were you. You forget that I have a law degree. You won't win."

André followed up with, "You should leave before we get security. We're capable enough to remove you, but I don't think any of these guys would like to touch you."

Jakes followed her progress as she stormed out of the restaurant and exhaled, relieved. His friends didn't say a word when they joined him at the table again. Jakes suddenly felt tired. He had enough and mumbled to André that he was going home. When he put his contribution to the meal on the table, he met Angie's eyes briefly. She quickly glanced away but not before he saw the brightness in hers.

Jakes wanted to explain, but he couldn't do it now and left the restaurant through the side door. When he heard a voice, Jakes stopped automatically. It wasn't the person he hoped for though, but Doc Matthews. The older man patiently studied Jakes before he asked, "How do you feel?"

Jakes only had to think about it briefly before he could smile, much to Doc's evident surprise, "Great, Doc. Thanks for your help."

The psychologist laughed relieved. "I take it that that was the woman who made your life hell. I'm proud of you, Jakes. I think we defeated your nemesis."

Jakes glanced at the restaurant and nodded, now more serious. "I think so too, doc. Now I need to overcome the other problem too."

"That will come, Son. Just persevere. This was the first step.

Jakes knew he was right. He might not be there where he might have been without Moira's influence, but if he could overcome this, he might overcome the next stumbling block. He could only hope that it wasn't too late.

ANGIE TRIED to make her smaller against the pillar and listened to the conversation between André and Daniel without even feeling guilty.

"Jakes is quiet today. Is he okay?" Daniel asked, concerned as they studied their friend where he was sitting alone on the stairs, deep in thought.

André quickly reassured his captain, "Give him a chance. Doc Matthews spoke to Jakes last night before Jakes went home. The knowledge that he stood up against Moira still needs to sink in, but that was the breakthrough we hoped for. If we can now convince him to stop his extreme loyalty, it will be even better. He deserves happiness."

Daniel laughed, "I think Moira still can't believe that Jakes stood up against her and then even laughed in her face. Geez, I thought I'll never hear Jakes laugh out loud again. It was awesome to hear."

The two walked away, and Angie couldn't hear the rest of the conversation.

She was feeling unnecessarily upset. She hadn't slept well, too jealous when she thought about Jakes and that woman last night. Now she found out that that was the bitch who made his life hell in the past. It was just as well she didn't know that last night. She might have started a catfight.

Her heart softened as she glanced at Jakes. He looked so alone, but she knew that was a misconception. She heard and saw how his friends supported him.

Everyone did, except her. She agreed to be friends but had avoided him since. It might be time that she accepted there wouldn't be anything else between them and took the friendship he offered. Maybe one day...

No, it wouldn't help to put her heart on that again. From now on, until she went home, she would be the friend Jakes needed. She would bury her feelings deep.

Having made that decision, she didn't prolonged and walked across to where Jakes was still sitting. She sank down on the step next to him. When he glanced sideways at her, she asked, "Are you okay?"

"Do you care?"

Angie flinched when the harshness of his words hit her. For a moment, she stared at him, not able to get a word out. She jumped up, ready to flee when he stopped her, putting his hand on her arm, "I'm sorry, Angie. That wasn't necessary."

Angie sank back on the step, waiting for him to speak. When he didn't, she asked, "I heard the woman at The Final

Whistle last night was Moira. I just wanted to find out if you are okay."

Jakes's eyes followed his big hands when he rested his elbows on his knees and threaded his fingers. He looked calm and confirmed it. "Yes, it was Moira, but I'm fine. I realised last night that she doesn't have a hold over me anymore."

"That's wonderful," Angie smiled, relieved. She lifted her eyes to study his face. His eyes still looked troubled, and she murmured, "You don't look fine."

Jakes turned to meet his eyes. "You're right. I'm not."

"Why not?"

His voice sounded gruff when he admitted. "It's you, Angie. I miss you."

"I miss you too. Jakes," Angie answered honestly.

"Then why do you avoid me? You said we could be friends, but I never see you. You go out with Rick and the other woman, but... I know you told me I had no right, but I'm jealous when you're with Rick."

"You can't expect me not to have other friends," Angie accused.

He rubbed his hands through his hair, "I know, but I can't change how I feel, Angel... Angie. I'm sorry. Can't we be friends and go out exploring, as we did in Denver? I can show you around as you did. We can..."

"Do you really think we can only be friends again?"

"Hell, I don't know, but please give me a chance. I can't... Please, Angie, I can't lose your friendship too."

Angie's answer was easier than she imagined. "I would like that. It will be nice to discover new places with you."

Jakes looked astonished as he stared at her. "Really?" he finally managed.

When Angie nodded, his smile broke through, the rare, full smile when his eyes and mouth joined in. She almost had to catch her breath when the effect of it caught her unaware before she could answer his next question, "So, tell me, what do you still want to do? What have you done? Have you been to the Cradle of Humankind or Hartbeespoortdam?"

"Slow down," Angie laughed about his sudden mood change. For the next hour or more, they stayed on that stairs talking. They were unaware of anyone else and therefore didn't see the satisfied smiles they elicited from their friends. It was especially Jakes' laughter that found his friends' approval.

ANGIE HADN'T THOUGHT it possible, but she had accepted that friendship was better than nothing. Now and again there was that awkward moment when they were both so intensely aware of each other that it would've been easy to give over to the passion and just kiss each other and get it done with. Neither of them did, however, and every day got a little bit easier.

The first week they spent most of Jakes' free time with Jesse and Jakes' teammates. On Friday night Jakes invited Angie, Jesse, and Rayno for dinner. They had a good time until Jesse put a damper on it with his announcement. They had finished eating but were still lounging around the table when Jesse cleared his throat and announced, "I should've told you earlier, but I only got an answer today. I'm going back with Rayno on Monday."

Her heart dropped with a bang into her shoes. Did it mean she also had to go back? She knew it didn't make sense because she was the one who hadn't been eager to come? Even a week ago she might have felt different but now? She didn't want to go back, but now she might not have a choice.

"Have you changed your flight yet? I mean, I probably have to…"

"You don't have to," Rayno reassured Angie. "You're welcome to stay in the cottage as we agreed."

"But..." Angie still protested, but then Jakes pleaded, "Please stay longer? Or at least until we go on tour. You haven't done everything you have planned yet."

Jakes was right. Maybe she had to do it now. Who said she would ever come back to South Africa?

"Jakes is right, Angie. I will feel guilty if you also end your holiday because I'm going back earlier," Jesse urged.

"Then why are you going back?" she asked him.

Jesse smiled, "To attend classes." He continued telling them that he knew now what he wanted to do with his life. After his discussions with Christopher Brooks, Jesse was going to change his career. He enrolled in a few intensive classes in Media and Communication. He had English and Creative Writing as subjects at university and that, with the new courses, he could prepare for a career as a communications officer like Christopher.

Jesse's excitement was contagious. Angie was so happy for her brother that this trip gave Jesse answers to what he had been looking for.

JAKES HAD SURPRISED her yet again. This time he not only surprised her but since it was their twenty-fifth birthday, he also included Jesse. He arrived at the cottage early on Saturday morning, bearing gifts and then promptly proceeded to make breakfast for them. He then announced that he had arranged a party that evening with his friends after their game against Pays de la Loire, the French club team.

Jesse's gift was a Buffaloes jersey with Jesse's name and number twelve on the back. That was not all. Jesse also got a signed rugby ball and photo of him, Rayno and the team, taken the day they trained with them.

Angie also received a jersey, but hers had Jakes' number eight on the back and with it a bouquet of indigenous South African flowers. Apart from the flowers and jersey he had given Angie, he gave her two smaller boxes. The one contained a photo album with photos of them he took in Denver and Keystone. The last package was much smaller and contained several charms for her bracelet, which Angie wore every day.

When Angie looked up, Jakes was watching her rather nervously to gauge her reaction. She smiled, and he returned it, spontaneously. That was her best gift.

Angie leaned over and kissed him lightly to thank him. It wasn't a long kiss. It wasn't even a romantic or sensual kiss. It was sweet, but it still left Angie aching for more. She didn't take it further, though she wanted to. She needed to be stronger.

THAT AFTERNOON they attended the game wearing their new jerseys. Angie was nervous as she had been every time Jakes played. Her fears were substantiated when Jakes caught the ball in the lineout close to the French' try line. He was supported by the two props, but when the French took his support out from under him, Jakes fell quite heavily on the ground. The referee blew his whistle when Jakes stayed on the ground.

Angie jumped up. She didn't even realise that she held her breath until he got up rather groggily. He still looked uncomfortable as he swung his arms and upper body to both sides before he slowly ran back to his position. Angie's legs felt numb when she sank back into her chair, her eyes fixed on Jakes. She even missed the try that followed.

From the ensuing kick-off after Matthew's conversion, Loire ran the ball wide. Jakes reached for the opposition centre, grabbing him by the shoulders. The centre slipped down, and Jakes' arm moved around his neck. When Jakes realised what was happening, he dropped his arm straight away, but it was too late. The referee blew his whistle for a high tackle and sent Jakes to the sin bin. His shoulders dropped as he stared at the referee while he gave his lecture, but Angie was convinced Jakes didn't hear a word. He knew the rules well enough.

He looked disappointed when he sat on the chair next to Michael to watch the game. He downed the bottle of flavoured milk that Michael handed to him and took deep gulps of the fluid. He glared at the field, and when the French scored a try, his head and shoulders dropped.

The moment he returned to the field, Angie could see Jakes was trying to make up for the ten minutes in the sin bin. The ten minutes resting helped him to come back fresh. He was all over the pitching, getting involved in loose scrums, backline movements and the attack. Jakes even stole balls in the loose scrums and tackled like crazy or making several meters each time he ran.

It was pure enjoyment watching him because it was evident how much he enjoyed it. Every now and again, he would grin, something that happened more often than before.

ANGIE SHOULD'VE KNOWN that things would change. It was inevitable. That attraction had always been there, hidden just below the surface, even when they tried to pretend it was only friendship.

Since Jesse and Rayno returned to Denver, Jakes and Angie spent even more time alone in each other's company. Once a week they would spend with his friends, but they spent most of the time Jakes wasn't at the stadium, together. Sometimes they would explore, visit art exhibitions or went out for dinner or a movie. Most of the time, however, they stayed at the cottage where Jakes cooked them dinner. While he trained, Angie painted.

Then Jakes surprised her with a trip to Cape Town. The Buffaloes had a bye that weekend and Jakes managed to convince Coach Brady to release him the Friday from training. They flew to Cape Town on Thursday afternoon where Jakes hired a car. It was already dark when they arrived at their hotel and had dinner at a restaurant close to the hotel. Angie only appreciated the setting the next morning when Jakes came to wake her up early to watch the sunrise over Milnerton Lagoon. The city was still quiet and peaceful, and the flamingos added to the beautiful setting.

When they turned to walk on the beach to the hotel, Angie pulled in her breath, awed when she got her first glimpse of the famous Table Mountain. The soft light of dawn painted the mountain a darkish purple. There wasn't a cloud in sight, and she had, therefore, a clear view. Her laughter exploded. She didn't even think of taking a photo as she drank in the beauty in front of them. When Jakes' hand touched hers, her fingers curled around his.

Things changed then. Simple touches like that occurred more often. Jakes still didn't kiss her, but the way he looked at her made her aware that it was just a matter of time.

It became more evident in the week after they returned from Cape Town. They spent every free moment together. They talked about things that really mattered. She thought she knew Jakes, but during this time, Angie got to know the man she always thought he hid behind his introverted personality.

That Friday night was the turning point. Jakes asked Angie to escort him to a wedding at the stadium. She didn't have to wonder anymore whether it was only her imagination that things had changed between them. The subtle touches and in-depth talks of the previous week, all led to this.

She might blame it on the romantic atmosphere of a surprise wedding. During the ceremony, Jakes slid his hand over hers and threaded his fingers through hers. When she looked at him in surprise, he held her eyes the whole time the couple said their vows. It felt as if he wanted to tell her something, but she was too scared to get her hopes up.

Her fears didn't stop her from enjoying the evening, with Jakes as an attentive date, holding her hand most of the time. When he later pulled her into his arms for a dance, Angie loved the tender way he held her. And then, when he took her home, the kiss was inevitable. Even when they pretended to be only friends, this had always been there, between them.

She didn't have to wait long for the kiss. As soon as Jakes closed the cottage door behind them, he stopped her from walking away. Angie noticed the intensity in his eyes as he studied her face. He lifted one hand and stroked his fingers over her cheekbone. One tip pushed a wayward curl from her face.

He whispered. "You are so beautiful that you take my breath away, Angel."

Angie struggled to breath when Jakes lifted his other hand to cup her face. His voice was hoarse when he added, "I can't fight this anymore, Angel. I don't want to be friends only. I want more."

Jakes kissed her then, not allowing Angie to ask what he meant. Coherent thoughts slipped from her mind. She gave herself over to the sensations caused by his touch.

When they had to breathe, Jakes buried his face in her hair, and his arms held her firmly against him. He looked reluctant when he let her go. He gave her one more swift kiss and whispered, "We need to talk, Angel, but not tonight. Come to my house on Sunday night for dinner, then we can talk."

When Angie nodded her agreement, he brushed his mouth over hers and whispered, "Good night."

When the door closed behind him, Angie knew things would never be the same again. There was no way they could only be friends.

CHAPTER TWENTY-ONE

J akes watched the faces of his teammates while they waited in the tunnel, waiting to run on the pitch. He hadn't seen them as focused and determined as they were today. It felt as if something had shifted, not only with him. He didn't know what it was with them, but he knew what had changed for him.

As they ran onto the field, Jakes glanced up for a split second into the stand to where Angie should be.

This game, he played for her.

Maybe he should do it every time, Jakes thought briefly when they walked off the pitch ninety minutes later. They had not only beaten the Welsh team with one of their highest scores of fifty to thirty-five, but Jakes had also scored two tries, one in each half. Both came after a scrum, but Jakes still had to work hard to deservedly receive the Man of the Match award. He didn't expect it.

.   .   .

ANGIE, Chloe and Jaylin were talking non-stop as usual while they waited for the players to join them after the game. When she felt a hand pressing on her shoulder. Angie knew it was Jakes. When she looked up, he surprised her and the rest of the table when he kissed her. There was a moment's silence, then a few catcalls, but Angie wasn't aware of that. She was only aware of Jakes' lips on hers, and the way his hand had tangled in her hair. He lifted his mouth and grinned. He then took the chair next to her, leaning back as if nothing out of the ordinary had happened.

When the chatter around them resumed, Jakes leaned into Angie. She felt his hand seeking hers under the table, and she smelled the fresh aroma of his shower gel. His mouth curled up in the corner in the way she loves. His eyes twinkled as he whispered, "I figured you would anyway kiss me to congratulate me on my game."

Angie lifted her eyebrows to tease, "You think?" but when she saw his sudden frown, she laughed, "Maybe." She was relieved when his smile reappeared, and it stayed there for the rest of the evening. She was aware of his friends' curious glances, especially when Jakes, for the first time, more openly showed his affections. He didn't hesitate to hold her hand or put his arm around her, not only that night but also the next day during a barbeque at Mark Bailey's house.

She was right. Things had changed, and Jakes wasn't shy to announce it.

FOR THE THIRD TIME, Jakes made sure everything was perfect. Angie went for a nap, and he, therefore, had time to get everything ready for what he had planned. When he did everything he wanted to, he went inside and changed into his swimming trunks. When they came back from the tour, it would be too cold for that, so it was one of the last opportunities Jakes had to enjoy these last, warm days of summer. He cleaned the pool, and when he finished, he took a welcoming dip. Jakes had already finished his swim, and his trunks were dry without any sign of Angie. He rehearsed his speech again, and in the end, he went through all his preparations one more time.

The weekend in Cape Town and the surprise wedding in their midst helped Jakes to decide. As soon as he had, he knew he didn't want to wait any longer. He didn't want to be friends with Angie anymore. He tried to show her the last week. When Angie didn't push him away, Jakes knew he had a chance. He had to use that chance now before they go on tour.

When he ran out of tasks, he went inside to change. At the bottom of the stairs, he hesitated. Instead of going to his room, he slipped into the guest room. Angie was still fast asleep. He stopped next to the bed to watch her for a few seconds without her being aware of it. His heart clenched, just watching her. She was so beautiful with her dark hair spread over the white pillow. She wore a top with spaghetti straps, and Jakes admired the legs exposed by her shorts, now sporting a tan she got since she arrived in South Africa.

He knew he was playing with fire, but he couldn't resist it. Instead of waking Angie up as he should've done, he stretched down next to her. He balanced himself on his elbow and took his time studying her. He lay close enough to feel the heat from her body.

Angie turned over to her side with a soft sigh, and a few moments later, her eyes fluttered open. Their eyes locked, and it felt as if time stood still. Angie smiled and murmured his name at the same time as she lifted her hand to touch his face.

Jakes felt his body's reaction, caused by her touch and her nearness. He stilled, too scared to move when Angie's hand moved down his neck, over his shoulders and his chest. He never thought he would love anyone as he loved this woman. He also never thought that he would need anyone with such intensity as he needed her now.

She broke eye contact to follow her hands. What did she plan? Did she even know what she was doing to him?

When her hands moved lower over his stomach, he couldn't take it. He had already clenched his jaw so hard that it hurt to stop him from doing what he really wanted to do. When her fingers wanted to continue their movement, Jakes quickly put his hand over hers and held it. She lifted her eyes to meet his when he breathed her name, "Angie, do you know what you are doing?"

"Am I doing it wrong?" she asked Jakes impishly.

Jakes grunted, "If you want me to make love to you now, you're doing it absolutely perfect."

Angie smiled, "That's what I want."

She pushed his hand away, then her fingers fluttered over his stomach again, lower until it reached the elastic of his trunks. Jakes groaned, but the groan was swallowed when Angie leaned over to kiss him. Her reaction surprised him, but boy, he was not going to complain. When her tongue slipped into his mouth. Jakes was lost. How could he say no when he wanted it as much as she did?

Jakes could not breathe. He was still not sure it was the right thing to do but with Angie touching him, he couldn't think straight. His uncertainty must have shown as Angie scuttled closer. She pressed her body close to his, slipped her one leg between his and her arm around his neck. Her lips pressed against his neck, brushing over his naked skin. She took her time to taste her way over his jaw, then nibbled at his bottom lip. When she slipped her tongue between his lips, Jakes knew he wouldn't be able to resist her. Not now. Maybe never.

He managed to exhibit a small amount of logic when he mumbled against her lips, "Only if you're sure, Angel. If you're not, please let me go. I otherwise may not stop."

Angie's eyes raised to meet his. Just before their lips met, she whispered, "I'm sure, Jakes."

Angie might be a virgin, but instinct drove them both. Hands and mouths made a slow exploration of bodies. While getting rid of their clothes, they get to know each other.

When he, at last, slid into her warmth, it felt like coming home. Their eyes held the whole time. They got lost in the messages they read in the other's eyes and in each other's bodies.

If this was a game, Jakes had lost it even before it started. He should've known that. He would've stopped if he could, but he couldn't. How could he, when Angie was so responsive in his arms? He couldn't, not when her beautiful naked body moved with his as if they had done it numerous times before. He definitely couldn't when they came apart in each other's arms in the most intense orgasm Jakes had ever experienced.

He knew why.

This was how it felt to make love to the woman you loved more than anything else in the world.

WHEN SHE WOKE up and saw Jakes lying next to her, Angie knew that this was the moment. She always knew that everything that happened before might lead to this moment but didn't know when. She also knew that whenever she lost her virginity, it would be to only one man.

She also saw his uncertainty when he realised what she

wanted. If she wanted him to make love to her, she would have to take the first step. And that's what she did. She felt his body's reaction in every kiss, every touch. Neither of them said the words, but he didn't have to. Angie knew he loved her. She saw it in his eyes when he made her his, softly and tenderly, knowing it was her first time.

Their bodies exploded in such an intense orgasm that Angie lost her breath when Jakes pressed his face in her neck. She felt his laboured breathing, but then he suddenly rolled off her and away.

Her breathing was just as laboured as his and only when she could breathe easier, did she open her eyes and turned her head.

Jakes lay on his back with his hand covering his eyes. Tension rolled off him, evident in the way he clenched his jaw. Angie had a sudden sense of foreboding. She could sense his withdrawal, even before he opened his mouth.

JAKES STRUGGLED to get his breathing back. Not only his breath. His entire world had changed with their lovemaking. He struggled to control his emotions.

Making love to Angie was the most incredible experience of his life. He would've loved to do it again, but it was a mistake. A colossal mistake.

That wasn't how he planned it. He should've been in control and did things the right way. All he had to do was to focus on the next few weeks. But no, he let one slip of a girl got so deep under his skin and into his heart that he lost sight of the big picture.

He forgot his promise to his friends and his team. He let everyone down but more importantly, he let Angie down. That was not how things should've happened. She deserved the romance and everything he had so carefully planned.

"Jakes."

Her voice was a mere whisper. Jakes heard it, but he couldn't look at her. She shouldn't touch him. If she was going to do it, he wouldn't be able to resist her. Not now, after he had a taste of how it would be to love Angie.

Hell, no. He had that taste before, but now that he knew Angie intimately, Jakes wouldn't be able to resist her again—yet he had to.

It was only until after the final in July. He must wait.

Sudden panic rushed through him when he heard the sheet rustling next to him. He jumped up, grabbed his trunks, and slipped them on without looking at Angie. Only when he was decent did he turn around to face her. Angie sat up. She had covered her body with the sheet, her eyes wide. Jakes could read the concern in them, which made him feel even worse.

To Jakes, his voice was gruff, and he sounded short when he pleaded, "I'm sorry. It was a mistake. I shouldn't have... Please get dressed."

He turned, but not quick enough. He saw Angie's face turn ashen, and tears brightening her eyes. He knew she didn't understand it now, but he would explain as soon as she got dressed, but he needed to get out of the room while he still could.

He couldn't stay here and have a sensible conversation with her when he knew she wore nothing underneath that sheet. It was way too tempting to slip back in bed and do it all over again. And again. He wouldn't be able to stop.

Jakes rushed out of the room, upstairs to his own and got dressed. He made sure he had what he needed before he went to the veranda to wait for Angie. Jakes had to think of a way to fix it. He hoped that by the time she joined him, he had found a way to fix it.

His fingers played with the jewellery box in his pocket while he paced up and down the veranda.

HER HEART BROKE into a thousand tiny pieces. Angie hadn't expected such a sudden turnaround so soon after his sweet and tender lovemaking. It hurts.

What did she do wrong?

She shook her head. No, squash that thought. She did nothing wrong. It takes two to tango, and Jakes had been into this as much as she was. She was tired of thinking she was at fault.

And, more importantly, she was tired of Jakes playing hot and cold with her. This wasn't the first time. When would she ever learn her lesson? She should never have listened to her heart.

Disgusted, Angie threw off the sheet and got out of bed. By the time she was dressed and located her bag, she was angry. She was mad at herself and at Jakes. At least the anger gave her enough strength not to plead with him. She refused. Angie left the house without seeing Jakes again.

When she closed the front door behind her and headed to the security gates of the estate, she didn't look back. She fumbled for her phone to call a cab when she heard a car approaching from behind.

Please don't let it be Jakes.

Now the initial anger was fading, she felt close to crying again. She ignored the car, but then heard someone calling her name. Grateful it wasn't Jakes she turned her head. She met Melissa's concerned gaze and stopped.

"Are you okay?" Melissa asked.

Angie shook her head. She hadn't even realised tears were flowing over her cheeks.

"Where are you going?" Melissa asked. "Let me take you."

Angie shrugged, "I don't know. Not to the cottage. He might come looking for me."

"Who? Jakes?" Melissa asked, surprised.

Angie nodded, "Yes, I don't want to see him. Can you take me to a hotel?"

"Come on, get in."

Relieved, Angie rushed around the car to the passenger side. After she fastened her seatbelt, Angie glanced at Melissa. Melissa didn't press for an explanation but only said, "You can stay with me. I won't let your secret out, but I think you should let Rayno's family know you're safe."

"They're away for the weekend. I'll let Jesse know as soon as I can change my flight. I want to go home."

"Are you sure? Don't you think that's drastic? You may fix it," Melissa tried.

Angie shook her head firmly. "No, not this time. I'm done. This time, he hurt me too deeply."

JAKES STRUGGLED to find the right words to explain to Angie why he acted as he did. When he felt ready at last, she hadn't come out yet. He glanced at his watch, shocked at the time that had passed since he left her. Maybe she had fallen asleep...

Fear gripped his heart, and he rushed to the guest bedroom.

There was no sign of Angie in the bedroom, or anywhere else in the house. Jakes searched for his phone, but all his calls to her went unanswered. He texted her, but he already knew it wouldn't help. Angie wouldn't answer his texts.

Jakes panicked. He tried to phone Angie again, then Rayno's mother, and Angie again, but neither of them answered. Maybe she was still on the estate? Suddenly more hopeful, he grabbed his keys, and for the next hour, he drove around trying to find her, but there was no sign of her.

Back at the house, he tried Rayno's mum again when he still hadn't any success with Angie. His relief when she answered, turned to full-blown panic when she told him they were away. Jakes drove to the cottage, but the lights were off. Jakes waited for almost two hours at the cottage without Angie appearing. Or maybe she was there and didn't want to speak to him?

When darkness fell, Jakes was desperate. He phoned all the nearby police stations and hospitals but still no sign of Angie.

He had only one option left. Angie would speak to one person. *He* might have an idea where she could be. Jakes called Jesse.

When Jesse answered, Jakes didn't know what to say. He didn't want to spook Angie's twin and told him she was missing.

He didn't have to worry about that, though. He didn't have to say anything. As he suspected, Angie had been in touch with Jesse. Jakes didn't blame Jesse for being angry with him.

No, anger was putting it mildly. Jesse was furious when he shouted at Jakes, "I don't know what you did this time, Jakes. I promise you, if you were close, I could kill you for hurting my sister. She's safe, but that's no thanks to you. She doesn't want to see you again."

"Jesse, please, I know I messed up. I need to explain to make things right."

"Jakes..." Jesse said, and Jakes' pleas died away. Jesse sounded bitter when he grunted, "Leave her alone. I shouldn't have asked her to come with me. I shouldn't have given her that letter, because then she never would've hoped."

"What letter?" Jakes asked, confused.

"The one I found in the wastepaper basket in your room at

Keystone. The one where you told her how much you loved her. Have you told her, Jakes? Face to face, I mean?"

Jakes closed his eyes and sighed. "No, but..."

"No buts. Leave Angie alone. You've hurt her enough. I don't believe you anymore, Jakes. I don't think you love her, or rather, I don't think you even know the concept of love. Otherwise, you wouldn't have hurt her as you had."

Jakes didn't know what to say, but he didn't have a chance. Jesse had already disconnected.

Maybe Jesse was right. Jakes had known it from the beginning, and he should've followed his instincts. Jakes told Angie's siblings he wasn't relationship material. He wasn't suitable for any woman, in particular not for Angie.

Jesse was wrong, though.

He knew what love was. And he knew how it hurt.

During that next forty-eight hours, Angie was grateful for the friendship she forged with Melissa. If it hadn't been for that, she wouldn't have been able to get through the night. Melissa gave her a shoulder to cry on at first. When she finished crying, Angie used the app on her phone to change her flight. She couldn't get a flight to Atlanta but got one to New York. A few days alone in New York might give her time to figure out her future. At home, her family would smother her with love.

Melissa also kept her up to date with Jakes' movements on Monday morning. As soon as Angie got Melissa's message that Jakes was busy with training, she went to the cottage to pack her belongings. She was back at Melissa's apartment before the team finished their morning session.

After she had a shower and something to eat, Angie worried again. What if Jakes found out she was at Melissa's apartment?

When she couldn't take it anymore, she called a cab to take her to the airport. She was lucky she could check in for her flight and went through security and passport control to the security of one of the airport lounges.

Only then she felt secure enough to breathe easier and let the tears flow.

CHAPTER TWENTY-TWO

J akes didn't know how he got home the previous evening after he spoke to Jesse. He couldn't sleep and walked around the house for hours, hoping Angie would contact him.

It was in the early hours of the morning that he went to lay on the bed in the guest room. There was a lingering trace of her perfume on the pillows and sheet. He held the cushion in his arms and breathed in the faint scent, but Jakes still didn't sleep. His mind kept trying to figure out how different he could've handled everything. He would keep on trying until he found her, he vowed in the early hours of the morning.

He looked terrible when he arrived at the stadium for early training. His movements were sluggish and tired, and he messed up his moves. Coach shouted at him, but Jakes couldn't pull out of it.

Every chance he got throughout the morning, he tried to phone Angie, but no luck. During lunch, he drove to Rayno's house, but the cottage was deserted. Jakes returned to the stadium for afternoon training still trying to phone. He got weird looks from his friends and the coaches.

After nine that night, Jakes knew he'd messed up too much. Angie's South African number went to voicemail. *The subscriber you have dialled is not available.*

When André confronted him the next morning about his appearance, he merely answered, "Angie is gone and no, I don't want to talk about it."

André might have told their other friends that Angie had left, because nobody asked him about it, and for that Jakes was relieved.

The rest of the week went by in a blur. Jakes didn't even remember how he got to Glasgow for their first match on tour against the Royal Blues. Although he tried as hard as he could, his heart wasn't in training.

His only contact with Angie was on social media. From that, he learned she was back in the States. On Friday night, he lost that contact as well when Angie blocked him from all her social media platforms.

ANGIE HAD SPENT time on her own before, but she never felt more alone than the time she spent in New York. She went through the motions of sightseeing but spent most of her time in the city's art galleries. It was in one of those galleries where the owner most likely felt sorry for her. She invited Angie to have coffee with her. She asked Angie so many questions, and when she heard that Angie also painted, she asked her to bring her paintings.

Angie had no expectations when she returned to the gallery the following morning. She had with her the paintings she finished while in South Africa. They were small, and being unstretched, she fitted them into her suitcase with ease.

Angie worried unnecessarily. Candice, the gallery owner, enthused about Angie's work. She invited Angie to exhibit them as part of a Young Artist's exhibition she planned for June and July. Angie left New York with a signed contract in her pocket.

For the first time since she left South Africa, she had a reason to smile, but her new-found positivity didn't end there.

Angie left two paintings in South Africa. One was for Rayno's mother, and the other one was the one she'd made of Jakes. She had asked Rayno's mom to give the painting she named *The Raging Buffalo* to Jakes when he returned from the tour.

Angie was unaware Rayno's mother delivered the portrait of Jakes to the stadium as they were going overseas and wouldn't be at home when Jakes returned. She was therefore stunned to get a phone call from Nicholas Carter, the CEO of the Buffaloes, a week after her return to Denver. Nicholas had seen the painting in Rachel's office. Her surprise turned to shock when Nicholas asked if she could do similar portraits of the first two captains of the Buffaloes. She would've been stupid not to agree. At least she wasn't and eagerly accepted the offer. Having met both Daniel and Damian Cooper, Angie couldn't wait to start.

Angie had enough to do while waiting for the dimensions of the paintings and the contract. She finished the painting of Rick. Rick was specific about what he wanted and sent several photos to her to find the right pose. Not nude, as she expected, but still shirtless, and looking dangerous. Rick might not make her heart beat faster, but he definitely was an attractive model.

Angie hadn't told anyone else why she left South Africa in such a hurry, but she had enough time to think about it. She couldn't blame Jakes alone. How could she when she initiated their lovemaking?

Would she have done it differently? Maybe. They probably still would've made love because that's what she wanted. She wasn't sorry that it had been Jakes who took her virginity. She loved him. She was sorry though that she hadn't confronted him and asked him why he pulled away. She had, as she usually did, avoided confrontation and fled. Now she kept on wondering whether she shouldn't have altered her reaction.

It was too late now. She had already waited too long to contact Jakes. And if she did, would the outcome not still be the same? Wouldn't he reject her again?

She wouldn't get the answer now. Maybe one day...

She now did what she knew best and put everything into her work. When Angie told her family she was moving to the cabin to paint, they protested at first. They didn't want her to be alone, but Angie insisted. The studio at the cabin was bigger, and she would need the space for the large dimension paintings. Jesse surprised her by convincing the others to leave her in peace.

Three weeks after she returned from South Africa, Jesse and Rayno even helped her to move to Keystone and set up her studio. Since she arrived, she had been productive. She had completed four paintings for the gallery in New York. Nicholas was excited about the preliminary sketches she sent him. According to him, they were all perfect. The portrait of Damian Cooper was now in its final stages, and Angie felt happy with it.

Jonathan and Claire contacted Angie the previous day to let her know that they were coming to visit on Friday night. The other two nights they would spend at a romantic getaway close by. Angie would've preferred to be alone, but she didn't have a choice. At least having Jonathan and Claire there, would help Angie take her mind off Jakes. She was tired of crying herself to sleep each night, thinking about him.

When Angie was painting, it was different, but at night,

when she was alone, she had too much time to think and to remember.

FOR THE FIRST time in his life, Jakes hated being on tour. To him, it felt as if it was what he would later dub as the tour from hell.

First games on tour were always tricky. The Buffaloes struggled in the first half. The pitch at Scotstoun where the Royal Blues played their home games was softer than they were used to. Not that it concerned Jakes. He wasn't playing. Coach had benched him.

Their next game was against the Irish Greyhounds in Limerick. It was cold, miserable, and the field muddy from the rain of the last two days, putting a damper on the squad. They couldn't find their rhythm. Tempers were flying, and like the previous week, they gave away too many penalties. The Irish converted six of those penalties into points, and the Buffaloes suffered their second loss. Jakes expected that.

Jakes again didn't play against the English Bulldogs in Worcester the following week. This time he was suffering from a cold. For the first time on the tour, the Buffaloes scored a bonus-point win. The fact he wasn't playing and they managed a win proved to Jakes he was the one jinxing the team.

For their last game on tour, they had to travel across the English Channel to play Pays de la Loire in Nantes. Jakes struggled again. He felt tired and sluggish and knew it was because of lack of sleep. It was already the second half, and they were behind. He bent, put his hands on his knees, breathing hard. His chest was burning, and every other muscle in his body too. He lifted his head, watching his teammates, and he could see they all felt the same.

They were all frustrated when the French scored a

converted try. After the kick-off that followed, Richie jumped high for the ball and tapped the ball back to his forwards. The ball passed through several hands before Jakes got it. He had only one goal, and that was the try line. He glanced towards his left for the next receiver. Before he could glance to his right, a large body slammed into him from that side. Jakes fell, with all the weight of the French number eight on top of him.

As soon as he hit the ground, Jakes heard the loud pop. A sharp, excruciating pain shot through his shoulder and arm. His opposite number must've heard it too as he rolled away. He tried to shield Jakes from the rest of the forwards who were ready to tumble down for a loose scrum. He shouted to the referee who blew his whistle.

Jakes had suffered many injuries in the past. Nobody needed to tell him he broke his collarbone. He lay still, too scared to move because he knew the pain would be excruciating if he did.

He opened his eyes when he heard Peter Sinclair and Michael speaking next to him as the young doctor tried to make him comfortable. Michael told him later he had been moaning the whole time that he had broken his collarbone. He knew there was a possibility that his part in the competition had ended. He would've liked to stay to the end.

Jakes passed out for when they braced him and turned him onto the gurney. When he opened his eyes, he noticed the concerned faces of his teammates and the opponents. They all stood and waited for the medics to push the gurney to the tunnel. Jakes heard the faint sound of the crowd clapping but nothing else.

He heard voices and felt the needle in his arm, and soon the numbing relief of morphine took over. He vaguely knew they took the X-rays, confirming his own diagnosis.

The flight back to South Africa that Sunday night was

something Jakes never wanted to repeat. He was under heavy sedation supervised by Dr Sinclair, but not even that had helped. He was still uncomfortable. He heard by then the team had lost and again blamed himself. If he hadn't broken their vow, the team could have won. After Jakes' injury, there was not enough time for the Buffaloes to get back into the game. They lost with nineteen points to twelve.

Dr Montgomery, the senior team doctor, had already made all the arrangements. On arrival in Johannesburg, they took him straight to the hospital in Pretoria. He remembered seeing his mum during the day. Through his medicated haze, he heard the hospital noises and voices around him. That same afternoon Jakes woke up drowsy, feeling the bed move, but he struggled to open his eyes. Jakes then felt the mask slipping over his face, and he fell into blissful darkness.

The next time he opened his eyes was to see his mother. Although she looked tired, she smiled with relief when Jakes opened his eyes. He only found out much later that he had an operation. The surgeon had inserted a metal pin to put the two halves of his collarbone in place. Jakes knew what it meant. He would have to wait six to eight weeks before he could start rehab on his shoulder. He still hoped to play in the Triangular Series and the World Cup, but he knew he would cut it close.

While he was in the hospital, his friends visited him whenever they had a break from training. That was until Friday when Jakes left the hospital. Instead of going home to Clarens as his family insisted, Jakes stayed in Pretoria. He would go crazy on the farm doing nothing.

The first game after their tour was a second-round match at home against the Royal Blues. Jakes sat in the players' box, watching the game. It seemed the Buffaloes liked to be back at home after a month-long tour. They celebrated by giving the

Royal Blues a hiding, scoring six tries. It resulted in a massive
51-11 victory for the Buffaloes.

Jakes was miserable. He should have been happy, but that
wasn't the point. That emphatic win proved to him how much
he'd messed up by sleeping with Angie. At least he would be out
for the rest of the Competition. He wouldn't jinx the team any
further.

After the game, he ambled to The Final Whistle. He
promised to meet the guys there, but he didn't know why he
bothered. He couldn't even have something to drink, as he was
still on medication. When the women drifted in, the reality of
Angie's leaving hit him like a brick in the chest. None of the
women spoke to him. They all ignored him as if he didn't exist.

His teammates were all in high spirits when they arrived.
They tried to pull Jakes into the conversation, but his heart
wasn't in it. He felt even more isolated when he noticed Daniel,
André, and Mark conferring with each other. Mark and Daniel
drifted off after a while, and André returned to his seat next to
Jakes.

Then it hit Jakes. He had given Angie up. He had pushed
her away for the sake of his team, but now it was all for nothing.
His teammates were going on with their lives, and he had
nothing. He didn't have rugby to keep him busy, but more
importantly, he didn't have Angie. Jakes sighed, dropping his
head in his hands.

Jakes looked up when he felt a hand on his uninjured
shoulder. Daniel didn't look at Jakes when he asked the women,
"Ladies, will you please excuse us?"

The women all looked as surprised as Jakes when the rest
of the team, with Christopher and Michael, got up, pulling
Jakes with them. Jakes didn't know what to expect when
Daniel pushed him into the chair at the head of the table in
the meeting room. The whole team was there. The senior

players, except Ryan, took their seats around the table. The rest were standing in a half-circle around it, all their eyes on Jakes.

Daniel spoke. "Bro', we all want to say how sorry we are for your injury. We miss you on the pitch, and we hope you recover soon."

Jakes didn't like to be the centre of attention and he flushed but more because of his earlier thoughts. He should have known his team wouldn't leave him.

There were murmurs of agreement with Daniel's statement. Before Jakes could reply, Daniel said, "But, this is not about the team, or about your rugby. We love you, bro' but we can't take your jabbering anymore. The last few weeks you've talked our heads off."

Jakes glared as Daniel's obvious sarcasm didn't go over his head. Jakes showed Daniel a middle finger, resulting in laughter. It soon filtered away when Daniel said, "Jakes, you're our teammate, our brother and our friend. We care about you, and we can't see you moping around anymore. Talk to us."

Jakes flushed, but his eyes searched the faces around him, and he knew it was time to confess. He cleared his throat and said, "Guys, I'm sorry. I must apologise."

He knew his face was red with embarrassment, but he couldn't meet their eyes. He looked down at his hands before he said, "I messed up and almost cost the team. I tried, but..."

He took a deep breath then mumbled, "Guys, I broke our pledge. I'm sorry."

Instead of the jeers he expected, the whole team cheered. Jakes looked up surprised, but all he saw was the amused faces of his teammates. "You guys aren't angry? I mean... We could have lost."

"Dude, you're the only one who lost," Mark smiled. Jakes knew he was right.

Daniel gazed at the other players, "I'm sure you're not the first. Right, Rick?"

Rick grinned, but he didn't have to reply. Everyone expected him to be the first to break the pledge.

Daniel turned back to Jakes. "Jakes, we know you. You're suffering since Angie left. We want to give you something as a token of solidarity."

Ryan, who stood behind Jakes, slid a standard European-sized envelope in front of him. Jakes' gaze flitted over his friends before he opened the envelope. The first document was his pledge, but over it, someone had written in bold letters, "Cancelled."

Jakes felt the corner of his mouth tug, but then he opened the smaller envelope and felt his heart lurch. Inside was a photo of him and Angie.

Jakes swallowed and fingered the photo. Richie must have taken the picture the day at Mark's house. Jakes had been standing behind Angie, both arms around her. He had bent over and kissed her on the cheek. She had leaned against him, lifting her cheek for his kiss, and a small smile softened her features. Looking at the photo, Jakes felt confident that, at that moment, Angie loved him as much as he loved her. That photo resembled two people in love. Of course, he also felt it later that afternoon when they made love.

He swallowed hard as he put the photo on top of the cancelled oath. There was one more document, and Jakes unfolded it slowly. He inhaled when he realised what it was: a return ticket to Denver. It would leave in ten days and would return around the time Jakes could train again.

Jakes looked up in a daze as Daniel swept his hand through the air, encompassing the squad when he explained, "The whole team have contributed to the ticket. Richie might have contributed the most, as half the money came from the swear jars," he chuckled. Before Jakes could reply, Daniel instructed, "You can say thank you to the rest of the team, then we can discuss it."

Jakes smiled and did what Daniel ordered. He thanked each of the guys as they filed out of the meeting room. Alone with his group of friends and Michael, Jakes joined them at the table again.

"Okay, let's see what we need to do. You have to see your specialist in a week, and after that, you should be fit to travel. We know your training and rehabilitation concerns you. Michael arranged with the Rehab Centre in Denver where Dr Summers will monitor you on the other side. André will stay in your house to look after it. Anything else?"

Jakes frowned. "The biggest one."

Daniel raised his eyebrow. He didn't have to say a word. Jakes answered, "Angie won't speak to me."

"What did you do? Why did she leave?" Daniel asked, straight to the point as usual.

Jakes flushed. "I know it may sound bad, but that's not what I wanted to say. You know, I think before I speak. Well, I didn't. Not then. I needed a few minutes alone... and then I would tell her that... but she didn't come out... and then... she left," Jakes rambled.

"Jakes," André said calmly. "Tell us what happened. Take your time. We're not here to judge you. We're here to help you."

Jakes fingered the rubber band around his wrist. These days he wore it as a reminder of how far he had come. He wasn't as distressed now as when he got a panic attack.

"It was that day after we were at Mark's house. I invited Angie for dinner. She asked to nap when we arrived at my house. I showed her to the guestroom, made sure everything was ready as I planned, and then went outside for a swim and cleaned the pool. Much later, I went to wake her. She looked so beautiful I couldn't resist it. I should have known I was playing with fire. I lay next to her, watching her sleep. Then she woke up. Just like that. When she touched me that was all it took..."

"You made love," Matthew surmised. "Uhm, was it bad?" he asked, surprised.

Jakes shook his head vehemently. "Geez, guys, please do not expect any details! I can't... All I can say that it was mind-blowing. Incredible. Geez, you don't have to tell me I messed up. I freaking apologised. Not for making love, but I apologised.... I guess... for messing up my own plans. I wanted to tell her about our pledge. I wanted to tell her I loved her, and I wanted to ask her to marry me. I thought if she knew about the pledge, she would understand why I wanted to wait to make love. I wanted to do it the right way. I had candles and champagne and..."

Jakes fiddled in his pocket. "I even had the ring," he said, taking out the jewellery box with his grandmother's ring he carried with him everywhere. Why he didn't know.

"So, why didn't you ask her?" Matthew asked again.

"I needed a few minutes to regroup. I went back outside and thought about how to fix it. A while later, I realised Angie hadn't come out. I couldn't find her anywhere, and she didn't answer my calls or messages. I phoned Jesse as a last resort. He told me she was safe and that I had to leave her alone. I couldn't understand it. I only recently realised how Angie must have interpreted my words, but it was too late. Angie had by then blocked me from all her social media."

It was quiet in the room for a long time until Christopher spoke. "Okay, I have an idea."

CHAPTER TWENTY-THREE

Would he always arrive in Denver with an injury? It almost felt like it! At least he arrived in more comfort the second time, eleven days after the talk with his teammates as his teammates bought him a business class ticket to Atlanta. They promised the same class ticket for Angie if Jakes could convince her to come back with a ring on her finger.

Jakes didn't want to think far ahead. There were still too many obstacles before he could get to that, but he had done all his research in the last ten days. If he had his way, Angie would return to South Africa with not only the one ring on her finger.

The last two days were nerve-wracking. Jakes wasn't sure if he could travel. His surgeon might have thought he had a weird patient. Jakes had been so relieved when the doctor gave his final approval, he had hugged him.

He didn't know what he would have done without his friends. He found out that evening when they gave him the tickets that Christopher still spoke to Jesse. It hadn't been easy. Jesse was reluctant to get involved in Angie's affairs again, but

Christopher managed to convince Jesse after a long conversation to give Jakes a chance.

Jakes pushed the trolley with his luggage through the crowd at the arrival hall with one hand. He was careful to protect the shoulder Doc Montgomery put in a protective wrap for the trip. He was looking for the sign for the cabs when he heard his name.

Jakes turned in surprise when he recognised Jesse's voice. Jesse didn't give him a welcoming smile, but he came, which was more than Jakes expected.

Jakes pushed his trolley towards Jesse, and when he stopped in front of him, he held out his hand. It felt like an eternity before Jesse took it and only said, "Jakes." No welcome or good morning or anything else. Jakes didn't blame him.

"Thank you. I didn't expect that you will meet me here."

"I'll take you to see my Dad, and then we'll have lunch with him and Jonathan. You can keep your story till then."

Jakes sighed. "Oh boy, I didn't expect to face the whole firing squad at once."

Jesse suddenly grinned. "Yep. Serves you right, man."

Jakes stopped and turned to Jesse. "Jesse, I didn't lie. I love Angie, and I would do anything to fix this. It's such a mess and a huge misunderstanding. All I ask is an opportunity to prove it to her. I made loads of mistakes. I told you I'm not good relationship material and probably not the best choice for your sister. I just didn't realise how bad I sucked at it."

Jesse nodded, and then he walked again without replying, and Jakes followed him. If this was bad, Jakes didn't want to imagine how the rest of his grovelling would go.

Three hours later, Jakes felt as if he'd played one of the hardest rugby matches in his life. The three men were stoic, giving no sign of if they believed him. They showed neither sympathy nor anger while he told his story, and Jakes didn't know where he stood. All he could do now was to ask and hoped he would get the right answer.

His gaze slid between the three men facing him. He took a deep breath before he said, "That's it. You now know everything. The only thing I still have to say... to ask is... If you believe me, and if Angie believes me and forgives me... If she's prepared to give me a chance... I ask your permission to marry Angie. Soon, that is. I can't bear to lose her again. I promise I'll do anything in my power to make her happy..."

All three of them were quiet, staring at him. Jakes felt his heart beating fast and his hands shaking, as he tried to take a sip of his now cold coffee. Jakes noticed the look they shared before Doc Summers held Jakes' eyes and muttered, "This calls for a beer."

Jakes stared at him. What did that mean? Was that a yes or a no?

Doc Summers suddenly laughed and held out his hand to Jakes, "Welcome to the family."

Jonathan added with a huge grin, "Well, if you can convince Angie."

Relieved, Jakes shook the doctor's hand, then Jesse and Jonathan's before he promised, "I will try my best, Doc. If she gives me a chance, I promise I'll try whatever is necessary to convince her," while Jonathan placed their orders. When they each sat with a beer in their hand, Jonathan proposed a toast, "To begging and grovelling and Happily Ever Afters."

Jakes accepted the toast, and asked, almost pleading with the three men, "I'm going to need your help to get Angie to give me a chance to explain."

Jonathan said with an enigmatic grin, "There's nothing like a captive audience."

Jakes frowned confused, and Jonathan laughed, "Okay, here's the plan..."

. . .

SHE WISHED they wanted to leave now. It was nice to have them here, but she was tired of keeping a brave front, not showing how much she still hurt. With Jonathan and Claire here, it brought back too many memories.

Her heart sank when Jonathan invited her for a drink at the pub before they left. Angie didn't want to go, but she hadn't left the house in days. An outing might do her good and agreed.

Jonathan promised that she could come home early but was closer to seven when Jonathan stopped in front of the cabin.

Claire greeted over her shoulder, but Jonathan got out and hugged her. His parting words confused her. "I know you're hurting, but things will get better. Someone told me it takes a strong person to apologise, and an even stronger person to forgive. Keep that in mind."

With those strange words, Jonathan got into his car and drove away. Angie stared at the departing vehicle, wondering what he meant.

Angie was still pondering over Jonathan's words when she opened the door and locked it behind her. Relieved to be alone, she had closed her eyes when she leaned against the door, but now she had a strange awareness. Something felt different. Something also smelled different, reminding her that she hadn't had much to eat today.

She opened her eyes and inhaled. Was she hallucinating? She quickly closed her eyes again. Her legs felt weak. Grateful that she hadn't moved away from the door, Angie leaned against it for support. She inhaled, forcing the oxygen to her lungs before she opened her eyes again. He was still there but now much closer than he had been seconds ago.

Jakes was close enough to smell his aftershave and see the uncertainty in his eyes.

She shouldn't look into his eyes. It was the vulnerability in his eyes that had drawn her to him in the first place.

Not heeding her own warning, she looked. Jakes' skin was pale, and there were dark circles under his eyes. He licked his lips as if he was nervous.

As her eyes drifted lower, Angie noticed the sling holding his shoulder in place. She should've expected it. She knew about his injury. Angie had told no one, but she'd learned how to stream his matches. She'd seen when he fell and lay still, and she'd thought her heart stopped beating. She heard later he broke his collarbone and had an operation.

Her eyes drifted up to his face again and saw he still watched her with that same intensity.

And then he spoke. Angie had to strain her ears to hear what he said. His voice was low and gruff, his accent so much stronger.

Angie didn't want to get her hopes up again, but the honesty in his voice and what he said, made her change her mind.

JAKES WAS a nervous wreck while he waited for Angie. This was his one chance to fix things, to convince her how he felt, and this time he had to do it right. When Angie had left for the pub with Jonathan and Claire, and they received the confirmation from Claire, Jesse and Rayno brought Jakes to the house. He had so much to do, and it would've taken him much longer with only one arm, but with their help, Jakes prepared everything.

Claire had texted him when they left the pub, and Jakes waited around the corner. When the car stopped, he almost bolted, but then the front door opened and closed. He didn't hear Angie's footsteps, so he came out of his hiding place.

He drank in the sight of her as she leaned against the door with her eyes closed. Her hair tumbled over her shoulders, and it contrasted with the pallor of her face. She too had dark circles under her eyes. The blue top she bought in Cape Town was now hanging over her slight frame, confirming that she lost weight.

She suddenly opened her eyes. She must have seen him as she stared straight at him. She probably thought he was an illusion because she closed them again. He hated that. He wanted to see her eyes.

Jakes moved closer, clenching the single red rose in his hand so tight he feared he might break the stem. But then he reached her, and for the first time in two months, he was close enough to breathe in her clean smell of water and lily-of-the-valley. He was close enough to see the sparkle in her eyes when she opened them again. He could even see her lips trembling, and her pulse fluttering at the base of her throat. That was when Jakes knew he might still have a chance.

But this time he had to do it right.

He took another step closer, holding out the rose to her and said, "I love you. I love you so much, Angel. I don't want to be without you anymore. I know I messed up but, please, give me a chance to explain, to make things right."

Jakes waited. Maybe Angie hadn't heard him, but at last, she stretched out her hand and took the rose from him.

"All I need to know is why?"

Her question was a mere whisper. Jakes didn't know what she wanted to know. "Angel, I have so much explaining to do, and I don't know where to start. What do you want to hear first? Why I hadn't told you before now that I loved you? Or do you want to know why I apologised after we made love? Or why I pushed you away time and again?"

"Why did you apologise?"

Jakes flushed. "Well, that's the easiest one to explain. I didn't plan to make love to you then. Don't get me wrong. I wanted to. I also wanted to tell you how I felt almost right from the start, but that's all part of the longer story. Why I apologised was moronic."

He stepped a little closer to her, lifting a trembling hand to lift her hair from her shoulder. "I had it all planned out, you see. I prepared a romantic dinner. I've set the table in the garden with candles and flowers and everything. I first wanted to tell you how much I loved you, and that I want to spend the rest of my life with you if you will have me. I would then have gone down on my knee to propose."

His breath shuddered. "When I got in the guestroom to wake you, and you touched me, all my plans flew out of the window. I couldn't resist you, Angel. I knew I should have been stronger, but at that moment... It was incredible. Amazing... Then it hit me. I haven't explained to you why I pushed you away at first. I would have told you that the team made a pledge last year to avoid women until after the final of the new competition. I didn't tell you I loved you. I didn't propose. I didn't apologise because we made love. I apologised because I wanted to do it right as I planned it. I got in a panic and rushed out to fix it. You see, if I stayed there with you, I wouldn't have been able to resist you. I waited and waited and then... You were gone."

He took a deep breath before he continued, "I'm sorry, Angel. I can be a pain, always planning everything to perfection. When things didn't happen the way I planned, I panic. It hadn't always been like that. It only started when I realised that if I planned carefully, I wouldn't get into uncomfortable situations. It was my way of controlling my life, but I took it too far. I'm working on it. I'm not a perfect guy, but I beg you, Angel, please give me a chance to make things right."

Jakes tried to wipe away the tears flowing down her cheeks, but she lifted her hand and put it over his.

She almost hiccupped when she smiled. "You just did."

Jakes stared at her, trying to breathe. Angie leaned forward, stood on her tiptoes, and kissed him. When she stepped back, she smiled, "I don't want a perfect man. I want a real man, who makes mistakes, as long as he can admit when he has. I only want a man who loves me for who I am. I want you, Jakes, because I love you too."

Jakes slipped his uninjured arm around her. He pulled her tight against him before his mouth claimed hers, kissing her as he dreamed of these past few weeks. He pulled away, pleading through ragged breaths, "Please repeat it."

"I love you."

Jakes suddenly laughed. He hadn't felt so happy and light in a long time. He looked down at Angie, who frowned, "We probably could've had this conversation somewhere more comfortable?"

Jakes chuckled and looked up. Angie followed his eyes and laughed, "Really?"

Jakes nodded, "Jonathan said I'll need all the help I can get. I reckoned a few sprigs of mistletoe might help. Even fake ones. I tried to be romantic because our first kiss was under the mistletoe, remember?" Jakes grinned as he led her to the family room with his arm around her shoulder.

"I remember..." Angie stopped in the doorway of the big room Jakes had transformed the room with the help of Rayno and Jesse. He set the table they used for games in front of the window and filled the place with candles and red roses. Soft music played in the background, and the rich aroma of food drifted from the kitchen.

Angie turned towards Jakes, misty-eyed, and he said gently,

"I still have so much explaining to do, Angel, so much to tell you. It may take a while. Do you want dinner first?"

Angie's stomach rumbled as if in reply, and Jakes laughed, "I guess it is dinner first."

"And after dinner, are you going to declare your love again?" Angie asked coyly.

"Been there, done that," Jakes teased back and laughed at Angie's indignant face. She punched his arm and probed, "Are you going to propose?"

Jakes pretended to think about it before he replied, "I don't know, but if I do, will you say yes?"

"I may," Angie grinned and stepped away from him. Jakes only hesitated for a moment. He remembered his friends' last-minute advice.

Forget well laid out plans.

Live spontaneously.

Jakes made a split decision. He fumbled for the ring in his pocket and stopped Angie before she could walk away. Angie turned around to face him, only to find him on one knee in front of her. Her laughter stopped, and fresh tears spilled over her cheeks.

Jakes swallowed hard. His emotions almost overwhelmed him, but although he struggled, he managed to get the words out. "I didn't know it then, Angel, but I fell in love with you the first day I met you. Every day since I fell a little deeper and will probably do so for the rest of our lives. You are the one who healed me, who keep my feet on the ground, who taught me how to laugh and love again. I love you, Angel. I want to share the rest of my life with you, loving you, protecting you and taking care of you. Will you marry me?"

Angie's "Yes" was immediate, tears still streaming down her cheeks.

Jakes' hand shook as he slid the ring on her finger. Before he could get up, Angie leaned down and cupped his face. Their eyes were bright, with tears and laughter. They looked at each other for long moments before their lips met to seal their love.

Jakes didn't even interrupt the kiss when he got up, pulling Angie against him.

Food can wait.

Explanations can wait.

This was far more important.

THE END

Note from the Author

In the series, Richie Campbell is a Scot from Glasgow who came to play for the Buffaloes. I rarely use these Scottish phrases, but to set Richie apart from the South Africans, I had to bring in a few, for example:

Aye - Yes
Wee - Small
Ken - I know
Ye - you
Yer -Your

The phrase *ga mae no dae that*, comes from a Scottish tv show called *Chewing the Fat*. Richie only uses it to frustrate Sarah.

Please also note that most of the series use South African/British English. In *Eye on the Ball*, however, there is a mix of American and British English such as Mom (for Angie) and Mum (for Jakes).

ACKNOWLEDGMENTS

I will be remiss if I don't thank my family and friends for their support.

I also need to thank my beta readers, who suffer through my first drafts.

A special thank you to Sarah Bullen, the Writing Room for her support and guidance;

Editor: CA Els

The following people and organisations prepared to answer my endless questions:

Stephan de Wet;

The Glendale Raptors; and

The Scottish Rugby Union

South African Society of Physiotherapy

More about the author

Having spent decades devouring romance novels, South African-born romance writer She published her debut novel, Eye on the Ball, and the first book in the Taste for Love series in 2018. She loves travelling and is an avid photographer, forever snapping pictures of her food and drink – much to her Husband's frustration. Francine is an enthusiastic rugby supporter who (once) even played the game but now prefers commentating from the sideline or n front of the television while enjoying a glass of her favourite wine.

Subscribe to Francine's Newsletter

Follow Francine on Social Media

CHARACTERS IN THE PLAYING FOR GLORY SERIES

THE SQUAD

RESERVES

HEAD COACH: TOM BRADY
ASSISTANT COACH: CARL BECKER
HIGH PERFORMANCE MANAGER: NATHAN SINCLAIR

MANAGEMENT AND SUPPORT

NICHOLAS CARTER
CEO

ADMINISTRATION	COACHING STAFF	MEDICAL SUPPORT	PHYSIOTHERAPY
EMMA COLE-CARTER DIRECTOR: FINANCE	PETER MATTHEWS DIRECTOR OF RUGBY	DR JAMES MONTGOMERY MEDICAL SUPPORT STAFF	MICHAEL BRADY HEAD: PHYSIOTHERAPY
CHRISTOPHER BROOKS DIRECTOR: MEDIA AND COMMUNICATION	TOM BRADY HEAD COACH	DR PETER SINCLAIR JUNIOR TEAM DOCTOR	SIMON KELLER SENIOR PHYSIOTHERAPIST
LISBETH (BETH) MEYERS (PA)	ASSISTANT COACH CARL BECKER	DR PETER MARSHALL TEAM PSYCHOLOGIST	DARIUS LATEGAN PHYSIOTHERAPIST
RACHEL DUNN PLAYERS ASSISTANT	NATHAN SINCLAIR HIGH PERFORMANCE MANAGER	CHLOE MARSHALL NUTRITIONIST	MELISSA ROUX PHYSIOTHERAPIST
	HANNAH BLAKE SPORT SCIENTIST		SANDY BECKER MASSEUSE

OTHER CHARACTERS IN THE SERIES

Angie Summers	- Artist	*Eye on the Ball*
Cara-Mia Frescoe	- Performing artist	*Playing the Field*
Damian Cooper	- Former Captain of Buffaloes	*How to Tame a Buffalo (Kick-Off, 3)*
Dan Mackay	- Brother of Sarah MacKay/Captain: Scotland	*Choices (On the Sidelines, 1)*
Elizabeth Blake, Dr	- Trauma doctor	*Concussion*
Jaylin Cooper	- Linguist	*Blood Brothers*
Jesse Summers	- Angie's twin brother	*Chances (On the Sidelines, 2)*
Jessica (Jess) Mackay	- Teacher	*Choices (On the Sidelines, 1)*
Jon Brooks	- Son of Christopher and Riley	*Obstruction*
Landie Schoeman	- Ballerina	*'n Man soos Pierre*
Lia Moorcroft	- Events Coordinator	*Chances (On the Sidelines, 2)*
Lynn Brown-Cooper	- Environmental Lawyer	*How to tame a Buffalo (Kick-Off, 3)*
Riley Adams	- Journalist	*Obstruction*
Samantha Brady	- Netball Player	*Playing by the Rules*
Sarah Mackay	- Elocution Coach	*Wrecking Ball*

Playing for Glory